To Johanna!
Thanks for
support.

Kam

MW01600788

Oct 25 26th;

BURNING
BARRIERS

Karen Moulder

authorHOUSE®

AuthorHouse™
1663 Liberty Drive
Bloomington, IN 47403
www.authorhouse.com
Phone: 1-800-839-8640

The story is based on real events, but the character names have been changed. Since this book spans over a twenty year period, much of the original dialogue and spoken phrases are not exact quotes, but remain as true to the original circumstances as I can recall.

Published by AuthorHouse   10/22/2012

First Edition: August 2012

ISBN: 978-1-4772-7537-5 (sc)
ISBN: 978-1-4772-7538-2 (hc)
ISBN: 978-1-4772-7539-9 (e)

Library of Congress Control Number: 2012918229

Collaborative writing by Darcie Duranceau
Edited by Cliff Carle and William Harris
Book cover design by Travis Pennington of Pro Book Covers
Photography by Myra Thompson and Lynette Mejorado

Dedicated To
ALL WOMEN FIREFIGHTERS
FIREFIGHTERS OF THE BROWNSVILLE
FIRE DEPARTMENT

And to
DARCIE DURANCEAU
Colaborative Writer
CLIFF CARLE
Editor, Copy Editor
CASSANDRA GUERRERO
Fire Inspector, Best Friend

ACKNOWLEDGMENTS

THANKS....

TO Darcie Duranceau, who was inspirational in bringing my story to life.

TO Cliff Carle for his never ending patience with me as I stumbled through this process.

TO Cassandra Guerrero, my best friend and biggest fan. She continues to fight the barriers that we both faced. She gives so much to everyone... most of all to keeping us and the community safe.

TO William Harris, my English Professor and friend, who showed me that I could write.

TO Mark Matthews, who inspired me to follow my dreams and has always been there for me. ;)

TO Bruce and Leona Moulder, my parents, who were always there to guide and help me even when I didn't listen.

MOST OF ALL...TO MY children Myra, Clint, David, Lynette, and Dylan who struggled along with me, yet maintained their pride, enthusiasm, and support in their mother.

CONTENTS

BURNING
BARRIERS

PROLOGUE

DESPITE ALL THE strength, all the fortitude, and all of the resolve Kate had found in her everyday life – in that single moment she was as helpless as a person could be. The second impact sent her head lurching forward; her chest strained against the vinyl cloth strap which held tight and, just short of her forehead meeting the steering wheel, whipped her back again with the same violent force. Kate could see that the car was still moving, but it was out of her control as it spun around, whipping her back and forth in her seat once more before all came to rest at a bizarre angle. The noise behind her was deafening as she fought to release herself from the shoulder strap. Her back ached as she twisted, pushing off of the front console for leverage, but she didn't care. She had to reach them.

In the backseat, now resting above her head, Kate's two youngest children dangled from their carseat harnesses. Both screamed in her face while she fought to release one and then the other. The car was standing, nearly straight up, nose first, in the ditch, which made it difficult for her to maneuver them. She had to lay the oldest, Lucy, against the back of the front passenger seat, while she unbuckled her infant son, Dustin, from his car seat. Then, carefully, making sure she was perfectly balanced, Kate pulled them to her and held them tight against her chest for a few seconds before attempting to open the door. Both front doors held firm when she tried to push at them to escape.

She had no idea how long it would be before help arrived. Experience had taught her that response times depended on numerous factors and could vary. Kate ignored the pain that was ravaging her back and neck. She set Lucy where she had rested her before while holding Dustin; gingerly she pushed her weight up with her legs so she could reach the rear door handle. After a moment of tugging, she felt it release, and the door fell open. There was a brief moment of relief, but she was not entirely sure how she was going to get herself, a three year old, and an infant of four months, over the seat and through the exit she had just created.

Just as panic began to show its ugly face and tears threatened to fall from her eyes, a familiar sleeve of black with a reflective yellow stripe reached in, touching her shoulder.

"Hey…It's Kate! …and her kids!" Roger, her fellow firefighter, shouted to the other men. He turned his attention back to her. "Are you alright? Stay still and we will get you out."

How odd it felt, the role reversal — she was not performing the rescue — it was she who was being rescued.

Once freed from the crushed metal box, Kate took in her surroundings. The driver who had caused the whole ordeal was pinned in his truck between two trees across the ditch from her, just shy of hitting a house. The red taillights, still working, shone brightly back at her. Her instinct was to cross the ditch and offer help, retrieving the man from his precarious perch, but even if they would have allowed her, the pain in her back drove home the reality of her limitations. Instead, Kate watched, offering kind words of reassurance to her scared children while they were set atop the white sheet-laden stretchers to be examined.

The adrenaline continued to drain from her body, and she found it more difficult to move of her own accord. The men, her colleagues, were forced to lift her up onto the stretcher. Kate cringed in agony. She looked up at them, motionless, head secured in a neck brace. From experience, she knew that look of concern that flooded their eyes. She had shared it with these men before, and fear pierced her to the core as she thought that she might never share anything with them again.

PART 1

IGNITING THE FLAME

"From little spark may burst a mighty flame." – Dante Alighieri

1

THE BACKROOM OF the church was lit with an eerie light cast from the thin plate glass window that provided a cold feeling despite the unusually warm conditions the day held in store. The cool gray walls adorned with simple but religious artwork seemed to grow as her eyes followed them from floor to ceiling until the small room felt more like a cave. The sensation made her feel small – young. She had felt the looks of disapproval from some members in attendance.

"Relax, Kate. This is your day, not theirs," her aunt Cathy, who was still very young herself, offered in loving advice.

"I know. I know," she sighed, glancing at the woman through the mirror. "I'm so excited!" The gorgeous young bride let a smile fill her small tanned face. Then her cheeks and the tip of her button nose blushed. She looked down, slightly embarrassed at how excited she really was, and brushed her small fingers over the dress. Despite what others thought about her marrying at the young age of fifteen, she felt perfect. The bridesmaids bustled about excitedly as they fitted themselves in yellow and lavender crepe and organza gowns.

Her mother's hands shook beneath lace gloves, attempting in vain to tie the perfect bow from the pale yellow ribbon in the hair of her other

3

daughter, Beth. The older – yet still young – mother of the bride, Leah, had a look of excitement on her face, which was that of a woman on "her" wedding day, and although Leah would not be the one ushered down the aisle to meet her groom, this really was the result of her planning – the wedding she never had.

"Thank you for letting me share in this." The words were sweet and sentimental; Leah had to look away so the mascara wouldn't trail down her cheeks.

From the decorations to the guest list, her mother had taken part in every detail. Kate's parent's marriage, an elopement, had lacked any formal luster, but had stood the test of time. Her father, the man who had swept up the beauty before her, would walk Kate down the aisle today and give her away to her own love.

Her own dress hugged her figure as she strode, head held high despite the relentless quiver in her stomach, to the full length mirror that hung lackadaisically from a thin wire and nail, tilted just enough so that her left foot was seemingly cut from the picture. The faux gold frame reflected the strange light of the room, causing her reflection to have a haloed effect and emphasizing her youthful face, which bore a natural blush that was more beautiful than even the most skilled beauticians could pull off. Russet ringlets framed it, delicately falling from the gorgeous loose bun that her aunt Cathy had lovingly and agonizingly fashioned atop her head. By anyone's standards, she was beautiful but with an air of innocence about her.

Today, Kate felt more special than she had in her entire life, a feeling that radiated from her through the fitted lace dress, a gift from a close friend – as opposed to an expensive designer model. She realized that most girls fantasized about their wedding day, planned each and every detail years before the actual day, although for her, it had never been that way. Kate had been a rough and tough tomboy, so the dream wedding fantasy that many girls shared was never foremost in her mind. Kate had always wanted to be a wife, but despite her delicate beauty, she was not the typical girlie-girl. She only cared that her loving eyes met his adoring brown eyes as she strolled down the petal-adorned aisle, and with that thought, a smile crossed her lips just as the crepe-clad duo came to stand by her – her sister, Beth, in yellow on one side, her best friend, Jane, on the other.

"You look beautiful...gorgeous," Beth said, fussing with Kate's veil. The choice of who would stand beside her on this day was a simple one. These were the girls who best understood her, who knew her secrets, who would enjoy the stories of her future as a wife.

"I love you guys!" Kate said, hugging each in turn.

"Careful, careful!" Kate's mother came running to reposition her veil, which didn't want to stay in place, again.

Together they were admired – three youthful beauties who had yet to even reach their prime, but each held a certain maturity given the situation and potential for teenage giddiness. There was an undeniable sense of elation beginning to fill the room; the three linked arms and made their way to the hall, to the over-sized doorway that led to a short opening between rows and rows of chairs that would serve as the clichéd aisle. As soon as they arrived at the entry – as if by pure magic – the piano began to play. Moments later, she was whisked away into a fairytale in which she was the princess, and the man who would soon call himself her husband was her prince.

She walked toward the man who held her heart, taking in the sight. Avery was dressed in a rented tuxedo, his black hair blending into the nape of the jacket so that the edge was nearly undetectable, and his deep chocolate eyes shown with a damp enchantment as his princess seemingly floated with a steady pace between the sea of chairs to join him. The walk to him, although technically very short – a mere thirty feet, was enough time for a girl to mature into a woman before him, and when she reached him, she felt the glow emanate from her jade green eyes, pleading that the rest of their lives be as blessed as that exact moment. Avery returned her silent promises and requests with a small nearly indiscernible grin and a squeeze of her small, but strong, hand.

Before the intimate crowd of family and a few friends, they said the sacred vows that would bind them together and begin a life unlike either of them had ever imagined. In that moment, it was the perfect union – meant to be – and as they strode hand-in-hand – Mr. and Mrs.

— past the smiles and happy tears of mothers and fathers, brothers and sisters, uncles and aunts, she felt on top of the world.

"I love you," Kate whispered to the man at her side.

"You look beautiful." Avery smiled lovingly at her.

The photos taken that day showed a too-young couple staring dreamily into one another's eyes with an immature love, but never would they accept others' claims that their love was doomed to fail. Kate felt, in that moment, that she'd spend the rest of her life breathing his every breath, celebrating his every achievement, crying his every tear, and sharing his every thought.

"All right everyone," Leah spoke loud and proud through happy tears still trailing down her face. "We will see you all at the reception."

They all convened at a small pavilion by the lake's edge. The lapping water created a soothing and rhythmic backdrop to an intimate and entertaining evening of cake and *hors d'oeuvres*, dancing and reminiscing, talking and dreaming. The gifts that had been presented to the new couple by loved ones in attendance were opened on the spot, for all to see, until terry cloth and crystal, loving sentiments on cardstock and kitchen necessities, created a small boundary between newlyweds and guests. She realized that this was not the celebration that many hoped for, but it was hers, and she adored every single second with those most important, soaking it up along with the loving glances and warm embraces of her love before heading off on their honeymoon at a charming Tiki hotel on the beach.

Kate and Avery had spent a long relaxing weekend in a suite which themed the colors jade and peach, and bamboo furniture. It faced the ocean so they were able to enjoy their breakfast on the balcony watching the sun rise and feeling the ocean breeze. They took long walks hand in hand along the shore in the evenings after dinner till the day came for them to return to their new life together as husband and wife in the mobile home they purchased prior to their wedding.

Although it had originally been her intention to remain in school and fulfill the requirements in order to earn her diploma, Kate found herself more and more often filled with the overwhelming feeling of being suffocated by these halls, by the suddenly naive actions of those around her, and by disappointment at not being able to help with their financial obligations. In the evening, sitting before him, working on the day's assignments, Kate felt as if she were indulging in child's play when compared to the actual work Avery did. As the days went on, these feelings came to dominate her so much that she began to lose interest in her schoolwork and spend more of her time caring for their home and for Avery than she did studying, completing assignments, or planning for and completing projects. She felt compelled by the world outside the brick walls, by the thoughts of living as an adult, by the dream of eventually having a baby.

2

I T TOOK VERY little in the way of suggestion on her husband's part before Kate found herself permanently disenrolled. Within a short period of time, Kate was also employed full-time at IHOP. Although not the most glamorous job, it was her first job, and she enjoyed the company of the other workers there. All day, the anticipation of receiving her first paycheck would work its way in, past the to-do lists, specials, and patrons' orders, but she fought to keep it together so as not to create any trouble for herself. Two days later, as Kate prepared to leave work, she realized that she would no longer be a "waitress in training." The thought of being a full-blown waitress, which meant tips, filled her with pride and excitement. Not only would she greet Avery tonight with the treasured paper in her hand, but they also could share in the happy knowledge that no longer would they have to survive on a single income.

Kate came home to him smelling of sticky, sweet syrup, and frying grease, and untied the long thin black strings of her apron and tossed it carelessly atop the pile of dirty laundry awaiting her arrival. Then, still dressed in her work uniform and with shirt precariously hanging half-tucked, Kate rushed to the kitchen to see Avery sitting at the table.

She came up behind him and threw her arms around his neck while unfolding that valuable piece of paper clinched in her hand.

"Look! Look! Look!" Kate bounced up and down on her toes.

"I see. I see. I see." Avery laughed, then flashed the large grin of approval that she so craved. He stood to embrace her, holding her tight as he swirled her around the kitchen only stopping to passionately kiss her.

The shift had been long, and she had left the house that morning after preparing his breakfast and packing his lunch. Nine hours later, her feet aching from the hours of trudging from one table to another, back and forth from the kitchen, balancing large trays of entrees, drinks, and yes, of course, waffles, yet giving no mind to her fatigue or any of her aches and pains, Kate cared only that she was enveloped in his arms, warm, safe, and cherished.

The setting was not romantic – a very small, very cramped kitchen that had not been cosmetically updated in many years– and Avery was not the rich and strapping prince of a young girl's fantasies, but in that moment she felt truly blessed to be exactly where she was and with the person who held her so tightly. She leaned in, and he kissed her as if it were the first day they met.

One by one their clothes began to fly across the room. Passionately kissing as they fell on top of their small bed, they wove in and out of the sheets, their bodies entangled so that neither had any clue where one ended and the other began. In that moment, their love, their happiness, their strength, was flowing through them and making them one. Together, they reached a climax unimaginable to the young woman she had been, and then fell back on the bed, drifting off in each others' arms.

Two months later, Kate was not as thrilled to walk through the front doors of the waffle house. It was 6:00 a.m., and although she should have been used to these hours, she couldn't shake her exhaustion. She hadn't been employed here long before her manager had introduced her to the early crowds, which represented a decent increase in her tip income. After all, it was a waffle house, and breakfast was, essentially, its *piece de resistance*. Nevertheless, it was becoming more difficult to build up the motivation to pull herself from bed. This day, it was especially true since she could barely keep her eyes open on the road. Her stomach churned as the scent of frying bacon and super sweet syrup hit her in the face as she entered. She had to fight the urge to pray to the porcelain goddess each time she served a tray.

3

"Honey you need to get yourself home and to bed," said the kind, slightly overweight waitress, Sonia, who had salt and pepper hair and wore large glasses. Behind the thick lenses, one could clearly see a look of concern.

"I'm just a bit tired today," Kate lied, but her pale face and black-ringed eyes gave her away.

"'Bout time to take the test," another less kind coworker said, as if invited to take part in the conversation. To the confused expression of her prey, the raspy-voiced, over-tanned woman crudely stated, "Seems you be knocked up, sweetheart," the last word slipped over the wily woman's tongue in a way reminiscent of a snake, "coming in here every morning, as if you risen from the grave." With that, the waitress turned on one foot and, in a single motion, slid an order pad into her apron, lifted a full tray of food, flipped her hair, and trotted off, very proud of her cleverness.

Meanwhile, the younger, potentially expectant, girl was frozen with an unfamiliar mix of emotions and feared she might faint where she stood. Kate leaned slightly until her fingers just touched the greasy stainless steel counter beside her, and then said under her breath, *"No I can't be. We were careful."*

Just then, the manager walked by and, seeing Kate completely devoid of color, led her through the backroom and to his office, where he immediately began dialing the phone. She saw his mouth moving, but in her current emotional state could not hear a single word of what he said. Moments later, he was ushering her out of the office.

Now his voice became audible. "…it's okay, Kate, we all get ill. Go home and get well. If you need another shift covered, give me a call and we will do what we can."

The man was gentle and warm as he led her out the front door and to her vehicle, smiling to customers all the while, providing them the assurance that someone would be with them momentarily. Kate welcomed the guidance. She was not completely sure that her mind would be able to properly lead her feet to the car without it.

"I…I need to go," Kate sputtered. He just smiled and nodded at her. Once in the parking lot and without the company of her kind superior, she was forced to regain enough sanity to navigate her vehicle away from her place of employment and to the nearby drug store.

Upon arriving at the drug store, Kate sat there fumbling with the keys, then stumbled out of the car, and somehow managed her way to the aisle that would hold the answer for her. Six dollars and a near nervous breakdown later, Kate was on her way home, happy that her husband was at work by this time, and she would have some time to come to grips with any news that may be unexpected before delivering it to him. Kate wasted no time, threw off her shoes as she walked, ripped the apron from her waist and cast it aside, then headed directly into the bathroom to assume a position that had never caused her so much anxiety before this day. Awaiting the response – though it only took a few moments – was pure torture. Kate paced, then sat, then stood and paced again, attempting all the while not to stare at the stick and wondering if the old proverb about the watched pot applied. When Kate finally had her answer, she almost wished she didn't. Her rude and intrusive coworker was entirely correct.

How am I going to tell Avery! She kept saying over and over in her head. Just then he walked through the door.

"Hi sweetie!" Kate smiled, not looking him in the eyes, walking over to hug him.

"Hi honey! What's for dinner? I'm starving!" looking around the kitchen as he hugged her.

"I haven't had a chance to start dinner yet. I need to talk to you and have been trying to figure out the right words to say this, but I guess there are none, so I will just say it. I'm pregnant..." she said as her voice trailed off at the end.

"What? Did you say you were pregnant?" Avery acted as if he didn't hear her, or didn't want to hear her.

"Yes, I'm pregnant. I just took the test, and it was positive," Kate said, not knowing whether to be happy or cry.

"How can that be? We were careful. I know you used the foam!" His eyes went wide with confusion.

"Yes I know. I don't know what happened, but apparently it didn't work." She was just as confused.

"We aren't ready for this. We're barely getting by now, and we don't have insurance." His head began to shake from side to side; then he walked up to Kate, enveloped her in his arms, and whispered in her ear, "Don't worry, Kate. We'll figure it out somehow."

Kate had always idolized her mother — the life she led, the fact that all her children loved her so. Now, it was her turn. Nearly seven months had passed since that day when she'd felt so weak, so feeble, so utterly surprised, and she'd since realized just how much she wanted this child. With every ounce of her being she craved to see the face of the baby within her, but this process had not happened without her fair share of trials and tribulations — the first of which had been the issue of money. It had taken a great deal of effort to save enough to pay the tall gray haired man, Dr. Gregory, who saw her for the first few months. He had been kind to her and gently instructed both of them on how to ensure that Kate was properly caring for herself and the baby while in her pregnant state. But his compassionate personality hadn't saved him from a malpractice suit that claimed his medical license and left her high and dry in her eighth month of pregnancy.

"What am I going to do?" The tears flooded Kate's eyes and fell like mini waterfalls, running down her cheeks, as she sobbed to her mother over the phone.

"It's all right. It's all right," Leah attempted to comfort her.

Moments later, Avery walked through the door to find her an emotional mess. He took the phone from her hand, said goodbye to his mother-in-law and hung up the receiver.

"I'll talk to my mother to see if she has any ideas. In the meantime, cheer up! We'll be in Dallas this weekend for your sister's wedding," He said, trying to take her mind off of what was ahead.

"I am happy for her, but it still hurts that she didn't ask me to stand up for her."

"Kate, you're pregnant! She was probably thinking that you wouldn't be able to," Avery tried to reassure her.

"I know, but it still hurts that she didn't even ask me." Kate tried to cheer up, knowing that she would be around her family, but the thought that she never measured up to her big sister always cut deep inside her.

4

KATE SPENT MANY nights crying on her husband's shoulder after returning from Dallas. She wasn't sure if it was her hormones, her situation with the doctor, or her feelings of inadequacy in comparison to her sister, but she couldn't find the joy that she should have had with the arrival of her first child.

At the suggestion of Avery's mother, they reached the decision to see a midwife for the delivery. Although this conclusion was not one that left Kate with much comfort, it had settled the problem, and she was reassured when Leah arrived from her new home in Illinois to stay with Kate through the delivery.

On this morning, a few weeks after Leah had arrived, Kate was awakened early to a strong gripping pain in her belly, which at first left her terrified, and then thrilled. She roused everyone else in the house and started packing items needed for the baby's arrival. Kate found herself sitting in an unfamiliar setting with the midwife and Leah, hours later, wondering why she'd been in such a hurry to wake everyone up.

The small house that they had pulled up to that day was a far cry from a hospital, and the differences only multiplied when they entered through the thick, wooden, windowless back door. The room they entered was very small and barely lit. The bed, which was the only thing that resembled any medical facility she had ever seen before, was pale blue-aqua and dressed in sheets that were white with strips of gold. The only window was obscured behind a hideous orange lace curtain, and she wondered if there was even a store that sold such an accessory anymore. At that moment, she felt a rush of nervousness and anxiety, wondering if there had been some sort of misunderstanding – was she standing in the middle of a birthing center, or an abortion clinic?

"What are we doing here? This is not a healthy place to have a child. I should be in the hospital…" Kate gasped.

"Relax, relax." Leah held Kate's hand and walked her to the bed in the center of the room. "Just lie down and relax. This woman is trained to deliver babies. It will be alright… we're here for you."

"This is not safe… this is not…" Another contraction forced her to double over, and she cried out, more out of concern for her situation than for the pain she felt. Despite her apprehension, moments later a short, round, dark haired woman entered the room. The middle-aged woman was kind and supportive and assured Kate that both she and the baby would be perfectly safe and well-cared for in that very room.

"Bienvenidos! Pees, make comfort." Through the heavy Hispanic accent, the tone with which the woman spoke made Kate feel at ease, and now, with the woman standing nearby, Kate lay half-dressed and able to time contractions closer than three minutes together.

Another round of pain came upon her, and she ripped at her mother's small hand wondering for a half second if she could break it, and then letting go of the thought when her own pain became more intense than anything that had come before. The midwife, moving past Avery, who stood at the foot of the bed, came to her when the pain had finally subsided. She took a moment to check Kate's status and gave her the go ahead – with the next contraction – to begin.

"Okay, you push now!"

Kate folded in half, terrified and filled with unbelievable pain. She screamed a guttural screech, and with each push, the pain worsened along with her level of exhaustion. Although her mother did nothing but encourage her, as the pains worsened, Kate's annoyance at Leah increased. She tried to fight the desire to scream at the very woman who had endured the very same torture while bringing her into the world, but she could not hold back her callous words and harsh demands.

"Don't touch me!" Kate screeched, violently pulling her hand from her mother's grip.

"I'm..." Leah looked down at Kate and quickly pulled her hand back. "I'm sorry."

All at once, an overwhelming feeling of remorse set in to accompany the lingering annoyance. Kate fought to make sense of the situation; to find sanity within herself, but given all that she was experiencing, she simply could not hold back that which was raging inside, and when she felt the hand of her mother once more, she recoiled, "I said, DON'T TOUCH ME!"

With each push, the baby's head was exposed momentarily, and then again it would disappear into the blackness within her. In despair, Kate cried out, "I CAN'T DO THIS!" As the words spewed from her lips, the rotund woman grew springs, jumped to the table and began pushing on her large round stomach. Kate began to feel as though she was in some savage foreign country where there were no doctors or hospitals, and people just did the best they knew how to deliver a baby. The thought of going to the hospital was becoming ever more real with each push of the crazed woman atop her, until...finally a rush of relief as both head and shoulders worked their way free of her body.

The scream that followed was both heart-wrenching and heart-warming. "Is a boy! No, is a girl!" the midwife corrected herself. Yes, after moving the umbilical cord from between the baby's legs, it was, in fact, a girl.

After the delivery, Leah stayed another week with Kate and her new baby girl before she begrudgingly headed back home. Her stomach ached, and Leah felt near tears saying goodbye to her new granddaughter.

Days later, she discovered that baby Mia was not to be the only addition to the family. Leah returned home to learn the reason for her weight gain and upset stomach was not from all the Mexican food she had enjoyed during her stay, but that she was pregnant yet again at the age of thirty-eight. Only seven months after Mia was welcomed into the world, her uncle – Kate's new brother – Justin, made his appearance.

Kate sang at the top of her lungs while swinging her ten month old daughter around, making her giggle heartily. When she sat her on the floor again, Mia made a sound that would have been incomprehensible to most, but Kate heard very clearly, "Again!" "Not yet, sweetie," Kate tossled the child's hair; "Mommy has to finish dinner first."

Kate twirled back to the pot on the stove, and the toddler clumsily followed suit behind. Together, they sang, or rather she sang, and Mia made sounds in time to the music, and Kate was happy. It was evenings like this when Kate realized that life was how it should be. When the meal was complete, she scooped Mia up once more for a second dance across the kitchen floor, which ended at a wooden high chair with a raised tray. Kate set the child in place and lowered the tray just as the song ended. Mia giggled once more, and her eyes shown with absolute happiness.

The financial situation had been growing increasingly more difficult since Mia's birth. Kate and Avery had decided it was best that she stay home to care for their child. But for this news, she was not prepared. Avery came into the room, and Kate noticed one hand held limply to his side, as if nearly defeated, but the other hand was drawn, armed, as if prepared for battle.

5

E'RE GOING TO have to move." Avery said the words so simply, so matter-of-factly, that Kate was almost inclined to walk to the bedroom and begin packing.

Instead, she muttered, "What?!"

Avery looked at her as if he were irritated that she did not just accept the statement. "We have to leave. I spoke with my sister, and she says that a friend has work for me in Houston. It's the only way."

"No. We're just reaching a good place and feeling settled here..." Kate couldn't hold back.

Avery looked down at the plate she'd just placed on the table minutes before he'd walked through the door and took a bite. He waited for her to continue, but she couldn't form any words that made sense.

This had been the only home Kate had known since leaving her parents' home. She was scared of making such a big move away from everything and everyone they knew. Her future felt unsure for the first time in her life. The good mood that had filled the air only minutes before was replaced with overwhelming uncertainty.

"Honey, it's the only way. I can't support the three of us on a mere two dollars an hour salary. We both know I can earn better wages there immediately."

In a very meek, resigned voice, Kate simply said, "When do we have to leave?"

"I'm giving two weeks' notice tomorrow," Avery said after he'd swallowed another bite of potato. "We can leave that Friday and stay with Faith and Randy until we find a place."

Kate shivered at the distressing thought that they must move seven hours away, but the fact that he wanted to be gone in two short weeks was just too much to take in. She fell into her chair and pushed the plate of food toward the center of the table. Kate sat there looking at Avery, her eyes asking if there was any other way. He returned a silent shake of his head. Avery reached out and touched her hand as a way of saying that it would all be alright, and she knew it would be, even if in that moment it was not. The three of them shared the last of the quiet nights that they would have for several weeks.

Although the initial shock had sent her into a state of uncertainty for that night and much of the next few days to follow, once Kate came to grips with the fact that they were moving, she almost welcomed the idea. The change of scenery might be good, and it would be nice to have her sister-in-law there to offer advice and guidance as they started anew. Certainly, Houston would provide them the opportunities they needed to make the life they had dreamed of for themselves, not to mention that their daughter would have the good fortune of growing up close to her cousins.

The house they pulled up to in Houston was large compared to the one they'd been living in. Faith ran out the front door and greeted them with a big smile and hugs all around.

"Hi. Hi. How are you? How was the drive?" Faith gushed.

"It wasn't bad," Avery answered for his family.

Mia, in the backseat, was squirming to get out and see her cousins who were following close behind their mother in an effort to join in the mini-celebration. After the chaos had died down a bit, the whole group moved as a congregation to the room that would serve as their quarters while living with their extended family. Though Kate had been rather nervous about the whole ordeal, she was now beginning to feel a bit more at ease, watching the children laugh and play as if they'd known each other for years.

In the weeks that followed, Kate enjoyed the company of her sister-in-law, who provided conversation and a release from some of the stresses of life. While they talked, Mia played endlessly with her cousin, Jessica, who was about the same age.

"Ahhhh...Ahhhh...Ahhh!" The screams of a child brought terror to her heart immediately. Kate and Faith rose to their feet in a hurry to reach the kitchen where the two girls had been playing. Jessica clutched a soaking wet towel in her little hand; the towel that had served as a barrier between the counter and the pot of boiling water that now saturated her little body. Jessica screamed again, followed by silence, then more screams as the hot water soaked clothes continued to burn her tender skin. Tears rolled down the young child's face. She stood frozen, not knowing what to do.

Kate stood by as Faith made quick work of removing the drenched clothing from Jessica's body, whispering words of comfort as she did so. Kate and Avery, seeing the torment on mother and daughter's faces, ushered the other children from the room, toward the glass sliding door, and outside to the backyard. Kate fought back her own feelings of helplessness, and could only watch as Randy rushed past them in a hurry to reach the phone.

"Hello, I need an ambulance at..."

Kate moved the kids farther into the backyard where they would be free to play while chaos descended inside. Through the windows, they helplessly watched the parents soothe the crying child and exchange looks of fear, panic, and possibly guilt. Kate felt awful for the couple who had been so kind to them, who had been too distracted by their presence to err on the side of caution. Tears welled behind her eyes as she saw the worried face of her sister-in-law and friend. "Come on kids,"

Kate addressed the little people at her side when the paramedics came storming into the house.

"I wanna see. I wanna see!" the cry came as the kids caught sight of the men rushing around inside.

The paramedics loaded Jessica on a stretcher and packed her down with ice; her continuing screams cut through the air, making every heart ache.

Kate and the two remaining children, along with her daughter, clung together. The small forlorn group watched Avery and Randy jump in the car and follow the speeding ambulance down the road. Kate looked down at her daughter, and in that instant realized how very fragile the child was.

The scalding water had wreaked havoc on the poor child's body, leaving severe burns on her chest, wrists, and ankles. Jessica was forced to stay in the hospital for a few weeks. During that time, Kate was happy to help around the house, take care of the child's siblings, Anna and Ross, and do all she could to ease the stress on her in-laws for the few months she was there at their home. What was once a one-sided favor was soon going both ways, and through the experience, the women formed a closer bond.

After those stressful yet cherished months, they finally found a place of their own. The small apartment at first felt cold and sterile compared to the "life" that was present everywhere in her sister-in-law's home, but slowly, bit by bit, Kate put it together and made it a home. The complex featured a pool that was soon the favorite spot of the mother-daughter duo, and most days the two of them could be found there enjoying the sun and water. This was a wonderful time for Kate, who was enjoying the special moments with her young daughter.

"Come on, sweetie. I see some chairs." Kate pointed to the vacant seating she had spotted as they were walking to the pool.

Mia tugged at Kate's hand, trying to make her move faster. Kate let the little hand fall; then set their towels out on the chairs. "Do you want to..." her heart pounded, "Mia! Stop!" In horror, she watched her two-year-old daughter run to the pool's edge and jump in without hesitation or caution.

6

"M IA!"

Mia didn't know the difference between the shallow and deep ends, and soon, Kate was running full speed after her.

At the edge of the pool, Kate quickly dove to the bottom to pull Mia to the surface. Mia choked on and coughed up the water that had filled her small lungs. Kate held her close, crying. "What were you thinking?"

The terrifying reality of what could have been passed through Kate, and she shook with fear. In that moment, she knew she had to take steps to protect her daughter so that this would never happen again. Together, the two went to the chairs.

"She's okay. Aren't you, sweetheart?" Kate tried to assure the others looking on. Then, under her breath, "I'm not sure that mommy is." Her heart was still pounding.

A few days later, Kate stepped into the pool with her daughter's hand held tightly in her grasp. She walked her out until Mia could stand with just her head above the water, and began to teach her how to swim.

It was the realization of the unbelievable bond that forms between parent and child combined with the knowledge that her husband's job was not entirely stable that caused her reaction a few weeks later. Kate didn't know whether to laugh or cry, scream or celebrate. The white pregnancy stick – once again – stared back at her. She imagined that it mocked her; asking if she needed to have a conversation regarding the birds and bees; if she had somehow forgotten, momentarily, how exactly this type of thing happened.

"I never even felt sick," Kate said aloud, as if somehow that made the pregnancy impossible. "How am I going to tell him?" She pushed a heavy hand though her hair.

Despite her overwhelming surprise, the sickness settling in the pit of her stomach, knowing that she would have to share the news with her uninsured and utterly unaware husband, there was an undeniable thrill rising in her. Mia had become the single source of joy in her life, her reason for waking in the morning, for smiling and laughing in the face of near financial defeat, and for holding on to dreams of better things to come. Another pregnancy, though unplanned, unexpected, and certain to cause serious financial strain, made Kate secretly happy. In that moment behind the bathroom door, she allowed herself a small smile.

As was expected, breaking the news that night to a man who never wanted children resulted in anything but happiness. From what she could tell, alerting a man to such things, when not expected, results in three distinct stages of realization. The first, of course, was utter disbelief.

"You're kidding me," Avery said, his eyes growing bigger, like a deer in the headlights. "You're kidding me," as if what had been said was something as foreign as an ancient language not yet translated by modern man.

"It's true." Kate assured him further by rubbing her hands over her belly.

Next was anger. This was the stage she hated – and feared – the most. Although this man she lived with, cared for, and loved was not one to raise a hand to her when angered, his eyes radiated an unspoken fury that was unlike anything she had witnessed in him before. It was also this stage that took so long to move on from. For with this news came the hate-filled words.

"What the hell, Kate? We've been using that same foam stuff you bought, right?

"Yes! Hello! You were there too."

"We cannot do this right now!" He stomped his foot down for emphasis.

She said nothing while he paced the floor.

"I don't know what we are going to do." He went to their bedroom and shut the door.

Yes, with this stage, as much as her outward stance was anything but meek, inwardly she felt every bit the child that her age suggested. Eventually – it was the case in both instances – he came out of this stage and moved into the third and final stage.

She imagined that there must be fathers-to-be who reacted differently, but as for her husband, he made a cold, hardened, "I've reached my decision," expression. He emerged from their room hours later with that look, accompanied by the words, "It's not the right time, you know, but we'll figure it out."

It was implied that the responsibility for the baby's care would be hers and would be added to those of taking care of their first child, laundry, cooking, cleaning, and – first and foremost – him.

The next morning, Avery emerged from the bathroom shaking his head. "I don't know how you expect me to pay for the medical care." He grabbed his lunch in one hand and jacket in the other. He left without another word or show of affection.

7

OF COURSE THIS was something Kate had considered, in great depth, but hearing the words out loud caused her to visibly shiver.

"I don't know either," she said to the void where he had stood seconds before.

Kate put the thought from her mind, temporarily, busied her daughter with a new toy – a gift from the girl's Great-aunt Cathy– and got to the phone, excitedly tapping the familiar number. Her mother, like herself, was filled with a wide array of emotions at Kate's current physical state, but by the end of the conversation, she'd not only provided the much needed renewal of excitement and happiness, but also eased some of the nerves revolving around the current lack of medical coverage. Leah suggested that Kate's grandmother might be able to assist. Now armed with her phone number, the still young mommy was comforted by the idea that she was still able to seek comfort from her own mother.

By the time Avery arrived that night, Kate had completely forgotten his complete lack of excitement at the news. Instead, she was filled with a renewed love for the man. It had been a long but excellent day that had left her filled with joy, which she longed to bestow upon him. After serving a delicious – and very special – dinner of homemade, cheesy lasagna, Kate was sure he would be relieved to hear the news her grandmother shared with her today. The kind woman on the other end of the phone had, at one time, been a midwife but was no longer practicing, so after having heard the news of her granddaughter's pregnancy and less-than-perfect financial status, she had immediately called in a favor.

When Kate received a return call from her grandmother that day and heard of the friend – a practicing midwife – who'd be willing to handle the delivery, she nearly fainted. Tears had rolled down her cheeks and worked their way between her lips, which formed a permanent and broad faced smile, to leave her mouth tasting sweet and salty. The relief that filled Kate overwhelmed her and radiated through her voice as she carried on a conversation with the older woman – her savior – for another half an hour.

When finished, she was left with the feeling of security that comes with being cared for by another, and moved immediately to the kitchen to begin working on dinner.

"Hi honey. How was work?" When he didn't answer, she kept talking, "I had a great day!"

Avery was surprised to be met by such warmth and kindness. Kate recognized the surprise in his face, and it made her smile before she reached up to kiss him, pulled the chair out for him, and served him the food with an excited shake in her hands. It was only once she had laid out food on Mia's plate, as well as her own, and pulled herself up to the table that she began to recount the events of the day. At the end of the conversation, Kate was met with the relief that she expected and, even though Avery didn't express the happiness she felt, she was glad that she could provide him some peace of mind.

Kate wasn't sure which she enjoyed more – the thought of seeing her new baby – or watching her daughter, who was growing like a weed, help pack the bags for their trip. Mia's small bag was overfilled with nearly every piece of clothing from her small white dresser, and all were clumsily wadded in the two-year-old's version of folding. Kate looked on, giggling to herself at Mia's antics, sharing the excitement and enthusiasm as her daughter fought to fold her own clothes and those she'd purchased for the long awaited arrival of the new baby.

"Are you excited?" She looked at her daughter, whose face became illuminated at the question.

"Yes! Yes!"

"We're going to have fun, aren't we?" Kate smiled at Mia, thinking about the two weeks that they would get to share with her grandmother.

"Yes! Fun!" Mia looked up with her big green eyes and the biggest smile on her round chubby cheeks that would melt any mother's heart.

It would make an interesting trip – a two-year-old and her nine-month pregnant mommy on a ten hour bus ride, but Kate wasn't overly concerned and looked forward to the shared experience with her daughter. She had used just a few dollars of their grocery money that week to purchase special snacks, juice, and an activity book. They could use the included crayons to color, and decorate pages with the pretty stickers. Plus, Kate had packed a small bag of Mia's favorite toys – two small dolls, a plastic bottle to feed them with, a play purse, and two storybooks. With this, they were prepared for hours of quality mommy-daughter time. They went to the kitchen to make a dinner for Avery that he could warm up when he got home from work. They each enjoyed a banana and peanut butter sandwich with a small glass of milk before Faith arrived to drive them to the bus station where they would begin their journey to Grandma's house in Dallas.

When the bus pulled up before them, they stood up from the bench where they'd sat perched in waiting; it was the most massive thing that the young child had ever seen; silver and shiny three quarters of the way down, its bottom section, however, was covered in dust from miles of travel on the road. A blue stripe ran the length of the side, containing a large, bold, logo of the transportation company. When the doors hissed open, Mia giggled with anticipation. Waiting behind a line of people to board, Kate's hand jiggled as Mia jumped up and down and excitedly jabbered in words indistinguishable. Mia, who was so wound up that she could hardly contain herself, would unlikely be sleeping for much of this trip. Good thing Strawberry Shortcake and Miss Piggy would make for good riding companions.

The tired and worn down traveling duo arrived at the Dallas bus station. Kate's back ached horribly from the long trip, and heavy bags added to an already tremendous weight around her mid-section; still she had lugged her young daughter half asleep from the bus until they were greeted by the warm, excited frenzy of helpful hands and happy smiles of her Grandmother Maggie and her Aunt Cathy. She was relieved of nearly all of the added weight as the two divvied up the load between them – her aunt quick to claim the small child.

From the bus station, it was only a short ride to the house where they'd spend the days or weeks until the baby decided to come. It was beautiful and quaint, the perfect grandma-type house. Despite Kate's weary, achy muscles, the excitement filled her all over again, and she was as spry as she ever had been when she sprang from the car with the two older women who collected her bags and Mia, and headed to the front door.

The house itself was small, but the lot seemed to go on forever. In the back, she could see fences which surrounded a number of relatively small animals, from this distance indiscernible, though she strained her eyes attempting to make them out.

"What?" Mia's face scrunched in her own attempt to see.

"Oh," sang Grandma, smiling endearingly at the child in her arms, "you've seen the goats already, have you?"

Mia nodded and smiled back.

Kate entered the house; her senses were overwhelmed, and the heightened emotional state nearly took control of her – the smell was sweet like homemade cookies; the decor was warm and inviting, and every surface seemed to welcome her, from the extreme plushness of the carpet to the Tiffany-style lamps that cast light in a variety of colors about the room.

"This is beautiful," Kate said, gently touching one of the homemade quilts laid over the backs of the sofa and chair; small figurines adorned wooden shelves throughout the room.

In the corner, by an old wooden rocking chair, was a large woven basket containing yarn in a variety of colors, a portion of which had been knit into the beginning of – what she assumed was to be a baby blanket in a rainbow of pastels.

"Thank you, dear." Grandma smiled lovingly at Kate. "You're welcome to use anything you see. Consider it your home while you're here."

Her grandmother led them quickly through the house – promising to give a better tour later – to a room set up for their stay. A four-poster bed demanded attention immediately upon entering the room. Its surface was covered with a beautiful arrangement of more homemade quilts and Afghans, which created a kaleidoscope – worthy color palette. In the corner was an antique wooden rocking chair that invited her daydreams of rocking her new baby and beside it a distressed oak dresser with brass pulls and a large tilt mirror atop it. The reflection Kate caught as she scanned the room was a happy one of three women standing close and a little girl with a look of absolute astonishment.

"We make a stunning group, don't you think?" Her grandmother's question made Kate smile.

"Yes. Yes, we do," she agreed.

The women stayed just long enough to be sure that Kate and Mia were settled in and comfortable and then adjourned to the kitchen with more promises from Maggie of a proper tour, fun, and storytelling beginning first thing the next morning. At that, Aunt Cathy said good night before shutting the door behind her to return to her home.

Her promises did not go unfulfilled. Maggie woke Kate with a light knock on the door just past seven-thirty in the morning. The long trip had obviously worn her out. Despite her expectations that excitement would lead to little sleep, this was the latest Kate had slept since well before her daughter's birth. She awoke happy and refreshed, eager to see what the day had in store for her.

She reached over to gently stroke her daughter's silky brown hair. Kate smiled down as little green eyes peeked out at her from behind lengthy lashes. For a few minutes longer, she just sat there and ran her fingers through the child's hair and hummed a lullaby. When Mia realized where they were, she jumped up with such enthusiasm that she almost fell off the bed. The two dressed to join Maggie in the kitchen.

They were met with a breakfast of homemade blueberry muffins, orange halves, and glasses of juice. Next to her plate was an empty coffee mug.

"Decaf, sweetheart?"

Kate smiled and nodded at her grandmother who had even thought to have decaffeinated coffee because of her pregnant state. This was heaven, Kate thought to herself as Mia began to tear into the muffin. Kate too tore the head off her muffin, added a dab of butter and enjoyed the first delicious bite.

After breakfast, the two were shown around the rest of the house, which was not much; it was only a small two bedroom home, but beautiful nonetheless.

"Come. Come. Let's go see the goats," Maggie gestured to the backyard.

Her grandmother's invitation caused quite a stir in Kate's little one.

"Yeah!" the cheer resounded through the room.

Along with petting and feeding the kids, Mia was thrilled to be taught how to hand milk the older animals. At first, Kate thought to use her pregnant condition as an excuse not to take part in the activity, but ultimately, she decided that it might be fun to try something new and so gave in, took a stool beside Mia, and tried her hand at the task as well. They laughed as Kate dripped some milk into the tin pail, and then Maggie showed them how it was done, and in long smooth motions managed to produce a decent amount of milk in only a moment's time.

Once they had filled the bottles with milk, they walked back to the house stopping to pick a few vegetables from the garden and enjoying the warmth of the sun.

"Would you like to go into town today, or would you rather stay here?" Maggie asked, and then added for Mia's benefit, "We could bake a couple batches of cookies."

That was the selling point, and they spent that day making homemade cookies that reminded Kate of her own childhood, and enjoying each other's company.

After twelve days of living this way, Kate had begun to feel at home, and she wished she could live her whole life right there, in the comfort of her grandmother's home. She loved to see how much Maggie enjoyed Mia and looked forward to seeing a similar reaction to her second child. However, she knew today would be different. As she woke, covered in a delicate afghan, she thought of how Avery would react to this environment. Nervous and anxious to see him, Kate rose from bed silently, careful not to wake Mia, and walked to the shower. It was still very early, and she was sure that Maggie would be in no hurry to use it.

Cathy had picked up Avery at the airport, and they arrived at Maggie's house a few hours later, just before lunch.

"Daddy!" the little girl screamed with excitement as Avery climbed from the car.

"Hi, baby!"

Both Kate and Mia ran to greet him.

"It's so good to see you." He turned to Kate. "...both of you." Avery hugged and kissed her on the cheek, then on the lips. To Kate's relief, this affection felt genuine.

Mia quickly grasped his hands, and despite his quiet protest, led him first to the goats in the back. Kate walked up as the young girl, leaning against her father, recounted the day that they'd milked the goats, laughing hysterically. Kate knew that he understood little or nothing of what the child said, but she figured he could wait to hear the story later. It was far too enjoyable to take in the image of her family standing among the small, bleating animals. Avery smiled back at her, seeming to share her thoughts.

Just shy of twenty-four hours later, Kate felt the first pang — a quiet reminder of the reason for being there. Another followed less than an hour later, making her visibly cringe and giving her away. At the urging of Avery and Cathy, Kate agreed to take a trip to the mall for shopping and walking, which might speed up the labor process. Although pain flooded her body with each contraction, stopping her in her tracks, the trip was not all bad. Cathy even made the kind gesture of buying a couple of small gifts, including a yellow lamb picked out by Mia.

"Here. Look at this! Oh, it's so precious," Cathy's voice reached an unmatched pitch as she got excited by the adorably tiny pink dress.

"Wrong color, I do believe," Avery commented and then laughed. "You should be looking at blues and greens."

"No way! It's definitely a girl. Look how she's carrying." Cathy pointed to Kate's bulging stomach.

"Oh, there are definitely enough beautiful girls already." Avery motioned to the group of women and his little girl walking with him. They all laughed.

A few hours later, back at her grandmother's house, Kate tried to hide her pain for Mia's benefit, but it was becoming increasingly impossible to do so. Squeaks and groans escaped her lips as another contraction gripped her midsection and sent her bending forward.

"AH!" the scream flew from her lips as warm liquid streamed down the inside of both legs. She ran to the bathroom, praying that none would hit the floor before her feet reached the cool linoleum. Only seconds later, Maggie knocked softly, and then handed her a bathrobe through the crack of the partially opened door.

"I'm placing a call to Daphne, dear." The voice was soft, calm and reassuring. "Don't worry about the mess. I can clean that up later. All that matters now is you and the baby."

With that, Kate heard the older woman's footsteps walk away toward the living room where the phone sat.

"I have some bad news," Maggie blurted out just as Kate was getting comfortable on the sofa.

At this announcement, Avery rose and came to be with her.

"It seems that Daphne may not be able to make it here in time." Maggie kept talking, quickly so as to avoid the terrified reaction for a few extra moments. "Another woman went into labor a few hours ago and is getting ready to deliver."

At this point, Kate felt nauseous and tears fell from her eyes. She looked to her husband, but he could offer no help. He too was horrified at the announcement.

"Don't panic, my dear." Maggie now took a different tone, one of exasperation. "If she doesn't make it, it's not as if I haven't done this sort of thing before. I'm perfectly equipped to deliver your baby."

Kate wiped her tears out of respect for this woman who'd taken her in, loved her and her child, and was prepared to care for her still in such a time of need.

Again, Maggie's voice softened, wiping Kate's head with a cool cloth. "It's okay, dear. Just think of your baby's beautiful little face looking at yours, and you'll make it through all of this with no problems."

Five hours later, the baby still enjoyed the comfort from inside Kate's womb. Kate heard a ringing in her ears and realized the sound was not within her head, but coming from the phone one room away as her grandmother rushed to answer it.

Maggie returned to the room with a look of relief. "Dear, you hang in there. Daphne is on her way. The other woman chose to go to the hospital at the last minute, so Daphne will be here soon."

Another hour passed before a very tall woman walked into the room. Her shoulder length black hair and glasses didn't immediately reflect her pleasant nature.

Kate screamed out, making the guest jump a bit before rushing to the bed to assess her situation.

"You should begin pushing now." The midwife laid a comforting, encouraging hand on Kate's leg.

Kate gave one big push and the baby's head popped out very quickly, not without pain, but the shoulders refused to budge. Kate was very near the point of defeat and cried out, "I can't do this! I want to stop. It hurts too much."

At that moment, Maggie took her hand and brushed Kate's hair away from her forehead. "You can do it, sweetie. Just one more push and your baby will be here."

The midwife, standing at the foot of the bed, was also encouraging her as Kate, completely drained of energy, muscled up one more very difficult push to give life to the most beautiful, not so little, baby boy that she had ever laid eyes on.

Finally being home with the children was a blessing. Kate found that she'd become very handy – crafting clothes for her family and cooking meals that her grandmother had lovingly shown her how to prepare during her stay. She even took the time to paint gigantic murals of Disney characters in the kids' bedrooms to bring more happiness to their lives. Everything was falling into place, and Kate was very pleased, even in the moments when life seemed chaotic. There was, however, one thing that she wished she could change about the situation – one thing that would make this life the one she'd always dreamed of.

8

THAT NIGHT, OVER a made-from-scratch meal, Kate brought the subject to her husband's attention. The children were quiet – newborn Casey asleep early and Mia busy addressing a new coloring book sent by Leah in a care package.

"I was thinking..." Kate knew she sounded tentative and wished it didn't have to be that way. "Now that things have settled down a bit, I was wondering what you'd think about me going back to school."

The last word hadn't left her mouth before Avery's face began to contort into a look she couldn't quite interpret, but she feared that it meant the worst. Her back straightened, and she began crafting her list of reasons should he decide to question her – or worse – deny her this dream.

Avery swallowed his bite of food as if he hadn't quite finished chewing, and the resulting lump was painful to choke down. "You're right." His reluctance was more than evident, but he did not waiver. "I promised your father that you'd return to school after we were married."

The excitement rising in her was too much to control. In a single motion, Kate rose from her chair and threw herself into his lap, embracing him tightly and repeatedly squealing the words, "Thank you!"

"You'll be able to keep up with this place and the kids, right?" he asked, but his tone implied that there was only one correct answer.

She nodded through tears of happiness, hugged him again, then went to hug her daughter, now looking on and obviously wondering about the emotional outpouring.

Classes started only a few weeks later. Kate had to rush around in order to get herself registered, get her class list, and purchase the correct texts in time; however, she was ready. On the first day, she arose bright and early to be sure Avery's breakfast was ready and his lunch was packed as usual, and then spent the day with the kids and cleaning the house just as on any other day. That evening though, Kate found herself rushing around with a baby on one hip and a toddler pulling the pant leg on her opposite side, she brought dinner to the table just before Avery walked in.

"Phew!" she said under her breath. It was going to work. A smile spread across her face.

Avery coughed and muttered something under his breath as well. She knew that he wasn't thrilled to be left in charge of the children that night, nor those nights to follow as she continued on with this venture, but she figured he might find that it created a stronger bond between him and his children. Kate sat to quickly eat with him before excusing herself with just enough time to drive to the location of her first class.

That is so much fun, Kate thought to herself on the way home that night, nothing like what she remembered of her past experiences. Although she'd done well in school, she'd never enjoyed a lecture like the one this evening. A good feeling enveloped her, and despite the mound of dinner dishes Avery had left for her, she rode that wave of happiness all the way to bed.

As the days moved on, she found it becoming easier to manage her time. Dinners were on the table in plenty of time, and she could even breathe between bites, rather than shoveling her food in and running out the door as on the first night. The routine was becoming second nature, and Kate loved every minute of it. She had time with her kids, and that was of the utmost importance to her, but she also had adult conversation, mental stimulation, and a sense of pride at doing something for herself.

Approximately three weeks into the program – just as the course was beginning to present a good amount of challenge for her – she awoke in the morning to find Avery already up and dressed. She checked the clock, wondering for one brief, very scary moment, if she'd slept through the alarm, but it had only rung the one time. She was not late. She gave him a quizzical look, which he obviously took as an invitation to speak.

"This isn't working." Avery fumbled with his belt.

She couldn't tell if he was actually adjusting it or simply using it as an excuse to avoid her eyes.

"This school thing is becoming a burden." He'd been complaining the last couple nights, but she hadn't taken it as anything more than him still adjusting to the change.

"What...do...you...mean?" The words were slow from her mouth. She wondered, for a second, if she was having a nightmare.

"It's not working!" Now his eyes met hers full on, and the volume of his voice jumped several notches. "I am tired of working all day and then coming home to watch the kids all night, while you traipse off to these classes."

There was a knot in the pit of her stomach that was growing by the minute. Kate felt that she might be physically ill. Yet, there was little sense in trying to argue with him. He'd clearly made up his mind about this matter, which was the reason for this planned attack while she was still half asleep.

"You're going to have to quit. Maybe you can go back when the kids get a little older." With that Avery left the room. She wondered if he cared at all how she felt about the matter. Even if he did, he had no intention of hearing it from her, or of changing his mind. And, with that, her dream world came crashing down around her.

9

I T HAD BEEN several months from that wretched day when she'd had to call the admissions office of the school – embarrassed, disappointed, and depressed – to inform them that she wouldn't be continuing with the program. Although life had gone on, it was not quite as happy and cheerful as it had been prior to her enrollment, and definitely lacked the spark of those few weeks when she'd been attending class.

The last few days had been worse still. She found that she was having difficulty doing daily chores. The children were running circles around her, and she had no desire to dress or make herself up. This morning, she woke feeling dreadful. Her body was so hot that she'd soaked the bed sheets in sweat, and when she stood, she had to quickly sit back down in order to avoid fainting. When she finally did get to the bathroom, her reflection was ghastly, and her attempt to brush her teeth resulted in five minutes of involuntarily emptying her stomach.

"Are you all right?" Kate flinched, not realizing that Avery was standing there a few feet from her.

"I'll make my lunch today," he growled. "Don't worry about it."

She sat there, hunched over the toilet for another ten minutes, working up the nerve to try walking again. Once mentally prepared, she climbed clumsily to her feet and started for the kitchen. Just inside the door of the small room, she made eye contact with Avery, then turned and ran back to her starting point.

He stopped in the bathroom again. "You look awful." The phrase was simply a statement of the obvious. His tone was cold and uncaring.

"I'm really sick. Can you stay home with me?" Kate said weakly, but before she could finish, Avery was shaking his head and offering excuses about busy workloads and deadlines to meet.

Fury intertwined with sickness in her stomach that day as she tried in vain to care for two small children between bathroom visits. All she could do, however, was to litter her bed with a few of their favorite toys and allow them to play beside her while she lay almost lifeless beside them until *brrrrrinnng...brrrrrrring...* She reached the phone just as the fourth ring blared. Head throbbing, Kate answered.

The soft voice on the other end sounded immediately concerned. It was Sandra from her church. "Are you alright, dear? You sound dreadful. Who is there to help you?"

Kate was embarrassed that her husband didn't care enough to stay with her, and answered, "I'm very ill, but Avery couldn't get out of work."

Less than half an hour later, Sandra was at the door prepared to help. Kate felt absolutely helpless and let Sandra lead her back to bed while her children were carried off to the other room to be cared for. Sandra came back in just long enough to inform her that someone would be with her each day until she got well.

By the time Avery arrived that night, she had slept for nearly four hours, interrupted only by her body's incessant need to vomit. She'd been fed warm broth, diagnosed with Asian flu, and had unintentionally opened Pandora's Box.

A few days passed with a throng of women taking pity on her in this time of need, and they continued to care for Kate and her children. Each night, when Avery arrived home, the last of the group would leave, and he'd angrily eat up whatever food they had left him for dinner. Although he made no secret of his embarrassment about the situation, it was she whose patience was being tried.

Even as she healed from the illness, took back the reins, and regained some of the weight she'd lost, resentment of Avery and his cavalier attitude grew within her. Although she continued to take care of him, the house – and, of course, their children – she found it difficult to hold a conversation with him or even be in his presence without becoming irritated for one reason or another.

Six months later, when Avery was laid off from his job, they packed to move once again, to relocate back to Brownsville, the city they'd originally settled in. Kate attempted to pack away her anger as well. She was determined to have this be a new beginning and a time to remember why she had loved this man in the first place.

10

SOME DAYS KATE wondered why her head simply did not explode. The kids were getting older now, and the construction business was slowing so much that some weeks they could barely afford the basic necessities to sustain life. Nevertheless, Avery pushed her to handle everything around the house and the care of their children, and still he managed to spend only the bare minimum of time with them.

"All I want is a little help!" she yelled at the door, which had slammed behind him.

This man who asked the world of her and gave little more than a paycheck in recent months, lifted not a finger to care for even the smallest details of his home life. This meant she was forced to run around the house collecting his dirty laundry, which was to be washed, hung out to dry, folded, ironed, and put away by her. Then, of course, she still had to clear the table after his meals, wash, dry and put away the dishes that he'd used. On the weekends, she maintained a vegetable garden, and she started to save them money, and cut the grass with the push reel mower Avery bought her to stay in shape. If not for her children, she thought, she might just go insane from the dreariness of her day to day chores. Fortunately, although a great deal of work themselves, her children were there and did things daily that made her laugh. She thought of Mia running through the house in her Wonder Woman Underoos, turning in circles shouting "Wonder Woman!" The thought made her chuckle, even as minutes before she'd wanted to cry.

Kate bent down to collect the wet towel that had been dropped where Avery had stood to dress for work half an hour before. Although she tried to be understanding of the depressed demeanor and cool tones when he spoke to her because of the stress revolving around his work, she couldn't overcome the frustration knotting in the pit of her stomach. It had started small when she'd been sick for all that time and Avery had shown no concern for her health and the safety of their children. Her frustration grew with each complaint he made about the state of the house, even though it was consistently spotless and each time he rolled over at night without even the smallest show of affection. There were very few romantic gestures made these days. The kisses at bedtime and when he left for work were basically a thing of the past, and he never showed any compassion or understanding after a hard day with the children or a night of little sleep when one of them was ill. It was as if she was expected to be his servant rather than his partner in life.

After a quick sweep of the house for the rest of the dirty laundry, she picked up Casey and made her way to the washing machine. Together with Mia, she let go of the bad thoughts and began emptying the freshly clean and damp laundry into a basket, then filled the machine again with a new load. For the time being, all was forgotten, thanks once again to small miracles. Soon, in fact, the second miracle awoke and joined them as they made their way to the clothesline to hang out the laundry.

The morning was cooler than usual, and there was a mist in the air as if it wanted to rain but couldn't quite muster the strength. Nevertheless, the fresh air was reviving for the spirits. Kate was slow to do her chores and allowed the children to play on the nearby swing set and slide before they returned indoors.

The day progressed in the same whimsical fashion, and she felt better as a result. Yet, that night, when the door swung open, she was instantaneously reminded of her level of annoyance that morning. It was too early for Avery to be home. He crashed into the room, full of fury, and proceeded directly to the phone without even so much as a glance in her direction. She strained to hear his conversation, but despite his anger, he was able to maintain composure and a very reasonable – albeit disappointing – volume with the caller on the other end.

"I have to leave." Avery said it frankly, as if he expected questions, but no argument. Before she could begin questioning him, however, he continued. "I have to go to Dallas and I cannot afford to move all of us again."

It had been only a few months since their last move, and she was relieved, in a sense, that he was not asking her to pack again.

"There's work in Dallas with my company. Not here. They've offered me the opportunity."

"But where will you stay?" She finally got a word in edgewise.

He just shrugged in response.

She knew he was concerned about the matter. They couldn't afford for him to have a place out there and maintain a house here. Kate felt a bit defeated at the news. The day of fun was over, and the real world was rushing in with full force attempting to drown her. "Let me make a call." Jane, who had stood by Kate's side a few years before on her wedding day, lived in Dallas.

Less than two weeks later, Kate found herself alone at the age of twenty-one with all the responsibilities of their home and two children. Every couple of days Avery would call, and they'd talk about what had happened since their last conversation. She couldn't shake the feeling that it was like talking to a stranger or a distant friend.

After the first few weeks, the situation grew unbearably worse. Though she strived to maintain the house the way that she once had, Avery's mother seemed to feel that it wasn't enough. When Avery did bother to call, more than once he had hung up on her when her words became flooded with tears. Then the phone calls grew further apart.

Although she had felt a level of frustration with Avery over recent months, she found that she missed him – more than she would have otherwise imagined. Each night he didn't call, she felt a twinge of anxiety. On a night when the emotions threatened to topple her, she decided to call the man she loved and missed, hoping he'd be missing her too, and the time apart would renew her spirit to get through each day and bring back the hope of being reunited with him in the very near future. She dialed the number of Jane's parents where Avery was staying. As it rang, and rang, and rang, she peered at the clock. *Is it too late to call?* The thought began to plague her. Kate imagined waking everyone in the house, and just as she was ready to place the phone back on the hook, she heard something. Returning the phone to her ear she heard, "Hello?"

"Yes, hi." Kate introduced herself and still frazzled, continued, "I apologize for the late hour. I was wondering if I could speak to my husband, briefly."

"It's no problem at all, sweetheart. We're usually up until eleven, but I hate to tell you that Avery isn't here right now."

Kate looked at the phone as if she was hearing someone else's conversation. It was ten o'clock at night, where would he be at that hour?

"Really?" Kate could hear the confusion and frustration in her own voice. Apparently, so could Jane's stepfather, Dan.

"Yes. I'm sorry." Dan hesitated a moment and then continued to speak. "It may not be my place to say anything..." Again, he paused as if weighing whether or not he really wanted to say whatever was on his mind. Though only fractions of a second passed, it caused her to feel panicked. "... but you should really get to Dallas as soon as possible."

"I can't do that, Dan. I have the kids and barely enough money to get by."

"Well, my dear, I'm afraid that if you don't, you might lose your husband."

The words stung like someone had slapped her across the face.

"I...I...I don't understand..." Her voice was shaking, but Kate didn't know whether to be mad, sad, or some other emotion.

"I hate to tell you this, but we have a friend staying here as well... she just split up with her husband. We've been letting her stay here until she gets back on her feet." His voice sounded sad, almost guilty. "Avery and Mary have been getting pretty close."

When Kate hung up the phone that night, her heart ached. While she was just hearing of the other woman, she knew in her heart that she was losing her husband, and she could do nothing about it.

Avery finally called two days later. His tone was short and cold, as it had been of late. Kate tried to engage him in talk of the children; she tried to explain how unhappy and lonely she was without him there, but he was curt and made excuses instead of returning her feelings. It hurt, but more than that, it made her angry.

"Where were you when I called the other night?"

Avery tried to play dumb, but she knew that he knew she'd called. Whenever she had called before, messages were left for him. "I called at ten o'clock that night and you weren't there."

"Oh..." His tone changed now, and Kate could hear the edge — maybe it was guilt, maybe it was anger. She couldn't tell exactly. "I needed to get out of here for a while. I just went for a drive."

"Who was with you?" In her heart, as a result of the words that were said by her friend's father, she knew.

"No one. I was by myself."

Kate shook her head, rolled her eyes and the anger filled her stomach and heart. She asked him about Mary, calling the woman by name so he would know she was onto him.

"I don't know what you're talking about!" Now his tone grew fierce and angry.

Kate didn't care. It was her who should be angry. She told him what Dan had told her on the phone when she had called that night.

"It's nothing like that. Yes, Mary flirts with me, but there is nothing more to it! How dare you accuse me!"

For a half a second she believed him, but then she remembered that he had not been home at ten in the evening in the middle of the week.

"Then why were you gone so late?"

"I already told you that!"

"Then why didn't you tell me about her before? Why didn't you tell me she was staying there too? Why were you hiding it?" She was angry. No, she was downright pissed.

"Because! I knew you would make a big deal out of nothing!" The phone clicked, and the line went dead. She held the receiver for a few minutes, just staring at it as if it held the answers she sought.

11

I T HAD BEEN several months since her husband had left them behind and only a few less since his communication with her had become unreasonable and distant. So, when her sister-in-law and best friend, Diedra, offered her a night of fun, she was hard pressed to come up with an excuse not to go. That was not to say, however, that Kate wasn't a nervous wreck about what lay ahead of her that night.

Her children were staying in the care of her good friend and neighbor, Christy, so she was not overly concerned about that. Kate knew that they would be well cared for in her absence and likely asleep in less than an hour after she left. It was purely for her own sake that she was worried. Even at twenty-one, Kate had never been to a nightclub of any kind, and here she was going as a third-wheel to one of the most popular places in town. Diedra, who was petite, busty, beautiful, and everything a man might wish for – insisted that they would be fine. She wanted Kate to meet the newest in her long line of boyfriends, and maybe share a drink or two.

Of course, none of that mattered when it came time to dress. She might not have been the highest maintenance as women go, but Kate was female, and that meant that at this moment she was in pure panic

49

over the complete lack of a wardrobe she had accumulated over the past five years. What was she supposed to wear to a nightclub? Her clothes were very modest, and her dresses were the knee length church going kind – and she didn't have the money to buy something new.

Brrrrinnnnggg…. brrrrinnnnggg… "Saved by the bell," Kate whispered, running to answer the incoming call. "Hello?"

"Are you getting ready?" It was the voice of her sister-in-law, the one who'd caused her this stress. Kate was formulating an excuse for not going when: "What? Don't tell me you're changing your mind! That's not an option," Diedra insisted.

"No, no…" Kate said, shaking her head a furious YES! "I just can't find anything to wear." Her voice sounded pathetic to her own ears, and she nervously twisted a strand of hair between her fingers. *This is ridiculous*, she thought.

"Oh, well, THAT I can deal with." And the line went dead. She looked at the phone puzzled, nervous, and then walked back to the bathroom to continue applying her makeup.

Just as she finished with the last brush of powder and was standing back to assess her work, the doorbell rang. It wasn't time for the sitter to be there; she hurried to the door, curious to see who would be standing behind it.

"All right, problem solved." The petite, but very dramatic woman pushed her way in, not waiting for an invitation. Diedra spoke hurriedly, "I brought two different outfits. You can choose, but I'm definitely thinking that the green one is going to be the better choice for your body."

Kate looked at the woman with terror in her eyes, but before she could say a word, Diedra stepped forward and held the clothes up to her. The first involved a mini skirt, and Kate immediately shrank away, making Diedra break into a fit of laughter.

"Yep, thought you might like the other one better," Diedra said, pulling out a far more desirable – yet still rather revealing outfit of skin tight jeans and a green v-neck shirt cut lower than anything she had ever worn before.

They got to the club a couple hours after the clothing debacle, and Kate was even more nervous than she'd been before they left the house. She felt exposed and wanted to be able to magically change the cut of her shirt. She thought, *What am I doing here?* She wanted to turn around, run, and never come back, but she didn't. Instead, she followed close behind Diedra as they walked through the front door where they were hit by a wall of smoke and loud music. The band was playing *Heart Break Tonight* by the Eagles, and upon hearing it, Kate felt a bit more at ease. It was the kind of music she liked. By the time they'd secured the small, round, black table in a back corner, Kate felt like she could almost fit in but eagerly welcomed the drink that was set before her.

The man who walked up to them during a break in music – the tall, dark, and handsome type, complete with a smile that seemed to ooze seduction when trained on the opposite sex – introduced himself, and bent to kiss the face of her companion before claiming the third of four seats around the table. This man, Alex, who she found intriguing, explained that he was the sound man for the band that was onstage – his brother's band.

Together, the threesome sat, drank, and listened to the music, enjoying each other's company well into the early morning hours when the club finally closed. Kate was thinking she was really happy she'd come out with Diedra, and in spite of her initial nerves, she had sincerely enjoyed herself until her thoughts were interrupted.

"Listen, I'm going to go with Alex," Diedra said with a wave to the man who'd accompanied them most of the night. "His brother, Fabian, can give you a ride home."

Kate's heart thumped madly in her chest, beating so hard she thought it might show through her shirt, which stretched tight against her. She lifted her hand and touched her chest to check. Just then Fabian joined them. Kate slowly slid her hand down to her stomach before extending it to his outstretched hand, shaking it firmly. The fact that he was very attractive only served to increase her level of anxiety.

She quickly and forcefully pulled her friend aside. "I don't think this is a good idea." She knew her eyes were wild and wondered if Diedra understood in their shared buzzed state just how serious she was about that statement. The answer quickly became clear.

"Oh, Kate, there's no need to worry." The words slipped out of Diedra's mouth as she flipped her hair, turning back to Fabian. "He's perfectly trustworthy."

Kate understood there was no sense in attempting to fight what was not perceived as a battle by the other party; she resigned herself to her fate, whatever it might be. After a brief introduction, her new escort, Fabian, said, "It looks as though I'm giving you a ride home?" With a nod yes, she reluctantly followed the complete stranger to his vehicle – pretending not to notice just how striking he truly was. He kindly led her to his car, opened the door for her, and maintained a pleasant conversation about his work as a high school teacher and nighttime gigs with the band. Meanwhile, she made repeated mental notes that she was still a married woman – even let it slip from her lips on one occasion when his hand innocently brushed her arm.

Once safely outside her home, she thanked Fabian, who had been so kind – so polite – and apologized again for the inconvenience.

He nodded, smiled, and thanked her for the company before driving away. A smile pulled at her face as she strode to the front door.

12

TWO EVENINGS AFTER her outing, she found herself in yet another heated conversation with the man she loved, the one she had married, the one who now lived hundreds of miles away, and apparently, could no longer stand to have a conversation with her. Kate thought of the happier times for a moment; she wanted to smile, but her heart was aching, and tears welled up in her eyes. She attempted to hold them back for fear that the children might notice, but her aching heart won over. They dampened her face, and soon she was sniffling and trying to quiet her own sobs.

Though she knew of his infidelity, she found herself feeling somewhat guilty as he turned the blame on her – accusing her of the very acts he had been committing for months. Kate made a mental note that the friendship with her sister-in-law had to be tempered, as Avery made reference to the man who had driven her home two nights before.

Though she was hurt and wanted nothing more than to have him there with her to feel the love of his embrace, instinctively she fought back, defending herself against his growing rage and accusations. This only served to anger him further.

"I'm done with this. I'm done calling. I'm done sending money to

a woman who's just going to use it to run around behind my back!"
With that last verbal slap, Avery slammed his phone down, cutting the
connection, and leaving her in disbelief and sobbing uncontrollably.

Hours later, after a night of no sleep, she felt calm enough to pick
up the phone again and – feeling pathetic and embarrassed – dialed her
parents' number.

Kate spent the next few weeks feeling sad, depressed, and alone, but
her parents had come through with a little extra cash so that she could,
at least, continue to provide the necessities for her children. She tried
each and every day to hide her pain from their children who didn't
deserve to be in this situation.

On Saturday, she stood in front of her television dressed in cotton
shorts and a t-shirt. In a few minutes her new favorite weekend exercise
program started. Kate had made it a goal over the past couple months
to complete a half hour workout each day, but had definitely come to
enjoy the weekend program better. She stood, excited to get started,
and to feel the effects of a good sweat – hoping that it would alleviate
some of the depression that was still filling her insides. As Kate reached
out for her first stretch, she was interrupted.

Brrrrinnnnggg… She ignored it and stretched again… *Brrrrrrinnnnggg…*
"Fine!" she screamed. The eyes of both her children followed her to
the phone.

The voice of her sister-in-law, Diedra, broke into her silence. "You'll
never guess where I am right now." The voice reminded Kate of
her husband's fury a few weeks before, and she felt herself tense up.
"Well…" The voice was now impatient and Kate snapped back to
present time.

"What?" Kate was confused.

"Guess where I am."

"I have no idea." She was slightly annoyed with Diedra for having
told Avery – even if this was his sister – that she'd been given a ride
home by another man…and in that instant, it clicked. "Oh."

"Yep. I'm at Fabian's house. I think you should talk to him. He
wants to talk to you."

Kate was about to argue that it was not a good idea. She knew it wasn't. Just look what had happened over an innocent ride home.

Diedra gave her no time to protest. "Hold on, he's going to get on the line."

Diedra giggled a sly little laugh, and the next thing Kate heard was a man's voice. It was deep and raspy, but riddled with a bit of a nervous quiver.

"Hello, sorry about that, Ms. Matchmaker in the other room gave me little choice."

Kate nodded, then realized that he couldn't see her and quickly added, "Yeah, she's an instigator…loves to do what she shouldn't." Kate felt his smile through the phone after hearing a slight chuckle, causing one to form on her own face.

Again, she found herself thinking that he was very talented at making her feel comfortable despite the awkwardness of the situation. His own nerves had passed as his voice was now smooth and pleasant to listen to. Kate felt embarrassed when she paused the conversation on more than one occasion to mother her children, who found some amusement at their mother's sudden interest in the phone. Mia was even trying to wrap herself in the cord – to emulate her own actions. This made Kate laugh, then feel slightly self-conscious, but the high school teacher apparently appreciated the mom side of her. Moments later she found herself smiling again.

"Would you like to go have a couple of drinks with us tonight?"

His question startled her but also left her feeling delighted. And having been falsely accused already, Kate decided to go for it.

13

A COUPLE HOURS LATER, she was greeting her friend, who once again had agreed to watch the children on short notice. Kate had felt a bit guilty asking, but Christy assured her that she was happy to do it. Then, seeing her laugh as the children came barreling full speed into her small frame, ecstatic to see their sitter, Kate was certain that the words weren't said with anything less than complete sincerity. She provided her friend the name and number of the place they were going before turning her attention back to Diedra, who'd arrived once again to dress and chaperone her.

The women climbed into the showy white Cadillac Eldorado and headed for the nightclub where they were to meet their male companions. Kate felt like she was living another woman's life for the evening. The thought both thrilled and terrified her. Never before had she been in this situation. Marrying and having children so young had taken this type of adventure – dating – out of the equation, but now here she was experiencing it for the second time.

Part of her was happy to be doing so, to be on her way to meet the man who'd been so kind, so genuine, and so intrigued by her on the phone. Yet another part of her felt horribly guilty and in betrayal of something sacred, something between her and another man – a man she still loved, even if he no longer returned her affection.

The place she walked into was bigger than the one they had gone to before and less bar-like. The "dance floor" was simply a small area designated by crudely laid brass floor transitions. This was a fact that no one seemed to mind, because as the night wound on, every inch of that space was covered with a mass of swaying gyrating bodies. She was fascinated by this and watched the dancers occasionally while drinking and enjoying the company of her newfound friends – one of them in particular.

Their conversations covered a wide variety of topics, and she found herself continually entertained. As the evening progressed, a division occurred at the small table, almost as if someone had magically placed a divider down the center. Before she realized it, she had the unbroken attention of a very good looking school teacher-musician, yet she wasn't nervous or anxiety ridden. She was happy, content, and willing to sit there having a conversation with him for the rest of the night.

At the end of the evening, she again found herself being escorted by Fabian to his car and away from her friend. Only, this time, she didn't fight it. She was happy to have his company for a little longer.

He climbed in beside her and smiled. His long fingers swept over hers before feeding the key into the ignition and bringing the car to life. Although the gesture was done with kindness and was not meant to imply anything further, Kate found herself wanting more of his touch. She wondered, very briefly, if it was this man or the lack of affection from any man – after not seeing her husband in months – that made her stomach do somersaults. At the thought, her face burned, and she carefully hid it from him as she turned in the direction of the passenger window, missing the sly smile that slipped across his face as he pulled out onto the road.

The drive to her place was fairly quiet. They had done the majority of their talking while at the bar and now enjoyed each other in near silence. Though she felt perfectly comfortable with this, Kate was growing more uneasy by the minute at the desire to touch him. She couldn't look him straight in the eye for fear that he would see her thoughts, so she kept her gaze slightly averted, as if taking in the lights of the city. As she contemplated these guilt-ridden thoughts, something brushed her shoulder, and she flinched; Fabian laughed. Then Kate laughed, realizing it had been his hand.

Now outside her apartment, she felt saddened that the evening was drawing to an end. Fabian studied her for just a moment, then before she had time to decide how to react, he leaned into her and they shared a kiss – her first kiss with a man other than her husband.

14

ER LIFE WAS not going the way she had planned. Several weeks and
many fights with her husband had passed since that night with
Fabian and the shared kiss. Kate knew she wasn't ready to be with
someone new but would never forget the warm feelings that came with
being with someone who actually found her attractive, interesting, and
worthy of his attention. She had spoken with Fabian on a few occasions
since then, and agreed to call him when she was available. But Kate
knew he would eventually be taken and would have long forgotten the
naïve girl who had bummed a couple of rides home.

She thought of what it might be like to be with Fabian. She'd spent
many a day and night coming to grips with the inevitable, which was
something she'd hoped to avoid. In the midst of her tears, she continued
laying folded clothing into bags and boxes.

It was time to go home, back to mom and dad, and face the fact
that her husband was not likely to return. It was strange, though, that
going home meant going somewhere she'd never actually lived. She
was moving to New Orleans, her parents' new place of residence, and
she felt out of place just thinking about it.

Her parents, though very kind throughout the ordeal, were beyond disappointed regarding the situation. They'd entrusted their "too young" daughter to a man who was now deserting not only her, but their children as well. Kate came to them a broken soul, constantly hiding her pain and trying to hold back the tears to protect her babies who were fortunate enough to be too young to fully understand the circumstances. Mia and Casey knew only that they were able to spend time playing with their four-year-old uncle, Justin, and a grandma and grandpa who liked to spoil them rotten, but also made their mommy feel sad. It wasn't her parents, of course, that caused her tears, but talking to them about the events would rehash the feelings of hurt, neglect and disappointment, and she would inevitably cry each and every time. Thus, it made sense that her daughter might think that it was her parents who caused her sadness.

One evening, after the children had fallen asleep in front of the television – Justin stretched across the sofa, Casey in her arms, Mia in her mother's – she saw her father, Brad, sneak away to the kitchen. He was gone for quite awhile when she heard his voice speaking in hushed, but very harsh tones. Assuming that he was speaking with Avery, and not sure what to do, she sat frozen to the spot, cradling her baby boy, drawing more comfort from him than he could possibly be getting from her in that moment. Her father never returned to the living room that night. Kate and her mother took the kids to their bed, and she crept away to her own – not that she would be able to get much sleep.

The next morning, Kate sat there staring at her father in utter disbelief. What he said as he dismissed himself without waiting for response left both Kate and her mother in silent shock. She wasn't really sure if she should be angry or thankful, insulted or relieved, but it did make her wonder if she had stepped into a time machine to an era when men arranged the lives of women with little or no concern as to how they might feel about it?

She could not make any sense of what was going on. The man who had wanted nothing to do with her – short of the occasional session of guilt or shouting match via phone – for countless weeks and months was now on his way to her parents' home. Avery was coming with the expectation that she would be packed and prepared to leave with him. Annoyed at his arrogance, she wondered if there was really any hope for reconciliation. Yes, she loved the man, but she also now hated him for everything he'd put her and their kids through, and he just assumed she'd willingly jump at his offer to settle their differences. She wondered how the other woman must be feeling. Kate went for a short walk to collect her thoughts before preparing for her trip – she had to go – she knew that despite her annoyance at how it had all been handled; it seemed she had no choice – it had been decided for her as though she were still a helpless child.

It took her hours – maybe even an entire day – to calm down enough to think rationally. Once at that point, however, Kate realized how much she really wanted this – the opportunity to go back to her grandmother's house to live where they'd felt so much love before. Perhaps there was still a chance for them? After all, she still loved him and could still be the dutiful wife and mother, so long as he was willing to say goodbye to Mary, and move them back with him – permanently.

Avery's mood when he entered the room was one of fake kindness. Kate felt the tension as soon as he entered through the door, though she stood across the room. His smile at her was forced and filled with a silent animosity which revealed his frustration and embarrassment about the situation. He did, however, seem genuinely happy to envelope Mia and Casey in a warm embrace, and for that she felt happy – and a small bit of hope.

She understood that he would be embarrassed, as was she when she first turned to her parents for help. It was not pleasant to admit that he had failed, and certainly he didn't like the idea that others thought him a failure as a husband and father as well. Kate's understanding nature allowed her to show him sincere compassion as they worked together to load bags and kids into the white pickup truck, which sat in the driveway waiting to carry them hundreds of miles away.

She hugged her mother tightly before getting in the vehicle herself. She really did want to go with him and try again, but she was sad to leave her mother, her confidant, her saving grace in this time of need. Kate wiped the tears from her eyes but not before her mother caught sight of them and reached out to give a squeeze to her arm as encouragement. As she turned to climb into the front seat, she caught sight of another exchange – slightly heated – between her father and Avery, and for a millisecond, she wondered what consequences would be in store for her this time.

15

THE RIDE WAS long and quiet, but still Kate felt herself energized as they neared their destination. It was strange to think how close she felt to her grandmother, a woman she'd spent very little time with as a teenager. It was more than that, though. This place held memories of happy times – the last that she really remembered sharing with her family, as a whole, and she hoped to rebuild, forgive, and forget. Kate knew that it would not be easy to do so, given all that had happened since the last time they were here.

It had been well over a year since they had pulled into this driveway, but at the sight of the house, the fence, and the speckled field, her daughter's memory went to work.

"Goats!" At the single word from Mia's small mouth, Kate laughed loudly, the sound filling the car and setting the children into a hyper state.

The day after their arrival, she made a delicious meal with the help of Maggie, which even included desert. The day had flown by; Kate was kept busy unpacking clothing and toys, getting the kids acquainted, and then perusing ingredients at the store that would work for the upcoming meals. After all the chaos, she was really looking forward to this time with her family – including the man she had not seen in months – and carefully arranged each plate until the presentation was perfect. When the table was set, complete with four seats and a highchair, she happily called in the troops.

As everyone sat to eat, her grandmother raised a glass, "To new beginnings."

The statement, followed by clinking glasses, made her smile inside and out. When she looked over to see her husband, Kate quickly discovered that he didn't share the same sentiments. Hiding his eyes, Avery ate his meal without saying more than was absolutely necessary, despite attempts by both her and Maggie to draw him into conversation. His mood hadn't changed since the car ride. If she couldn't get him to talk, there was no hope. At that realization, she found that her food did not taste as good as it had when she'd been preparing it, and the joy within her was getting lost behind a growing feeling of anguish.

Kate climbed into bed beside Avery not knowing what to expect of the night. Avery took her in his arms for a little while before drifting off to sleep.

After a restful night next to him, she woke with a renewed hope. They were to visit her friend Jane and her parents whom Kate had not seen in some time. She quickly got ready and checked to see that Avery was doing the same. She tried to feel that familiar spark when she caught sight of him changing, but was saddened to know that much of it had disappeared as a result of all she had gone through in recent months. She hung her head for a moment and sincerely hoped that the time with friends would bring them to some common ground.

When they arrived, Jane came running to greet her with a hug. Kate felt like a kid again in the embrace of her long-time friend. Though she had wondered if there would be some strangeness between them as a result of her husband's actions, none was present. Jane walked her into the kitchen where she was preparing some snacks; Avery was ushered in the opposite direction toward a television tuned to the "big game".

After a few moments of reminiscing, another woman joined them. With thin features, long dark hair, and dark eyes, she strode assertively toward them and worked her way into the ongoing conversation. Though she seemed sweet enough, there was something about the woman that simply did not sit well with Kate, and she instantly felt uncomfortable. A look from Jane told her all she needed to know.

Thoughts swirled in her head of her husband talking, laughing, and more with the woman. "I want to go," she whispered to Avery when they were alone in the corner of the room.

He just looked at her with an odd expression.

"I want to go. I feel uncomfortable here. She…" Kate was careful to motion in the woman's direction without making it obvious to the others in the room, "there is just something about her that rubs me the wrong way. She seems insincere, and I don't want to be around her."

His reaction frightened her. He stood, turned to her, and in a hushed but harsh voice scolded her. "You don't know Mary and cannot judge her. She is a very nice person with a good heart."

Had it been any other person, perhaps Kate would have not thought anything of his protest, but now she was sure that something was awry. She gave Avery a dirty look that said, *I know that I do not trust her, and I am pretty certain I know why.*

"I'm not judging her. I just don't want to be here with you and her together. Take me to my grandmother's house." Her request was no longer up for debate; she demanded, "I want to go…NOW!"

On the ride back, Avery looked angrily straight ahead at the road in front of him and said nothing.

As soon as they were safely in the driveway, she could no longer hold back. "You were with her! Weren't you?!"

Avery immediately sprang to a defensive stance, but still he said nothing. He glared at her, daring her to say anything more.

Kate defied him, "You had sex with her! And then you take me there to meet her?! Why?! What's wrong with you? Why would you do that?"

Avery still said nothing. He hopped back in the car, gunned the engine and sped away missing her by inches on his way out.

She couldn't control the tremors in her body as she sobbed. Her finger punched the ten digits, and soon she heard the familiar voice. Kate couldn't bring herself to act calm. Rather than saying hello, she immediately started crying again. "Mom!" The word was barely understandable through her tears. "Mom, I want to come back home..."

"Why? What happened?"

Then Leah was quiet and listened as Kate explained the situation. "...we haven't been intimate. We slept in the same bed, but that was it..." After a few breaths and a useless attempt to quell the tears, she continued, "...and now I find out that it's true...his reaction to my dislike of Mary said it all...and he drove off and left me here." Kate knew that she sounded weak and small, like a child, but her heart was breaking into a million pieces, and she needed the comfort of her mother.

Her mother's sympathy was very apparent, but still Leah tried to encourage her daughter not to give up entirely. "Just talk to him. Ask him what he wants, what he expects of you and your relationship. It may be the only way to get the answers you're seeking."

"I don't understand why he would come and get me and the kids if he didn't really want to make our marriage...our family work," she said with defeat in her voice.

When Kate hung up with her mother that night, she still felt depressed, but stronger. Upon Avery's return, it was obvious that he didn't want to be there with her. Finally, she had found the courage to address the matter with him, but she almost wished that she'd left the topic alone. She now had Pandora's Box wide open, and as fabled, there was no closing the lid.

Kate and Avery went outside to talk away from the children so they would not hear the screaming match that would inevitably follow. It was unlike any argument they'd had before. It was filled with animosity, hurt feelings, and a rampage of accusations – the only emotion not present...love.

The next day, as Kate's sobbing continued in the privacy of the small guest room of her grandmother's house, she heard small voices playing in the living room; she heard Maggie placing a call, and she heard her husband agreeing. She was going back to her parents' home; her marriage was over, and Kate felt she was the only one who didn't have a say in it. She had no way of financially supporting their kids, and she was being pawned off on whoever would take them.

Two days later, Avery drove her and the kids to the airport. Emotions were high, but they'd managed to be civil with each other. Kate checked her bags and was headed toward the gate when Avery stopped her.

"I...I just want to say how truly sorry I am for the way things have gone since your arrival," he said with a sad look of hopelessness. "I'm having trouble saying goodbye. I'll miss you and the kids. I..."

"I know. This is not how it was supposed to be...but we'll be fine," she said without conviction.

"I got you something you said you'd always wanted." Avery pulled a box from his pocket, and choked on his words, "I know it doesn't make up for any of the hurt I caused, but I thought I could at least give you something nice."

She opened the box and saw the pearl necklace. Her eyes welled up with tears. "Why? Why would you do this?" The loud speaker announced that her flight was boarding. "I...I have to go." Closing the box was like closing the door on Avery and the life they shared. Unsure she had done the right thing, Kate put it in her bag, grabbed the children's hands, and walked away, not looking back.

16

ACK IN HER parent's home, time passed, and the hurt lessened. After a few months, Kate had to return to Brownsville to collect the remainder of her belongings, and her mother agreed to come along. They had packed her things and visited with friends for a few days. After arriving at the airport for their return flight, and checking their bags, they stood near the gate that would lead them back to New Orleans where she'd start a new life with her children as a single mother.

Kate heard her name and turned to see a small man. His hair had receded until it reached the point of a thin line around the base of his head and over his ears. Even that was thinning. Dressed in a drab gray suit with a faded maroon tie, he looked unhappy to be standing there.

"Yes, I'm Kate. Can I help you?"

He handed her a large yellow envelope. "You've been served. A decree of divorce was filed with the court and is enclosed in this envelope. Please sign stating that you're in receipt of the documents."

Kate stood bewildered as the small man patiently waited for her to open the envelope, look at the papers, and sign the acknowledgement. She scribbled her signature in disbelief, then watched the man disappear into the crowd.

She lowered her eyes back to the papers in her hand, staring at them for a moment, when the tears began to run down her cheeks. She was amazed that there were any tears left after everything she had been through. Again she heard her name. Though scared to do so, she looked up and saw the last person she ever expected to see.

"I'm sorry." Avery's face was full of regret. Hers registered shock and awe. "Maybe we can work it out in time." He attempted a smile and reached to touch her face, but she moved away from him. "Go with your parents, stay single, and take care of the kids. I'll call you and we'll talk."

She glared at him. "Are you kidding me?" She wanted to tell him to go to hell. She wanted to punch him. She wanted to make him hurt like she did. "You just served me with divorce papers! There's no turning back now! JUST LEAVE!" She dropped into the airport chair as if the words had used every ounce of remaining energy. He walked away, and out of her life.

Not long after that day, she was forced to return to Brownsville yet again for the divorce hearing. Avery, who had never wanted children, was bringing a custody battle into the mix as well, forcing her parents and children to come along.

Anger burned in her soul as the man, who'd promised to love her forever, and stood in the airport asking her to work it out, was now standing before a judge swearing her to be an unfit mother.

Behind her, she heard the whispering voice of her mother. It held a rage that she'd seldom seen in all her years of life. "I have to get out of here..."

She couldn't hear the rest, but knew that it amounted to her mother cursing the man to whom she had entrusted her daughter and had once welcomed into her family.

Kate and Avery were called out by the judge in a highly meaningful manner. Her attention was snapped back. "Please join me in my chambers."

One of the bailiffs came out and escorted them to the back. She felt now like she wasn't only facing one of the most wretched times of her life, but was also being treated as if she were a criminal.

Once within the small room and away from the eyes of onlookers, the judge looked them both in the eyes. "I need to know before we proceed, if you truthfully feel that this marriage is over. Are you certain that you cannot work it out between yourselves?" He looked to her first.

"Your Honor, I have tried. I have tried everything. I even went to Dallas with him to work it out. My husband and family mean everything to me." She swallowed hard. "He hasn't even tried, and I don't feel there's any hope left."

Avery was standing there like an impatient child waiting to speak when the judge turned to him and repeated the question once more. His words rushed out in a flurry of hatred and anger.

"You've tried? Ha! I sent you money. I took care of you. I went and picked you up from your parents. What have you done? You..." His onslaught was about to continue when the judge interrupted him.

"We are done here. I am granting the divorce."

The bailiff returned to the small room and escorted her and the man she had once loved back to the courtroom. The child custody portion of the proceedings continued and immediately she knew that what was ugly...was about to turn repulsive. Accusations were spit like tiny balls of wet paper in the classroom. Fingers were pointed at each and every member of both families. The words were not only ridiculous, but hurtful, and would last well beyond this trial. Stories of his brother, who suffered from mental illness, were brought up, and though she knew it was necessary to play her part in this exposing war for the protection of her children, a part of her felt troubled for saying anything. Her brother-in-law, Scott, who was younger than Avery, had battled schizophrenia for years. Shortly after they had married, they'd received word that he had gotten worked up and stabbed his other brother Charles.

When, at last, the day was done, Kate finally received the news she'd been wishing for. The judge had granted her full custody of Mia and Casey. Her parents and her children were by her side as they left the courtroom, but her mother turned back when she heard the voices of Avery and his mother behind them. Her father was tugging at her mother's arm, but she turned to address him. "You! You should be ashamed of what you put your family through today."

Avery's eyes were stone cold and still full of the fury that had been present in the courtroom. Nothing more was said, but she knew she'd never be able to see that man in the same light again. Kate left Brownsville once again, but this time the life that she'd known was permanently left behind as well.

She'd arrived with her children in a new state, her education incomplete, and she was jobless. Without her parents she would have been lost, so each day, despite arguments about the direction she should take, she thanked her lucky stars for the man and woman who had raised her, still loved her, and were willing to be there in this time of need. In return, she vowed to do her best to make a path for herself, one that they could be proud of. Contrary to her mother's urging that she should be looking for another man to marry and take care of her, Kate tested for and received her G.E.D. She set forth to further her education, determined never to be put in this situation again, to never have to be dependent on anyone to take care of her, to never have to turn to her parents again for their help.

Going to college meant having to rise at six o'clock each morning, prepare Mia for school, help with the cleaning, then head to school for six full hours. It also meant coming home in the evening and spending a little quality time with her children before sitting down to complete homework assignments and study for exams.

Within two months, she'd conquered the schedule and was ready to take on more. The new part-time job, which involved tracking inventory at several local stores after business hours, would relieve some guilt and financial burden from staying with her parents since child support was so minuscule. Kate would now be able to help with the expenses. Regardless of her feelings of accomplishment, it also meant that she'd now have to leave her children a second time – in the evening – to go to work until midnight.

About six months into the new schedule, she awoke to a hand tugging her nightshirt. Kate reached down to touch the arm of her moaning little boy and realized immediately that he was far too warm

– hot. The feeling of drowsiness that had been very present was now gone. She scooped Casey up and rushed to the bathroom to find the thermometer.

"Mom, Mom..." She tapped Leah's arm trying to rouse her. When the eyes of her mother finally flickered open, Kate breathed deeply. "I have to take him to the hospital."

Casey was lying limp in her arms, but groaning in discomfort. Her mother was quick to her feet, and soon the three were out the door leaving her father, Mia, and little brother Justin home. The drive seemed horribly long as she watched the glassy eyed boy fuss in his car seat.

"Go ahead, take him in. I'll park the car and be right behind you." Her mother looked nervous, which made Kate's own heartbeat race. She carried Casey through the doors and met a nurse at the front desk. Kate was much younger than the thin blonde haired woman in blue scrubs who sat and droned on, asking question after question about her son. As patiently as she could manage, Kate hurried to answer each question, explaining that she'd given him ibuprofen earlier for the fever. Kate and Casey were finally escorted to a room where she felt heartbroken seeing her baby on a gurney being pushed down the hall by hospital staff. Kate hurried her pace so that she could hold Casey's hand as they walked. *Click...click...click...*the wheel on the gurney was all that could be heard as they continued down the long hallway.

Two nurses helped to make Casey comfortable. He looked like a small doll in the all-white hospital bed that out-sized him by a large margin. Dr. Stevenson came in to assess his condition. Kate tried not to get emotional when they stuck him with an IV, took his temperature along with his other vitals. Alone with her son and Leah, who had found her way to the room, Kate sat with a large sigh grasping Casey's hand, careful not to disrupt the IV that was taped there. They had assured her that his temperature was at 102 degrees and that with a bit of fluid – the drip of the IV – he would be fine. Half an hour later, another nurse, short, thin and in pink scrubs, entered the room carrying a large basket of containers, syringes, and tape. Kate cringed, knowing that Casey, who had screamed so at the IV being inserted wouldn't handle the thought of more needles well. Her concerns mellowed when the nurse simply attached a tube to the end of his IV and through that was able to get the blood needed for the tests they intended to run.

"All right, little guy," the nurse said gently, "I'm out of here. You get some rest."

Casey smiled up at her meekly. His cheeks were flushed, and his eyes were glassy, but still he recognized the kindness she'd shown. Kate swallowed hard to keep her emotions at bay. The nurse had no sooner closed the door behind her when a technician walked in. Before saying a word, he took the chart from the foot of the boy's bed and read it as if some critically acclaimed novel.

"Hello there…Casey," he addressed the boy by name and explained that they needed to take pictures of his insides to make sure he was healthy. Then, raising the rails on each side of the bed, he used his foot to release the break underneath and began to move it toward the door to take him upstairs to the imaging area. Kate was thankful that they allowed her to join him in the large, cold room as they took the X-rays they needed.

"How's it look?" Kate asked the technician.

"I am not allowed to say, but Dr. Stevenson will be looking at them very soon and will get back to you with the results as quickly as possible."

Although annoyed at his response, her practical side insisted that the answer made sense from a liability standpoint. She accompanied a lethargic Casey back to the room where Leah was waiting.

Casey was no sooner settled in bed when the nurse returned with a thermometer once again. "101 degrees…good."

The words were a comfort to Kate as she sat in the chair, rather exhausted. She looked up at the small, simple clock hanging on the beige wall just outside the room.

"Mom, you should probably head home. Dad will be getting up soon to leave for work, and Mia and Justin will also be up wanting breakfast before leaving to school for the day."

Her mother agreed, and soon she and Casey were left alone together. "I love you sweetie," she whispered before kissing his head and returning to her seat. For a long time, she just sat there staring at the wall, exhausted, but too worked up to fall asleep.

At last, stiff from sitting so still, Kate stood, paced the room a couple times, then came back to check on Casey, who was sleeping. She reached down to recover his little body with the blanket, but something was not right. He was too warm. It had only been a short while since the nurse had taken his temperature, but she was sure it had skyrocketed again.

She pushed the red button to call the nurse, and when prompted spoke her concerns. "I think his temperature has gone up quite a bit." As she said this, the boy moved and groaned without fully waking. "Please..." she could hear the fear in her own voice, "I think you should take it again."

A few minutes later, the nurse strode in. She checked the drip but had no thermometer in her hand. Kate looked at the nurse with confusion.

"His temperature was just taken..." the nurse explained, "he was at 101, which was lower than when he was admitted. The IV should help to stabilize it."

Kate felt frustration and anger flowing through her veins. "It should be, maybe, but it's not. He feels much warmer."

The nurse shrugged, then touched his head and immediately went to go get the thermometer. As if by flipping a switch, as soon as the nurse removed the thermometer from the child's ear, he began to convulse.

Scared to the core, Kate reached for his hand and yelled, "Do something! Call the doctor!"

The nurse tried to soothe her but also admitted out loud that Kate had been right in her instincts. Casey's temperature had reached 104 degrees. Acting quickly, the nurse paged one of her coworkers to bring ice packs and upped his medication via the drip.

Casey was screaming under the cold of the ice. Kate did her best to calm him until his body temperature had dropped to a reasonable point and the nurse removed the ice packs. As soon as the medication took effect, he finally stopped shivering and slept peacefully once again.

"Hi, it's me." She was nervous to be talking to Avery, and the thought that it would have once been the source of her comfort only further upset her. Kate's voice shook as she spoke. "I wanted to let you know that our son is in the hospital. He's running a very high fever. They're trying to figure out why."

His tone was harsh and cold in response. "I knew you weren't taking good care of him. You should've been..."

Kate didn't wait to hear the rest and interrupted him, "I will keep you updated." She'd done her part by telling him, and now she had to protect herself by hanging up.

It wasn't until three days later, when she'd reached a point of mental and physical exhaustion she wasn't sure she would ever recover from, that Casey was finally well enough to go home. Though Kate was glad to have him well once more, she was angry that with all the technology and equipment at their disposal, the doctors were unable to determine a cause.

Before he was released to go home, Dr. Stevenson pulled her aside. "I thought it best to tell you that all signs pointed to malaria. His spleen was enlarged on the images, and given the high fever, it seemed to be the culprit, but the tests came back negative." Her forehead crinkled with a look of confusion; she nodded, unsure of what to say in that moment. "Be sure to bring him back if the fever returns."

Without wasting any time, Kate reached for the phone in her mother's kitchen, dialed the number, and spoke fast, not allowing Avery time to respond. She said her piece and hung up before he could say a word. "... he is home and doing well. I will let you know if anything changes."

Her hand still clutching the dead receiver, Kate shook her head knowing that Avery never even called back to check in or to speak with his son to see how he was doing. She sighed heavily and returned to the room where Casey lay watching a cartoon and drinking some juice. She kissed him on the head and hoped with all her might that he'd never scare her like that again.

A few months passed and life returned to its normal pace. Kate smiled as she continued to work, thinking about all she had accomplished, moving on with her life even though her muscles ached, and she was beginning to feel the exhaustion setting in from the schedule she was keeping.

Her boss ambled over to her. Paul was a pleasant looking, kind man, but more than a few years older than her. Still, she enjoyed speaking with him and had come to look forward to their interactions over the past few days. Paul smiled, reflecting hers, which now grew a bit in intensity. Kate, suddenly nervous, pushed her hair behind her ear. Tonight though, his mannerisms had a different way about them. He was a bit shaky when he handed her inventory sheets, and his eyes gleamed in a way she hadn't noticed before.

"Um…" Paul started to say something and then stopped, turning away. Kate looked at him quizzically, waiting for him to continue.

"Uh…" Paul started again, and then finding his words, seemed to thrust them out so he didn't have to carry the burden of them any longer, "I was wondering if you'd go out with me this weekend?"

Her smile returned again, but was accompanied by a reddening of her cheeks.

"I'd love to," she said. "but I need to see if my mom will watch the kids for me first, and let you know."

17

H ER PARENTS WERE not overly supportive of her new relationship. Paul was twenty years her senior, and her boss, but Kate continued to date him. He took her to fancy restaurants, making her feel special and worthy of the foreign environment. In fact, she enjoyed him so much that it lessened the blow that came with the news that her ex-husband had remarried – a mere eight months after their divorce was finalized. He called asking to see his children. Avery's work schedule did not allow him to leave for a long enough time to come to visit them in the eight months since their divorce. He offered to pay for her to bring the children back to Texas for a visit with him and his new family.

Kate agreed and took a short break from work, school, and the growing bond between herself and her boss.

The trip to Texas which would bring her face-to-face with Avery was not one that she looked forward to, but she knew she could handle it. Kate had done a lot since he had so callously excused himself from her life that she felt he might perceive her differently – perhaps even realize how very badly he had short-changed her – and that made her feel confident. His new wife, on the other hand, was a source of much stress as Kate led her children to his door.

In the face of initial discomfort, the trip went well – the only real difficulty was the repeated calls from her new male companion. With each ensuing conversation, Paul's tone was becoming harsher, more heartfelt; her failure to answer every one of his calls brought up accusations of being with another man, and her disappointment more real.

Kate was saddened by the path their communications had taken while away. As soon as her children were settled at her mother's home once again, she went to Paul's house to talk. He opened the door as she was just about to knock. Kate could see his face was awash with anger.

"Why didn't you answer my calls or return my messages?"

"I wanted to wait till you were calm…" she began.

"You were with someone else…weren't you?" His eyes became wild and glassy.

"No, there was no…" Before she could finish… *Wham!* His hand landed so hard across her face that it knocked her into the wall. *Wham!* She felt the sting to her face, and again her head hit the wall, but this time she fell to the floor. Before regaining her composure, Kate began to feel a similarly painful and burning sensation in her abdomen, then to her back and next her legs.

"You whore! Do you think I was here alone waiting for you? HA!"

Her mind was unable to comprehend what was taking place, just that she needed to get away from the barrage of angry kicks. She rolled out of his way and climbed to her feet. Her body screamed in agony as she ran from his fury, out the door, through the hall, down the stairs and to the door of a neighbor she had met only a couple of times. Desperately, she knocked, screamed for help, and fell in the door as it was opened for her.

When Paul found her, his knocking on the door was so hard it shook the shelves and pictures in the home of her kind savior, who yelled to him that the police were on their way. Of course, given her absolute embarrassment at the situation, Kate wouldn't allow such a thing to happen and instead placed a call to her brother.

When she caught sight of her brother arriving, she quickly hobbled out the back door and rushed, sobbing into his arms. Ronnie held her only for a brief second before protectively escorting her to her small car, which she drove on a quick path back to her parents' home with her brother in tow.

Kate suddenly felt small and childlike again, confused and unable to protect herself. She trusted another man — this man, and he hurt her. Though her face, head, back, and legs throbbed, there were very few visible signs of what had occurred that day. Rather than bear the sight of her parents' pity and disapproval, she snuck in the door and to her room without seeing them.

The next day she sat, mentally bruised and battered, in front of her parents and told them of her newest plans. No longer could she drag her kids through the torment of her rebuilding her life and put them through the financial burden. After what had happened, she felt so naïve, and not mature or experienced enough to make the best decisions to be the mother she wished to be — so she was going to send them to live with their father for a while. She'd seen the way he was living, met the woman who had stolen him away, and knew that, although he had disappointed her, Avery was in a more stable position at the moment to provide for her children. Even as she said the words to her parents, they were meant to convince her. Kate's heart was breaking yet again, and though this decision left her feeling even worse than the separation and divorce, she knew it was the only way she'd be able to get her life in order — without placing any further burden on her parents — while providing Mia and Casey a safe and happy home.

While she was still convinced she was doing this in the best interests of her children, she moved to the phone and made the call. She held it together just long enough to make the arrangements, then broke down and sobbed again — something she had done far too often over the past few years, only this time it was more devastating.

The day that her ex-husband came to get the children was the most difficult she would ever face. She couldn't watch him walking away with the only source of happiness he'd ever provided her. Kate hugged her children, kissed them, told them she would come to get them soon, and then she walked out to her car. Kate chose not be there that day. She couldn't bear to see him take her children, not knowing when she would see them again. She thought back on the day when she'd held such high hopes for them, the day she'd looked into Avery's eyes and heard him utter the words that had meant so much to her then – but had fallen short since – "I do."

18

EVERY MORNING THE reflection that stared back at her from the mirror was too drawn, too pale, and too old to be that of a twenty-two year old. The late nights of worry combined with the agony of missing her children were weighing heavily on her, both mentally and physically. Kate had decided shortly after their departure that she needed to get away from her parents' house as well. A call to her former sister-in-law and still good friend, Diedra, back in Brownsville, had given Kate the courage to pack everything that would fit in the small sedan, which wasn't much since Avery had kept everything they owned for his new bride.

She was ready to head back to the city where she had last known happiness. The thirteen hour drive had provided her time to focus on the goals at hand. She needed to find an apartment, find a job, and create a life that would allow her to provide a loving and safe environment for her children.

Now that she had her own apartment, Kate felt proud that she was starting her life on her own without the help of her parents or a husband. It was a quaint one bedroom, which was starting to feel more like a home once she found some affordable furniture to fill it – many garage sales later.

It was now time to find a job, which was her reason for being up so bright and early. She had three interviews scheduled for that day and felt good that she might be employed before week's end.

Kate dressed in a knee-length, blue pinstriped skirt and a white button-down blouse, and headed out the door to her first interview. It was a restaurant. She had done this before – soon after her wedding – and felt she could easily do it again.

When Kate arrived, she straightened herself, checked her appearance once more in the side mirror, and strode confidently toward the double glass doors that served as the main entrance. The hostess wanted to know how many were in her party and nervously Kate giggled. "No, I'm here for an interview."

The girl sputtered something in Spanish that Kate didn't understand and was off, apparently to find whoever was in charge of interviews that day.

"Hello." The man's voice was deep, but when she looked up at him she was taken aback. The voice did not match the description at all. He was not any older than her and nearly as petite. In fact, she thought, his arms might be smaller than her own. Smiling in return, she shook the man's hand and was led to a small corner table to begin her interview.

The feelings of confidence that had followed her through the door were now backing their way out, abandoning her.

"We need someone who is fluent in Spanish. We serve a large Spanish-speaking crowd. Even some of our employees in the back cannot speak English well. You would never be able to do the job sufficiently." He stood with a frown.

Kate could see that this was her only drawback as far as he was concerned, yet it was a huge one. She too stood and thought at least she had two other interviews.

When she arrived home that evening, she was feeling lower than low. The day had resulted in one denial after another and all for the same reason; knowing she wasn't going to be able to learn another language overnight, Kate felt downright defeated and sick. Even though it was not anywhere near bedtime, she sank beneath the covers and hid from the world wondering how she could be living in the United States and not be able to find a job without speaking Spanish.

Kate awoke the next morning, feeling ghastly. Her mouth was dry her head pounded, and she felt seconds away from losing the contents of her stomach. Kate stumbled to the kitchen, made some coffee, and swallowed some ibuprofen. She sat down at the table with the newspaper sprawled across the top. After a few minutes of scouring the job ads, she began to feel slightly more human; she rose to find her pen and began circling some positions that sounded worthwhile.

It took another week and a half of searching when she showed up at the mall for an interview wearing a very respectable pair of black dress pants and a short sleeve beige blouse she'd borrowed from Diedra. Regardless of how many store managers had turned her down, she knew that she was qualified for this position. *How hard could it be?* Kate thought as she strode right up to the man who seemed to be in charge of the Hallmark Gift Shop, maintaining complete composure.

Kate extended her hand to the short rotund man. His hand felt almost swollen as she shook it and his breath stunk of stale booze. She wondered how it was that men like this could get ahead in life, while she was forced to struggle so. She introduced herself and told him that she was here for the interview. He just smirked, pointed to the back of the store, and muttered something in Spanish. Hairs stood on the back of her neck as she tried to calm the feelings of anxiety and frustration rising within her.

A girl behind the register, a few years younger than herself, having overheard the conversation, pulled Kate aside explaining that she had introduced herself to the wrong man.

"You don't want to cross paths with that idiot drunk. I'll go tell the manager you're here." She turned and walked to the back of the store.

A few moments later another gentleman strode through the racks of the gift shop with a piece of paper in his hand, stopping once to pick up a stray magazine that had slipped from its designated spot. He replaced it and continued toward Kate as if he knew exactly who she was. He looked down at what apparently was her resume, called her by name, and then shook her hand. He was a relatively attractive man and several years her senior. Gray hair had started lightly filling in around his temples. His eyes were a deep brown – almost black – and they shone each time the fluorescent lighting hit them. He wore a navy blue suit with a yellow and white stripped tie, which made her feel underdressed, but his mannerisms were kind, gentle, and welcoming. He escorted her to a table in the nearby food court and began asking her the typical interview questions.

It only took a few moments for him to get to the question she dreaded the most: "Puedes hablar español?"

Although she couldn't speak Spanish, she knew the term well and shook her head from side to side. Seeing the familiar look of disappointment and fearing that she may never find employment at this rate, she quickly snapped to her own defense.

"I know, I know. I understand that you would like to hire someone who speaks Spanish and that I'll be at a disadvantage, but I can assure you that if you give me a chance, you'll not be disappointed." She paused only long enough to catch her breath. "I'm a hard worker and I need this job. I'm honest and trustworthy. I'll be here on time and do the job that needs to be done the way it should be done, and I'll learn the Spanish I need to know to assist your customers."

At her words, a small smile lifted one corner of his mouth. "I might regret this, but I believe you can do the job. You can start on Monday. Be here at 9:00 AM."

Kate was so thrilled she felt like jumping, cheering, and hugging the man, but somehow she managed to keep her composure. She smiled, thanked him, vigorously shook his hand, and again assured him he would not regret it.

19

IT WAS ALMOST Christmastime, and she was falling right into place with her new job. Her days were filled with stocking shelves, waiting on customers, gift wrapping and demonstrating how some of the gifts operated for people as they came into the store. She actually had fun, like a child, playing with and demonstrating the toys. She was finding it easier to speak with people and for the first time in her life was not what others would describe as a "shy person".

Selena, who had saved her from the booze-riddled man who first greeted her, was fast becoming a friend at work. They'd giggle and joke each time this same guy would hobble his way into the store – which was just about every day.

They also shared stories about their lives. She told Selena some of the horror stories that had been her lot in recent years, and confided how badly she missed her children. In return, Selena would tell her about problems at home with her mother. A stern mother was something Kate could relate to, having come from a very strict and religious home herself. Kate offered guidance and support to the girl, happy she was the one to give it this time.

One night after work, Kate was sitting in her small apartment, and there was a light knock on the door. As she went to answer it, a second knock much harder and faster made her jump. Kate, suddenly nervous, peered through the glass peep hole to see a young girl with long dark hair staring back. When she opened the door, Selena rushed through the opening and in a dash explained that the late arrival was related to another, more harsh argument with her mother.

"Can I please stay here?" the small voice pleaded, and Kate felt sorry for the girl who now seemed even younger. "I can't go back there. Not now."

Kate understood what it was like to be distraught after an argument and have no place to go, so she took Selena in.

Kate actually enjoyed the company. They watched TV, ate popcorn, and just chilled in much the same way she'd done with her children many nights in the past. Selena quelled the ache for them a bit, so Kate sat back and enjoyed the conversation.

The next morning, Kate sat over her coffee – her guest was still asleep on the couch – when the phone rang. Not accustomed to early morning calls, it startled Kate. She shot out of her seat and sprinted to the phone, then realized that the situation didn't really call for such measures. "Hello?" She answered, a bit more relaxed.

"Do you know where my daughter is?" The words were spat at her, and Kate was happy that the phone was there to separate her and the caller. It took her a minute to make sense of the statement, and then she realized that the woman on the other end was obviously Selena's mother.

"Yes, ma'am. She stayed here last night. She came over rather late and was upset."

"Well…" Now the voice was completely hostile. She could almost feel it reaching through the phone to strangle her, "you better get her home or else I'm calling the police. She is under eighteen and you're harboring a runaway."

20

WHY? WHY ME? I'M A good person and only trying to help out a friend, Kate thought, shaking the girl awake.

"Ma'am...please don't do that. I could have turned Selena away and left her to be out on the streets, but I took your daughter in 'cause she needed a place to stay."

"I'm sorry! Thank you for taking her in, but she needs to come home immediately."

After a few moments, her guest was awake, the mother was calmed, and the two were discussing their problems over her telephone. At least Kate could breathe knowing she could enjoy the remainder of her day off now that she wasn't going to have to deal with the police.

When Selena handed her the phone back, Kate looked at her quizzically. "Mom wants to talk to you." And then the girl was off to the bathroom.

"Hello?"

"Hi." The tone that greeted her this time was much more kind. "I just wanted to apologize for how I reacted before. I was very upset and concerned about my daughter."

Kate could understand that. She thanked the woman for her apology and agreed to bring Selena home. After that, she intended to sit in her small apartment and enjoy the quiet. She needed it.

The next day at work had been rather uncomfortable, but by lunch time Kate had decided to make peace with the situation and inquired about how it had gone with her young friend's mother. After sharing a bit of the story, Selena promised never to put her in that kind of awkward situation again, and their friendship was restored. Kate felt good that at least one of the relationships in her life was so easily shifted back on course.

Today, however, was Sunday, and she was not going to be in any hurry to talk with anyone – or for that matter do anything, except relax and drink a cup of coffee with the morning sun peering in on her while reading the newspaper. After a few minutes though, she spotted something in the Help Wanted ads that made her sit up. It had been months since she'd lost her initial hope of finding a fulfilling position that could lead to a wonderful career and the opportunity to create the life she'd always dreamed of.

Kate had been called a tomboy many times in her youth; she considered herself to be rather tough and resilient, especially for being such a petite woman, and there was no doubt she was as stubborn and driven as any man, but was that enough to make it as a *firefighter?* She sat, studying the text for several moments and contemplating what it would mean for someone like herself. Then, momentarily embarrassed for considering something so out of the ordinary, she quickly moved on to the next page and continued scouring the ads. None of it was sticking, and after reading the same sentence for the third time, she flipped back to reread the advertisement. It stated the job was open to women and minority applicants. She thought for a moment and then flipped the page yet again to another article, then back once more before setting the paper down and heading for the shower.

That small section of newspaper tormented her for the rest of the day. Kate pictured herself making the money she needed to bring her children back home with her; and this position would allow her to not only provide for them but to spend more time together. She also considered the positive feelings that must come with rescuing a small child or elderly person from a burning building. Then she tried to imagine herself carrying a huge coiled hose over her shoulder and attempting to swing an axe to break down the door of a burning building. Back and forth her mind went for hours that day, and well into the next.

The entire next week was no better. Kate found herself mentioning the advertisement to her young friend at work, and pondering it during each lull in her work shift, at bedtime, and first thing each morning. Finally, when the mental anguish of thinking so hard and long about one topic began to truly eat at her, she contacted the office of the Civil Service Director to speak in more depth about what the job would entail. The man Kate spoke with told her that she seemed to be an ideal candidate to take the exam, and that it would determine whether or not she would be considered for a position.

Though at the end of the conversation she was no surer that she was physically prepared for something so intense, Kate found herself thinking of it as more of a possibility and less of a daydream. Two days later, she drove over to the building where the office was located, climbed the concrete stairs, and made her way to the office of the director to put her name on the list of test takers. She was the two hundred-eighteenth person on the list and there were still a few days left for sign ups. Her hopes were not high.

Kate visibly shook as she arrived at the convention center a week later, to find hundreds of other people there for the same reason. After standing around for a half hour, a tall stout man announced that the exam would have to be given in two shifts due to the large number of applicants. He announced that everyone with last names starting with letters between A and M would take the exam first.

Kate felt butterflies in her stomach realizing she would be in the first group. She got in the line to enter the building; thinking her nervous fidgeting might show her to be weak, she struggled to get her nerves in check as she took in her surroundings. The room was large, and the walls stretched far above her. The concrete floor echoed her steps as she strode to the check-in table. It was not a desk, but one in a series of informal folding banquet tables. At each table was an officer with a list of signees registered by a number for each test booklet, and overhead were large posters displaying intervals of the alphabet meant to direct people by last name.

Kate found her table and soon it was her turn to speak with the man seated before her. He was very young – she found herself wondering if he had even finished high school yet – but he was ruggedly built beneath his navy blue issued uniform.

"Hi! My name is Kate Matthews," she said, looking directly into his eyes.

"Hello Kate. Please select a seat at one of the tables directly behind you. Make sure you read through the instructions before the test begins, but do not open the test booklet." His voice was profoundly baritone – in a much rehearsed manner – probably because she was far from the first to enter the room.

The formal atmosphere was doing nothing to slow the rapid beating of her heart. It pounded in her ears and her footsteps echoed once more as Kate made her way to a seat two rows deep into the sea of tables.

Though she attempted to read the instructions provided to her, Kate couldn't concentrate on her task as more and more applicants filled the tables around her. The room was packed – every seat taken – as an amplified voice filled the air.

"Welcome. We'd like to thank each of you for your interest in becoming a firefighter and wish you the best of luck today. Exam sheets are now being handed out. Please remove all belongings from the table, except for your number two pencil. Please leave the written portion face down until instructed to begin. Thank you." With that the older gentleman who had introduced himself as a company officer, ran a hand through his silver and black hair, whispered something to one of the other men present, and walked from the room.

With the back of the testing papers staring at her, Kate's palms began to get moist, and she could feel goose bumps line her arms. Yet, as soon as she was instructed to begin and was able to flip the paper, her nervousness was replaced with a ticking clock, and Kate could think only of the questions and her answers.

PART 2

FLICKERING FLAMES

"A small spark neglected has often kindled a mighty conflagration."
Quintus Curtius

21

ONE WEEK LATER, Kate nervously climbed from her car, up concrete steps and through large, heavy wooden doors. As Kate grew closer to her intended destination, a knot was forming in her stomach and a thin layer of moisture at her brow. On the wall was a gold engraved plaque: "Civil Service Director" with an arrow pointing down a long corridor. Kate had followed this same path before, yet felt as if she were completely lost. She obeyed the sign and came to a growing mass of people, huddled around a single sheet of paper, clumsily taped to the wall. Kate tried to be patient, waiting for one after another before her. She couldn't help but notice that very few walked away looking pleased. In fact, out of the twenty or thirty people before her, Kate had only seen two or three who appeared to have received a passing grade. Anxiety gripped at her as she got closer and closer.

Once Kate reached the front of the line, she took the single step and peered at the paper. Although a short note at the top of the paper mentioned that there were 300 test takers and less than ten percent of those passed the exam, Kate apprehensively scanned the sheet for her test number. There it was, next to the number two hundred sixteen. Kate followed a line straight across to the other side of the paper, where she saw a single word… "Passed".

She wanted to jump and let out a cheer, but for fear of hurting the feelings of those around her, Kate held the emotion in. Then the true weight of the outcome sank in. Fearing that her legs would soon give out beneath her, Kate strode quickly to her car where she sat and began to comprehend what she had just seen – smiling broadly, giggling nervously, and shaking her head in disbelief. She was actually on the list – a list of "eligible to-be-hired" for the fire department. Kate was thrilled to not only have passed the test, but to have done so well amongst so many taking the exam. Her hands were shaking on the steering wheel; she felt a nervous wreck at the mere thought of what this could mean for her. Kate started her vehicle, and headed home to share the news.

The phone call from the fire department's Human Resources did not immediately come, as Kate had hoped it would, and a couple weeks later, she found herself filling out yet another job application. This time, Kate was led past a front desk and several exam rooms to a cozy office in the back. The room was very masculine in design, with two upholstered burgundy arm chairs facing a large mahogany desk complete with a high back leather seat. Kate found herself calmer than she had been in interviews of the past. The older gentleman who walked in was dressed in charcoal slacks and a light blue button-down shirt under a white lab coat embroidered with his name, Bob Kendall, followed by the initials "D.D.S." Dr. Kendall's hair was short and dark, but streaks of grey at the temples and the small lines about his eyes gave away his age. Dr. Kendall was very kind and pleasant to listen to, and she imagined that the patients he saw enjoyed the stories he might tell.

The interview went well and her lack of a second language did not seem to be a cause of concern for Dr. Kendall. As soon as the last word slipped from his tongue, "The position is yours if you want it?" Kate agreed to take the receptionist position. She left the office on cloud nine; pride welling at the fact that Dr. Kendall felt the trust to take a chance with her.

Time went by quickly working in the office. Although it had been difficult to master at first, due to her lack of experience and Spanish-speaking capabilities, Kate enjoyed the people she worked with and didn't mind the long hours. One of the Latina women, Melinda, who worked there, had taken her under a wing, providing guidance when it was needed and friendly conversation on breaks. About a month into her position, Melinda invited Kate to join her on a double date, of sorts.

"My boyfriend's brother, Drake, is very handsome. He's single, and has agreed to let me fix him up for the upcoming family *Quinceañera*." The grin that adorned Melinda's face was filled with a mix of pride for recognizing that the two would likely "hit it off" and self-consciousness at the thought that Kate might say no. Kate happily agreed to attend the Mexican celebration, and although she liked the idea of getting out and meeting new people, Kate felt a bit strange since she had not even met the young girl being honored. It might be nice, Kate thought, to have a day out with others near her own age, but her pulse raced each time she contemplated going on a date with a man she hadn't yet met.

Unlike her outings of the past, this time Kate used what little extra cash she had to buy an outfit that suited her tastes, and also her figure. The skirt and top were light-weight and airy so they moved with her as she walked. They promised to further enhance her moves should she dare take to the dance floor that evening. Kate felt beautiful readying herself for the day's events, and smiled genuinely at the reflection of herself in the mirror applying a light coat of lipstick.

The man who awaited Kate, in the backseat of the four-door sedan, which pulled up in front of her building, was just as he'd been described. Drake was average height and adorable. His hair was jet black and shined like silk in the sun. His eyes were so dark in color they almost appeared entirely black at first glance, and his demeanor resonated warmth and kindness as he climbed out of the car to greet her and assist her with the car door. Kate held a bit of hope for the evening to come.

The ride to the large hall, where the family celebration was to be held was filled with conversation and laughter. Kate felt an instant connection with the rest of the foursome and was perfectly at ease to be herself.

Upon exiting the vehicle, they were hit with the intense Texas heat, and Kate was grateful she had chosen to wear something so lightweight.

Once inside, Kate met many people, all of whom were thoroughly enjoying the affair. In fact, it took her nearly an hour to figure out who the honored girl was because of the level of commotion and excitement in the room. Drake was kind and gentle as he introduced her to people and translated for her when some spoke in Spanish. Kate liked his company, the feel of his hand on her lower back, and the way Drake smiled at her when she told him stories of her life and children. Kate felt so at ease with Drake that she was not as reluctant as she normally would have been when his father dragged her to the dance floor to participate in a traditional Cumbia dance.

22

THE EVENING TURNED to night far too quickly and Kate was sad to climb back into the vehicle headed for her apartment. At least Kate had the few extra minutes of his hand on hers, discreetly, as they sat side-by-side and took part in the four-way conversation.

The man Kate had met that day had made her happy like she had not been in many years, and Kate agreed to continue seeing him. Even after four months of dating, each time Drake arrived to pick her up, Kate would feel her insides flutter with excitement.

Today Kate was going to be alone until Drake got off work. She intended to tidy up the apartment and take full advantage of her rare time off, while daydreaming of what the evening would have in store. For the first two hours of the morning, that's just what Kate did, until the sound of the doorbell sent her sky high. She laughed at herself for being so jumpy, and then moved to the door to welcome her visitor.

Kate looked out at a man dressed in a casual suit and tie that she didn't recognize, but he knew exactly who she was and addressed her by name, while someone else – a woman – walked up beside him.

"Yes, I'm Kate," she said. "Can I help you?"

"I believe so. I'm here from the City Personnel Office. I'd like a few minutes of your time if you wouldn't mind."

Her mind raced as she realized what this might mean. "Please come in."

Kate stood back and let the man and woman into her apartment, nervously scanning it to be sure it was presentable. It always was, but for some reason Kate felt self-conscious. "Oh here...have a seat." The words left her mouth rapidly when Kate realized she'd been caught up in her own thoughts for an indeterminate amount of time and had yet to offer them a place to sit. It had been eight months since Kate had passed the exam, and she'd put the thought out of her mind, and now, in her living room, stood officials from the city discussing the possibility as if it lay just around the next corner. Could it be that what was once a far off dream was becoming a reality?

"Ma'am, I assume you know why we are here?"

Kate nodded in acknowledgement.

"There is another opening in the fire department, and you are next on the list to fill it."

She sat speechless.

"I'm here to speak with you because you need to fully understand the ramifications of your decision should you choose to accept the position. You will be the first woman to join the fire department. This means that you'll not only work with all men, some of whom may not be overjoyed at the change, but you'll also be plunged immediately into the limelight. As soon as the information is released, the media will want your story."

Kate looked at the man attempting to process what he was saying. She didn't know whether to giggle because this would mean much more money, and the chance to make a good life for herself – or to be nervous about the decision that was being placed in her lap. Not only would Kate be facing a highly dangerous, physically demanding job that would require her to stay overnight with a room full of men, but now they were telling her that she would be doing it – for better or worse – under the scrutiny eye of the media. If Kate failed, everyone would know about it.

The two officials seemed to be attempting to offer some guidance and support as they filled her in on the rest of the details. Before leaving, they told her to give it some serious consideration before reaching a decision.

Although she went through the act of weighing her options, Kate knew deep down that this could be her way of getting her children back. She sat, dumbfounded, for quite some time before she thought to seek out the advice of loved ones.

23

THERE WAS REALLY no decision to be made. This non-decision was the first step in capturing the life that Kate longed for, a job that provided benefits, a better paycheck, and time with her children.

Kate was the biggest mess, emotionally, that she had ever been on her first day, while getting ready, excited then nervous, anxious then nauseous – a rollercoaster of mental states. Kate was thankful that no one was there to see her off in the morning. She climbed into her car and steadied her hands by white-knuckling the wheel.

When Kate arrived downtown at Central Fire Station, she saw two news vans, each equipped with cameras and a reporter, and nearby stood a small group of rookies, all male, who looked just as nervous. Kate climbed out of her car, quickly realizing that the chaos was because of her. She was approached by not one but both reporters and the associated cameramen followed close behind.

Kate could barely think straight as one reporter informed her that she was about to be interviewed for a front page article in the Brownsville newspaper. Kate had never faced anything like this before and had certainly never been asked to answer questions about her life for the general public to read. Yet, somehow, Kate pulled herself together and spoke calmly with the tall, thin, and gorgeous man who addressed her.

"Where will you sleep?" the man said with a grin on his face and then added, "How do you feel about staying overnight with so many men?"

The questions seemed too personal, too intimate, and far too much to handle given her already shaken state, but somehow Kate managed to skirt those she wished not to answer and gave decent responses to those that were acceptable. Within minutes, the chaos had died down along with some of her nerves. It was almost a blessing in disguise as Kate entered the fire house for the first time with a feeling of confidence that wouldn't have been there had she not tackled the reporter's barrage of nosy questions.

Once the media had left, Kate and the other rookies were driven around to the various stations and introduced to the men on duty by Training Officer Garrett – a tall man, very well built for his age, gruff in tone, and a huge nose. Most of the firefighters greeted them in a pleasant manner. There were those few who made jokes indicating they were not accepting of Kate's intrusion into their world.

"When are you cutting your hair?" a short man with a disgruntled look on his face called out. He appeared as though about to pop out of his uniform as he spoke up from behind the kitchen counter.

"That's enough, Joe!" T.O. Garrett glared at the man.

On the return to the Central Fire Station, Kate and the rookies were introduced to and shown how to don and connect an SCBA (self-contained breathing apparatus). T.O. Garrett showed them the SCBA refilling station and how to use it. Although the day was not physically demanding, it was very eventful and mentally taxing. Kate was excited her new career. Her work schedule would be five days a week from 8:00 a.m. to 5:00 p.m. while training; and after training was complete, Kate would be assigned to shift work where she would pull twenty-four hours on duty and have forty-eight hours off.

For training, Kate and the other rookies reported to Central Fire Station. She arrived the next morning greeted by a new crew of firefighters. Most were curious to meet Kate, while others voiced their opinions concerning her capabilities with snide comments when Kate was given temporary turnout gear which included a coat, pants, boots and a helmet.

"You need to go to Tots and Teens to order your turnout gear. You're drowning in that coat," Dan, a large guy with black hair and big bushy eyebrows said as she tried on the coat. The rest of the men broke out laughing.

Kate felt uncomfortable, but she laughed along with them to appear that his words didn't shake her. Then she gave it right back to him, "Did you go to the Jolly Green Giant store to get yours?" The men laughed again as Dan stood there with a dumbfounded look on his face.

"Alright, that's enough. Let's make Kate and the other recruits welcome." T. O. Garrett shook his head as he led them to the front of the garage. "Let's go. We're driving out to Station Seven."

Kate and the other recruits rode along to Fire Station Seven; they studied the manuals on the equipment. After more hours of study, they had lunch and then back to even more studying before they were picked up and returned to the main station. They continued with this schedule while familiarizing themselves with the various fire stations for the remainder of the week.

Friday had finally arrived, and Kate looked forward to spending it with her new beau. Kate hadn't seen Drake much since accepting the position. The whirlwind had swallowed her up whole, and she had been entirely too busy during the day, exhausted at night.

This was a special occasion, one that had been discussed between her and Melinda for weeks, and Kate was excited to share it with Drake. It was another family outing, only this time it was a picnic and barbecue, much like her first date with him, yet on a smaller scale. It was going to be held at the house of one of Drake's friends. Kate had met Rob and his new wife several times and truly enjoyed their company. Along with the original foursome from their first date, there were to be three other young couples joining them. The hosting couple had a nice pool, so everyone brought a bathing suit and looked forward to a wet and wild afternoon.

Drake pulled up in front of her apartment in his brother's car fifteen minutes early. Kate watched at the window – wanting him to come in while she finished getting ready – as Drake climbed out of the vehicle holding a single rose. A smile pulled at her lips and Kate rushed back to the bathroom, so as not to get caught spying on him.

Drake came right in – she knew he would and had left the door unlocked for that reason – and walked right to the bathroom, knowing that Kate would still be primping. Drake kissed Kate on the cheek, handed her the rose, and told her again how very proud he was of her career. From that moment and throughout the rest of the day, Kate glowed with the light of someone who was truly loved and accepted.

Though Kate's private life was taking a peaceful, easy stride for the first time in years, her professional life was in the very bumpy stages. There were eight weeks of training to endure; some were spent in the classroom, and the rest demanded true physical endurance in the field.

Kate received extra attention because she was a woman, and she was constantly made to prove herself capable of the position. During one of her training classes, the instructor doubtfully asked, "Do you really think you're capable of extricating someone from a fire?"

"Yes I could, and I would find a way not only using my strength, but my intellect." Kate straightened up in her seat.

"Okay! Harry why don't you come up and help Kate demonstrate to all of us that she's capable of carrying you out of a building." The instructor pointed at the larger than average sized man sitting two rows over.

"I have to see this! You can't lift me," Harry said sarcastically, rising from his seat.

Kate threw on her turnout coat that had been draped over her seat, walked up to and turned her back to Harry. "Give me your arms..." she firmly grasped his biceps over her shoulders and slowly leaned forward lifting Harry onto her back. "Relax!" Kate ordered, and walked across the room with Harry, eyes bulging wide, on her back. The rest of the men burst into laughter at the sight of what could only be compared to an ant carrying a huge bread crumb on its back.

Kate lowered Harry to the floor releasing his arms, turned to the instructor. "Now I will show you what I'd do if he was unconscious."

"Okay! Go for it!" He sat there in amazement.

Kate looked directly at Harry. "Lay on the floor as if you are out cold." After Harry complied, she whipped off her turnout coat and threw it on the floor next to him. Kate kneeled next to Harry and rolled him onto the coat. She stood, grabbed the collar of the turnout coat, and dragged him across the room. Everyone, including the instructor, laughed, followed by loud clapping.

"I guess you showed us all!" the instructor stood as he continued clapping.

"Like I said, it's not all about being physical, but also using your brain." Kate stood tall, feeling she had won them over, though she wasn't so sure about Harry, who continued to wear a wounded puppy expression.

"This is what training is all about…being prepared and knowing what to do when a situation arises. Well done, Kate! Now let's get back to the lesson so we can finish on time," the instructor directed the class, looking over at Kate with amazement and a smile.

Kate forced herself to pay close attention to every single second of every lecture – no matter how dry a speaker may have been – and would follow that up with hours of study at home, to ensure she understood each and every term, technical procedure, every piece of equipment, and what they were used for.

In the field, Kate made an effort to work harder than the other recruits she trained alongside. Kate carried her fair share of the weight when practicing with multiple sizes of charged hoses, working quickly and methodically when attaching or removing nozzles.

The next morning, Kate and the other recruits reported to Central Station where T.O. Garrett informed them they would continue their training in Harlingen for the rest of the week. It was a thirty minute drive to the training field where they would get their experience along with other recruits from surrounding towns.

They would learn rappelling at the training tower today. Upon arrival, Kate was introduced to some of the other recruits, and the other training officer, Robles. Kate donned her turnout gear and climbed the four flights of stairs in the tower along with a few other recruits. Although a little winded, Kate showed no fear – despite what she might have been feeling as she stepped out on the ledge. She regained her courage, looking down at the men below who she knew were waiting for her to fail. *I will show them I can do this. I can do this!* Kate took her first jump, held tight to the rope, then her next jump, then another until she landed on the ground below.

"Way to go, Kate!" someone yelled from the group, peering out the window waiting their turn.

Kate stood unhooking the ropes, looked up and shouted back, "Piece of cake!" with a smile on her face. Once everyone took their turn, a few of the recruits from other cities, who had joined them, wanted to take pictures with Kate. She felt honored that they'd asked and stood proudly beside them.

That night, Kate went home to massage and ice her sore and bruised muscles, tape blisters, and soak her aching feet. Yet, the next morning, she awoke with a determination to be nothing short of great. Kate would not be defeated after working so hard to make something of herself; she would see it through, no matter what it took.

The following day, Kate reported again for the long ride to Harlingen where they would learn to operate the Jaws of Life. Kate was a bit intimidated by the day's tasks. The equipment was very heavy and quite large and bulky to handle. They arrived at the training field where she saw a group of men surrounding a wrecked car. Kate and the other recruits suited up in their turnout gear, put on their gloves and helmets, and joined the group around the car.

The instructor explained how to set up and connect the jaws and then demonstrated how to properly insert the jaws to separate the door from the vehicle. He looked around at the group locked his eyes on Kate, and smiled. She immediately felt a knot in the pit of her stomach. *Don't pick me...please don't pick me...*rushed through her head. Just as she tried to casually look away...

"Kate...why don't you come and show the group how it's done?" T.O. Robles raised his voice so all could hear.

"Sure...alright," Kate squeaked out and moved closer to the vehicle trying to exude confidence.

T.O. Robles moved to the side and handed off the Jaws of Life to Kate. As she grabbed hold, she realized just how heavy it was, but tried to act like it wasn't.

"Okay....place the jaws here in the door jam by the hinge to get the best angle," T.O. Robles instructed.

"Okay!" Kate replied, positioning the jaws.

"Now push down on this lever..." pointing at the trigger on the jaws, "and push it down slowly to open the jaws, separating the door from the body of the car."

"Okay....do I have it lifted high enough?" Kate tried to keep her voice even as she struggled with the weight of the equipment.

"Yes. You're doing fine. Go ahead and start." The instructor stepped back.

Kate pushed the trigger and the jaws began to open pushing against the metal, making a loud crunching noise. Kate felt the burn in her arms, holding the massive piece of equipment while it forced the door from the vehicle. *My arms feel like they are going to be ripped off. No... think positive! I can do this!*

The door popped from its hinges, throwing Kate off balance, but she quickly recovered. She felt proud she'd stood her ground and did what was asked of her. Kate had deftly moved the jaws to the other hinge when she felt a tap on her shoulder.

"Uh...Kate?" T.O. Robles said. "Okay...great job! Let's let someone else give it a try."

"Sure!" Kate released the trigger and handed it back to him.

Kate stood studying while each rookie took their shot at working with the jaws. When they finished up, they disbanded for lunch. Some went home, while Kate and her group went to eat at the local sandwich shop. They all met back after lunch for the water rescue training at the local swimming pool that had been reserved for the afternoon. Kate was a bit uneasy at the thought of wearing a swimsuit around these men. It was hard enough to prove to these men that a woman could be a firefighter, but now she would not be able to hide her femininity. Kate was not looking forward to the comments or possibly catcalls she knew were inevitable.

Kate walked into the dressing room, changed into her modest one piece swimsuit, and wrapped her towel around her waist before going out to join the rest of the recruits. She walked out to the pool, sure enough, to be greeted by whistling from some of the men.

"Alright, that's enough. Everyone into the pool." T.O. Robles barked.

Kate took off her towel and jumped in along with the rest of the men as T.O. Robles brought in a water rescue board.

"First we're going to learn how to properly retrieve and stabilize a drowning victim on the rescue board. I want you all to pair up. One of you will be the victim and the other will be the rescuer." T.O. Robles then began demonstrating. He made his way around to each group and gave hands-on instruction.

The afternoon went by quickly, but it was a refreshing way to stay cool in the afternoon's hot sun. Once training was over, Kate and the others sat around for a cool drink and then drove back to the main station. Kate got in her little blue car and headed home where she took a long hot shower, put on her fuzzy slippers, and made herself a nice dinner before collapsing on the sofa from exhaustion.

Kate awoke early as she had done all week, but today was Friday. She was happy the weekend was almost there, and she would have time to rest. After her morning coffee, Kate drove to the Central Station to meet with the recruits and T.O. Garrett. The morning training would consist of learning to handle a butane gas tank fire, and in the afternoon they'd extinguish an oil pit fire.

They arrived at the Harlingen training field and met up with the other trainees from the town. Kate recognized some of the men from the last time she was there. "Hi, John! How's it going for you?" she called out, excited to see someone who had made her feel accepted.

"Hi, Kate! Goin' great. How 'bout you?" John stood there with a wide grin on his face.

"Me too. I'm a bit nervous to finally work directly with fires, but yes, anxious to get started," Kate said with trepidation.

"Don't be! It's controlled. You'll be alright...I'll be there," John laughed.

"Thanks, John! I feel so safe now," Kate said with a hint of sarcasm. She heard her group called next to suit up. She put on her helmet and gloves, walked over, and stood with the group.

T.O. Robles gave the okay to start the fire. Flames began shooting out of the large two hundred gallon butane tank, and the hoses charged with water. Kate, along with three other firefighters, picked up the one and a half inch hose. She stood just behind John, who held the nozzle, and helped advance the lines while controlling the flame. Kate was frightened by the dangerous situation but held her ground and did her part. A third man, Dave, grabbed the wrench from his pocket once they were close enough, walked past Kate and John, and quickly worked to shut off the valve. The fuel supply was cut, and the flames were gone immediately. They shut down the nozzle and laid the lines down for the next group of trainees.

After the other two groups took their turn, they all took off for lunch at a pizza restaurant and then met back at 1:00 PM for the oil pit fire training. They were suiting up in their turnout gear when T.O. Garrett walked up to Kate with a grin on his face. "The media is here. They're covering the training...and you, Kate," pointing them out across the field. "They'll be taking pictures as well..." looking back at Kate, "front page story!" he laughed.

"Great! No pressure to perform at my best! Is there?" Kate frowned. She patted her helmet and walked over to the group of trainees and T.O. Robles.

"Sir, where do you want me?" Kate put forth her confident smile.

"I want you up front with me, Martinez, and Smith," he said pointing the men out in the group.

"Okay." Kate's composure immediately plummeted after hearing she would be in the front. *Yeah, no pressure here.*

"The pit will be set on fire in a few minutes. Help the men get the hoses in place," T.O. Robles instructed her.

"Yes, sir!" Kate belted out, heading over to the men. She helped them connect three separate lines. Each line consisted of six fifty-foot sections of two and a half inch diameter hoses with a two foot long double handled nozzle.

"Kate...get the nozzle and attach it on the middle hose," Martinez shouted as he continued connecting the hoses.

"Sure thing!" Kate went to retrieve the nozzle.

As she worked, her mind was racing with concern for the outcome.

"Okay, take your places everyone, the pit is about to be lit," T.O. Robles shouted. Everyone rushed to grab the three hose lines set up to combat the huge pit fire.

WOOOOOSH!! The massive black oil pit now had twelve-foot flames rising from it as thick black smoke began to swirl around it, masking the danger.

"Open your lines on fog!" T.O. Robles shouted. "Advance slowly."

There were five rookies and one experienced firefighter on each line as they advanced through the dense smoke. The water was flowing from the large nozzles in a fog stream that acted as a shield, protecting them from the intense heat and massive flames.

Although Kate was directly behind T.O. Robles, she was still very intimidated by the wall of flames and smoke, struggling to hold on to the large powerful hose. Even though the shield of water protected them, she could feel the heat on her face even through the shield of her helmet. They worked methodically as a team through the blackness to cut down the fire until it was extinguished.

Kate, along with the rest of the trainees, was not only exhausted but soaked from her own perspiration, and her face was black with soot. All, however, stood proud of their accomplishment as they posed in a group for the newspaper cameraman.

Once they were rested and had finished patting each other on their backs, T.O. Robles shouted, "Time to break down the lines. Get a move on!" Kate and the men looked like ants scattering, as they detached, rolled up, and put the hoses back on the trucks.

The ride back to Brownsville was very quiet. Everyone was exhausted from the day and fighting hard not to give in to sleep. Finally, they arrived at Central Station; Kate and the other recruits looked like zombies as they climbed from the truck.

"See you back here bright and early, Monday," T.O. Garrett instructed the group, followed by a number of sighs and grunts. "Monday we'll be taking it easy and studying from the manuals to give you all a rest," he added.

Kate headed for her car, feeling as though she might pass out from exhaustion. She was relieved that she had the weekend to relax and get a breather from the physical training.

On Monday, during a short water break, Kate was approached by a group of veteran firefighters who were talking as if she had been in a conversation with them all along. Kate was a bit intimidated, at first, being surrounded by men, older than her by five or more years, outweighing her by fifty pounds each, and towering a good six to eight inches over her head. Kate's initial reaction was to shrink back toward the water cooler where she had just filled her cup. As they attempted to mentally knock her down, to test her resolve with stories of their strenuous training, Kate reminded herself that improved training was the nature of the business, and she would be better qualified with it. She felt fortunate to be there and knew she was strong enough to take most of what was handed her. Kate thought, perhaps they were intimidated by her, a petite woman – a mere five foot three inches – doing all that they were able to do. That thought gave Kate strength, and she stepped with conviction toward the center of the men.

"Well then, I should be plenty prepared to work alongside you fine gentleman very soon." With that, Kate pushed through two of them and back to her group, smiling back at them. It felt good; she felt good. Kate would show them she could do this, and do it really well.

The weeks of training had progressed, and the general skeptical attitude toward Kate eased up a bit, but her nerves began to take hold again. T.O. Garrett – only wanting to ensure that each candidate succeeded – informed them that he would begin taking Kate and the new recruits to real fire calls to observe veterans in action.

On this dreary rainy morning, Kate was happy and content to study instead of being outside doing the strenuous training, but shortly after lunch was over, the alarm sounded. A small twin engine plane had crashed in a field nearby.

"Get suited up in your gear," T.O. Garrett directed the trainees. "We're going to go along with A Crew to the scene. A plane crash is not a common occurrence for the department, but it's one the department is trained and equipped to handle. Head downstairs. We'll be following along in the pickup truck."

Kate, along with the other trainees, suited up in their turnout gear and climbed into the rear of the department pickup truck. The sky was grey, and drizzling rain brought a damp chill as they drove to the crash site. Upon arrival, Kate noticed a small plane across a muddy field. Actually, it barely resembled a plane at all. The white and blue striped body had been torn to shreds in the violent landing; one of the wings was completely ripped off and now lay twenty feet behind where it was meant to be attached; the other was balancing delicately atop the wreckage. The fire that had been blazing before the rain had begun to fall was now just smoldering near the center of the plane, and smoke billowed in a single column which grew for twenty or thirty feet overhead.

Kate's legs quickly felt the burn with each step as she trudged through the thick, black, sticky mud that now filled the large field. Yet, she certainly wasn't going to complain about being slowed. It was bad enough, from a distance, to see the pale lifeless bodies in the wreckage. One man was hanging by his feet, which were lodged in the aircraft's window. His upside down face and vacant eyes stared straight out at her as she approached him. Also, his lifeless companion sat still buckled in the pilot's seat, and as Kate walked around the plane, she could see his body crushed within the cockpit. Kate glanced toward his head, not really wanting to look but unable to turn away. She noticed the softball size hole in the side of his head.

Kate stood there paralyzed by the sight; her heart was thudding in her ears so loudly she couldn't hear her training officer shouting at her. Kate could only hear the words in her own mind being replayed over and over again...*I don't know if I can do this.*

As she continued to circle the plane, the mud caked to the bottom of Kate's boots, making it difficult for her to walk. The borrowed boots were a little too large but had to suffice until her department issued boots arrived. With each step, her left foot slid out, causing her to lose her balance. Everyone laughed when one firefighter chirped, "Tots and Teens! Tots and Teens!"

Kate just smiled, gritting her teeth, and did her best to laugh along with them while continuing her struggle back to the truck as instructed by T.O. Garrett. The veteran firefighters remained on scene and began their extraction of the two dead men from the airplane while waiting for the coroner to arrive and pronounce their deaths before the funeral home came to retrieve their bodies.

The ride back to the station had Kate cramped in the truck cab, more than uncomfortable in her muddy turnout gear. When Kate climbed out of the truck, she stood as tall as she possibly could, and strode without hesitation straight toward the group of men she'd be working with. She tried not to draw too much attention to herself, all the while thinking, *How can I not? I'm a woman who is not welcome here in this man's world.*

"Hey, Kate! See you back here on Thursday," Robert, a firefighter who worked with A Crew, shouted across the truck bay, tipping his hat to her with a grin. Kate looked at him puzzled.

24

KATE...FOLLOW ME OVER to the office to sign your paperwork. Your training is complete, and you'll be put on shift work as a rookie firefighter with the A-shift starting Thursday." T.O. Garrett motioned her to walk over to the administration building next to Central Station.

"Hi, Kate!" Vivian, the secretary, smiled shuffling the papers on her desk. "Take a seat. I need you to sign a few forms to be sent up to payroll." She peered across her desk at Kate. "Looks like you survived your training. You ready to stay twenty-four hours with those guys you worked with today?" Vivian cracked a mischievous smile.

"It was tough, and I'm looking forward to working...but not quite sure about the guys next door." Kate let out a laugh, picked up a pen and began signing her life away.

"Well, good luck, Kate!" Vivian reached across the desk to shake Kate's hand.

Kate walked out to her car; a huge smile bloomed on her face. *I can't believe I'm finally starting work as a real honest to goodness firefighter.*

Kate drove home with mixed emotions: excited that she'd completed her training, but uneasy about working a twenty-four hour shift, and sleeping in the same room with a group of men all night. *Stop thinking about it! It's part of the job,* she ordered herself.

For twenty-four straight hours, Kate would be with these men who greeted her as she entered the garage and then at the top of the stairs as she entered the dorm, and again in the kitchen area. Some were clearly less pleased to see her than others.

Kate expected this attitude from some: the men who snapped off a quick hello, stated their names, and returned to what they had been doing prior. However, the remaining members of her new crew seemed kind and offered to provide answers to any questions Kate might have during her tour.

Here in this wide open space was a kitchen complete with large cafeteria-style tables lined up with stools attached, a living area with a television and couches, and a series of twin beds along the outer walls set up like dominoes, with just a few feet separating them; the staircase in the center of the room, and a pole that led to the garage below. The more Kate saw of the barracks where she would be spending many nights in the near future, the worse she began to feel. Kate knew that she was the first woman, and so far had dealt with that fact quite well, but suddenly the ramifications of her decision came crashing down around her.

There was a single bathroom – which once entered matched the room they had just left. It was large and open. There were three sinks, three stalls, and three open showers that provided no privacy. When Kate turned around, she saw that there was not even a lock on the main door. Though Kate fought the urge to look away, her eyes were pinned to the lock-less door. The man who escorted her explained – perhaps seeing her obvious mental anguish.

"The city should've issued sleeping shorts for everyone, provided a privacy screen for around your bed, and had a lock installed on the door," he said apologetically to Kate who was still staring at the absent lock in dismay.

Should have, but didn't, instinctively crossing her arms in defensive manner. *Too late, I'm here to stay for the night. Gee, I can't wait to see what else awaits me.* She did her best to clam down and let go of the sarcasm that was at the tip of her tongue.

"Thanks! I think?" she said with a short laugh, and determined to make the best of the situation, then returned to her new crew in the kitchen.

The day went by quickly. The men showed her the ropes and gave instructions when needed as they did the day's chores. By lunchtime, Kate was starving. In her excitement that morning she had left with only enough appetite for a few bites of yogurt. She was very happy to have good food at lunchtime, which was offered to her by one of her comrades. Kate was caught off guard to find that these men seemed to understand cooking, and she was downright shocked to see them take turns cleaning their plates when they had finished their meals. Though she had not spent a great deal of time around men other than her ex-husband and now her newfound love, Kate was certain that she'd never heard a friend talk about how good her man was at cooking meals and cleaning the house. Strange as it was, it felt right. These men knew what it was to work as a team.

Kate felt comforted by this discovery and was a bit more at ease by the time they moved on to their afternoon chores. It was "house" day, which meant that Kate and her colleagues were in charge of cleaning the station from top to bottom. At one point, while she scrubbed and scoured, Kate looked up to see another man – someone she did not recognize – enter the room. No one seemed to be alarmed by this, so Kate figured it was not out of the ordinary, and yet the man had walked straight in and without saying anything, as if he owned the place.

"Hello..." started the unknown man. When no one responded, he continued, "Okay...I am here to make Kate feel more welcome." He turned and walked directly to the bathroom. When he returned, in his hand – Kate hadn't noticed it when he had entered – he held a screwdriver. As Kate looked at him, he caught her gaze. Her face reddened.

"All right, all," he stated in a loud voice, "the bathroom door now has a latch hook lock on it. Give your new comrade some privacy when she needs it." He did not offer her a smile, nor did he wait for any response. He simply turned on his heel and walked down the staircase.

Though she should have been relieved at this turn of events, Kate somehow felt more uncomfortable than before…like she was working harder to remove an invisible stain. No one said a word about the lock. The night progressed as if nothing had happened. For that Kate was grateful. Yet the awkwardness that apparently only Kate was aware of was about to get even worse.

Their dinner was done; they had conversed, and she had heard many interesting stories, and even managed to regain complete composure after the interruption in the day; but now many of the men were headed for their beds. Kate tried not to look, but found her eyes wandering toward the uncomfortable sight of one man after another dropping his pants and jumping into bed in nothing more than a thin pair of boxer shorts – or worse, tighty whities. She placed her turnout pants next to her bed, which were pulled down over her boots so she could put them on quicker. Kate then climbed into bed, wearing her full uniform, and wondering what had happened to the promise of issued shorts for bedtime. She dozed off to sleep, but not before hearing the words circling in her head: *At least they aren't completely naked.*

SHHHHHHRIEEEKKK! SHHHHHHHRIEEEEEEKKK! Kate jumped out of bed, momentarily forgetting where she was. The alarm was so loud, so shrill, it took her straight out of a dream and planted her feet on the ground before she could even get her bearings.

25

OME ON, ROOKIE. It's your first call. Time to show what you're made of."

Kate was amazed at how calm the voice was that spoke to her as she leapt into her gear. Kate looked up to see the man – in only his underwear – methodically doing the same. Kate avoided eye contact and quickly turned away. Her heart was pounding; she was excited, nervous, and still half asleep as she ran after the men toward the...toward the... the pole.

Oh no! Kate saw it and knew what she had to do, but hadn't had the on-duty practice she wanted. Kate was still a bit foggy and couldn't wrap her mind around how to properly grip the thing as she slid down. Kate wrapped herself around it, gripping it tightly. She held in her screams of agony, with both hands burning as she rode the pole the whole way down to the lower level. When she reached the ground, Kate covertly peered at her hands, not wanting the guys to see the mistake she had made.

OUCH! Dammit! Fortunately, her embarrassment overrode the pain as she looked down at her bright red throbbing hands, but Kate climbed up in the truck and began preparing herself mentally to do the job that she was meant to do.

It wasn't more than seconds after Kate had boarded, weighed down with the heavy breathing apparatus, that the truck sped away from the station. She was amazed at how quickly and efficiently it all took place. Kate felt her heart race even faster and wondered for a split second if this was really happening and if she could do what was needed.

The short ride to the location of the fire was not short enough. Her mind reeled, playing out all of the possible scenarios that could occur once they arrived. Kate said a silent prayer that she would not crack under the pressure. People were depending on her. Kate reminded herself that she was trained – well trained – to do this. She managed to put her nerves on the back burner and found her inner wall of determination. Kate climbed down from the truck when it rolled to a stop outside the three story red brick building in the square by City Hall. The downtown building housed a bar on the first level and small apartments on the other two levels.

Through several windows on the second level of the building, flames flooded the air and shot straight up over the roof. It was as if she was dreaming the image because the rest of the surrounding buildings seemed perfectly intact. Smoke heaved up into the sky and the tiny residue floating in the air filled the path of the fire engine's headlights with an eerie shimmer. They were the first engine on the scene and everything happened quickly; yet Kate had taken in every detail like a motion picture. As she helped the men unload the hoses, Kate thought she heard something. It was faint but she could still make it out.

Kate yelled out to the superior officer, "Captain Carter! I hear someone in the building."

"What? Are you sure? I didn't hear anything. Where?" Captain Carter shouted back with a look of concern.

"The window at the corner of the building. I could barely make it out, but I know I heard someone." Kate pointed in the general direction.

Captain Carter immediately ordered a crew in to sweep the building. Three firefighters donned their masks, turned on their air, and climbed the ladder to the second story window. They entered, one after the other, creating a human chain, and then breaking it just inside. Kate waited with baited breath for an injured adult or scared child to be carried out by one of her heroic counterparts, but it didn't happen. They came out empty handed, shaking their heads "No."

Captain Carter turned and shot a look at Kate as if to say, *How dare you put my men at risk...rookie!*

Kate went back to the hose prepared to fight the blaze. But...there it was again.

Kate heard the same faint cry from inside the burning walls. She froze to listen, feeling like the boy who cried wolf. When she heard it again, Kate dropped her hose and ran to the captain once again.

"Captain Carter! I heard it again. Someone is up there in that room. Please believe me! I'm not making it up. It was barely audible, but I heard someone yelling." Kate stretched out her arm with her forefinger pointing to the corner of the building where she was sure the cry had originated.

Captain Carter looked at her for just a moment, and then said, "Kate, they already went in and found nothing."

"I know, but I'm sure I heard someone up there. I'm not making this up. Please? Have them check again," Kate insisted with as much conviction as she could muster.

"What did you hear?" Captain Carter looked up at the building.

"It sounded like a man moaning or a muffled cry for help. I'm not certain what was said but I am certain I heard someone."

Captain Carter regrouped the men and sent them to the room Kate had pointed out. Again, Kate waited, hoping for them to return with someone in their arms – for the person's sake more than her own.

A cloud of smoke emerged ahead of the men and Kate couldn't see them at first; as the air cleared, Kate saw the hurried actions of men trying to save a life. There he was, a frail and elderly man. His arms fell behind him as he was placed on the stretcher from an ambulance that had just arrived. Kate stood still for a moment, holding her section of hose. The smoke swirled around her. The sky, which would have been pitch black, was brought to life by the flames that were now engulfing this man's home. The powerful hose in Kate's hands felt like nothing more than a mere garden hose when she saw him move, just slightly, and on his own accord.

On her way back to the station that night, Richard spoke above the roar of the engines, "When we went in the first time, we searched the room. We checked above and below the bed and found no one. Then on the second sweep, we heard the faint moan and pulled the mattress from the bed. There was the elderly man, curled up. He'd buried himself between the mattress and box spring to protect him from the heat and smoke..." He turned to Kate and continued, "It's a good thing you insisted we go back in or tomorrow they would have found him dead."

She blushed. "I...I just did what needed to be done...but I'm really glad that he's alive." Kate tried to hide it from the men, for fear of coming across arrogant, but she was filled with the joy of helping to save a life and swelled with pride on the inside.

Kate worked alongside the men to prepare the truck for the next call. Though she should've been exhausted, adrenaline was still coursing through her. While they worked, Kate listened to the men talk about calls of the past, about their home lives, and of their plans for the upcoming weekend. Kate enjoyed their banter and felt happy to be there.

Captain Carter took notice of her as she worked, then walked up to her. "You did well, tonight." He smiled at her. "Thanks to you, that man will live to see another day. I don't know how you heard him over all that noise, but lucky for him, you did."

26

KATE REVELED IN her successes over the next few days at home. She felt good; she felt pleased she was doing something right. Kate liked her new schedule, which allowed her time to go grocery shopping, clean the house, prepare and cook real meals, and get in decent workouts. It even allowed more time with Drake, which was great. Things were going well – personally and professionally – and Kate could not contain herself.

Two days after her first fire call, Kate returned to the fire house. She leaned slightly to one side under the weight of the small duffel bag that hung over her shoulder. Kate had learned the first day that the men pitched in to buy groceries so everyone could share in the meals together. She decided to pick up a few things that might come in handy. The canvas strap of the bag cut into Kate's shoulder as she climbed the stairs to her new second home. Many of the men there that morning were the same ones Kate had worked with before, but she was introduced to a couple new faces.

Everyone was in a relatively good mood for being at work, and Kate thought how rarely that happened in the other jobs she'd worked. Even in the dentist's office, which was a pleasant place to work, the employees would rather have been doing something else. Here it felt like the men were just hanging around with a group of friends rather than a structured job. Kate hoped that one day she would fit in the same as the men all did.

This day progressed much the same as the first. Kate was quiet most of the time, listening to the jokes told by the men around her as she did her duties and studied maps. Kate brought magazines and a book with her for that evening after they finished their chores when there was no more work to be done around the station. It was "yard day", mostly spent outside the station, cleaning the grounds, sweeping away debris, cleaning the outside of the windows, and similar tasks. Although Kate realized it was still early to decide one way or the other, all in all, she thought she could really come to enjoy the job.

SHHHHHRRRRIEEEEK! The alarm sent Kate sky high. A couple of men chuckled as Kate fought the involuntary blush that was rising in her cheeks. They all ran to suit up, and this time, when Kate reached the dreaded pole, she was prepared. No burnt hands this time. Kate wrapped her legs and held loosely with her hands while gliding down, moving quickly at the ground in time to get out of the way of the next man down. Kate's gear did not feel as heavy this time, nor was she startled to see the commotion and to be a part of it. Kate calmed herself through deep breathing as the truck roared away from the station.

The men rode silently beside her, and Kate's mind drifted back to when she was a child. It was the first time she had ever laid eyes on men like these, dressed in all their fire gear. Kate recalled the mix of fear, wonder, and excitement that came when she saw them climb from their truck, pulling their hoses into her very own backyard where her younger brother, Ronnie, had accidentally set fire to their father's boat while playing underneath it with a box of matches. It had been a foolish move on her brother's part but had provided memories she would never forget, and now, she had come full circle.

The house they were called to was burning rapidly. Flames spewed from windows and doors. The roof seemed alive as smoke danced across it on its journey to the atmosphere. Close by, neighbors watched in horror as the house transformed into a massive orange glow. The houses on either side of the spectacle were tickled every so often by the fingers of stray flames. Kate, along with the men, jumped off the truck and prepared for what looked like a nasty battle. The smoke that hung in the air was thick, and men were sent to push the forming crowd farther back from the scene.

"Kate, aim your line at the house on the right!" Captain Carter yelled out, pointing at the two story house that was closest and most likely to be ignited by the teasing fire of the main blaze. At first, the task seemed an easy enough one, so she didn't don her air mask, but as the smoke grew thicker, Kate's lungs fought for the air they craved.

Though it was the middle of the day, the sky was grey like dusk, the ground littered with smoldering embers that were once pieces of deck, wall, and roof. Kate's chest ached from the effort of trying to catch her breath each time a light breeze pushed the pillar of black fog away. She struggled to hold the hose in place to ensure that the house would not become the next victim of the greedy inferno.

It took six hours to get the flames under control, but the other houses never caught. Kate had done her job, but still she felt lousy. After breaking down the lines and loading them on the truck, Kate climbed on board. The ride back to the station made her feel nauseous, and with each small bump and turn, Kate felt that she might lose it.

With the truck safely in the garage, Kate was up and ready to get out, knowing she was going to have to help prepare the truck for the next call. Kate tried to muster some strength, some resolve, but none would come. When her feet hit the garage floor, her stomach reached her throat and Kate ran up the stairs, which seemed endless, thinking she wouldn't make it to the bathroom in time. Hunched over the white porcelain seat, Kate threw up everything she had in her. The smoke Kate had breathed in had been wreaking havoc with her body, and she didn't even know it. Finally, when there was nothing left, she stood and cleaned herself before going down stairs and back to work.

Kate felt horrified and terribly embarrassed, vowing never to speak a word of what had just happened. She would not let these men think her weak and unable to do her job. Though her body still screamed in protest, Kate went to work on the truck in silence when she should have been on her way to the hospital.

Once they retired upstairs that night, one of the men jokingly referred to her: "Two times on duty and two major fire calls. That's what I call a jinx. Looks like you're the jinx of the A-Shift!" He laughed and tossed a kind smile her way as they headed to bed.

Although the night had not been pleasant, Kate was getting experience so that someday in the near future, she would be the one showing a rookie the ropes. Kate allowed a small smile to creep across her face.

27

URING THIS PERIOD of learning on the job, the relationship between Kate and her new love, Drake, had matured significantly. Kate now openly referred to Drake as her boyfriend, and they spent nearly every free moment together. Kate enjoyed his company, his attention, and his love. She felt a bit tense when talking to him about her active duty and what that meant – specifically the living and sleeping arrangements during shifts, but Drake assured her that he was okay with her job. Though Drake was supportive and understanding, Kate didn't quite know whether or not to believe him. Several times in the weeks since Kate started active duty, Drake had brought up the very same topic. She'd learned that when someone continues to talk about something, it's usually because it is bothering them.

Again, this evening, as they sat – her back against him – on the couch in her small apartment, Drake mentioned her "home away from home." Kate smiled up at his, but was intently studying his face for signs that Drake may be lying to her – or worse, to himself – about his level of comfort with her profession. Yet what Kate saw in his face was something completely different from what she expected. It wasn't anger, resentment, or annoyance. Drake appeared to be nervous. Kate realized she'd been completely caught up in her own evaluation, and turned her attention back to Drake's words.

"...those guys get to spend the night with you."

Kate felt her defenses building.

"I'm your boyfriend, and I think that it should be me who you live with." His words were not said with malice or jealousy. Drake's smile at her was warm and inviting, and Kate felt herself welling with delight.

"So...I think we should move in together," he finished.

Kate hugged him and fought back the excitement. Her life for the past few months had been filled with moments of accomplishment and love, and now it would be full-time. Rather than watching a movie, like they had intended, they spent the evening looking through the newspaper for larger apartments listed for rent. They cuddled, compared notes, and talked about the days to come.

Two weeks later, Kate had just come off another twenty-four hour shift at the station. Her new nickname had proven true: she'd spent most of the night battling a pretty fearsome blaze – adrenaline was pumping once again, coursing through her body and keeping her going.

Kate met Drake as planned, just outside a two-story brick building not far from the center of town. It was not what Kate would call her dream home, and there was no fancy architectural detail to mention, but the building looked well maintained, with lush landscaping. Kate was still dressed in her grey shirt and slacks, thick black leather belt and shoes that served as her daily work attire, when she joined Drake and followed their guide through the front entry and up a level of stairs. Just inside the door was a small hallway that led to a nice sized living room and connecting kitchen. The rooms were open and airy and would give her the freedom to easily move about. Off to one side was another short hallway that led to a small bathroom and not one, but two bedrooms. All of the rooms smelled of fresh paint which coated the walls in neutral tones. The kitchen was small, but provided plenty of cupboard space for her cooking utensils and food to feed a family. It was the cleanest, nicest apartment they'd looked at by a long shot, and it fell well within their budget. Though Kate fought to hide her excitement, it evidently bubbled out of every pore. She found it difficult to keep her feet on the ground when Drake smiled at her with an approving nod.

Pride came in knowing that she was fulfilling her dreams and the happiness Kate felt inside brought a satisfied smile to her face. Kate imagined her children running, playing, laughing down the hall from one room to another. Kate squeezed Drake's hand a bit tighter at the thought. They were not able to stay long, so they went ahead and filled out the application right then. Neither of them questioned that this was the place for them to begin their lives together. Before Drake left that day for work, he held Kate tight, looked into her eyes and said, "I love you, Kate!" And then, he kissed her deeply.

Since starting her new career, Kate's belt had more slack and her pants were far less fitted around the thighs and buttocks, yet she weighed more. The added muscle came in handy when packing up her belongings for the move. Kate made quicker and easier work of this task than ever before thanks to her new physique and sense of endurance, as well as her excitement over the move. This represented a change for the better – an improvement in her life, and for that Kate felt blessed.

It took Kate all day Friday to pack the remainder of her belongings, so that on Saturday, with Drake's help, they could make the move into their shared home. That night, over a box of takeout Chinese food, Kate realized just how exhausted she was. A quick scan of the apartment revealed large stacks of unorganized and unpacked belongings, and Kate knew she was looking at a long week ahead. She wasn't sure how she'd muster the strength for the next day – another work shift – but knew that she would; she always did. With that, Kate set the box on the coffee table, sat next to Drake and lay her head back against his shoulder with a sigh of both tiredness and contentment.

Kate couldn't pinpoint the exact moment when she had made the decision, but she knew she was ready to bring her babies home to be with their mother again. "I think it is time for Mia and Casey to come home. What do you think, honey?"

"We have the room, and things are stable financially. Yes, why not? I would love to have them here with us," Drake nodded in agreement.

"It would make our home and family complete. I miss them so much," she sighed. "I'm just not looking forward to calling Avery to discuss it." She let out an even bigger sigh.

Though she was afraid of the conversation that lay ahead, after having reached an agreement with Drake, Kate picked up the phone and dialed the number of her ex-husband. The conversation, as she might have imagined, was tense.

"No Kate! They're stable here and part of our family," Avery tried to convince her.

"This arrangement was only temporary, till I got on my feet, and you knew it. I have custody, and I want them back with me, now that I can support them. I want them back, Avery, and I don't want to go to court over this," Kate fumed.

"Fine! I don't have the money or time to fight you on this. When will you be picking them up so I can let them know and have them ready?" He sounded defeated yet relieved.

"I will have to call you back once I've made all of the arrangements."

"Okay." The receiver went dead.

"Avery?" Kate turned to Drake. "He hung up, but he agreed." A smile filled her face as she put the receiver down and hugged her man.

"That's great! I'm glad he didn't put you and the kids through another drawn out court battle." Drake took her face in his hands and kissed her softly.

"Me too," Kate whispered.

Surprisingly, one of the most uncomfortable calls Kate had ever made – though it left her feeling emotionally drained – went better than she expected.

After a brief celebration with Drake, she sat back down and realized she was not quite done with her ex yet. Though Avery had listened to her and agreed over the phone, Kate had no way of knowing how he would react when she actually showed up at his door, which she had every intention of doing.

The flight to Dallas had not been a long one, but it had left Kate tired, most likely due to her mind playing out every possible scenario she could imagine when she arrived to pick up her children the next day. For now, though, Kate let go of the thoughts, the fears, the anxiety, and focused on returning once again to the home of her dear grandmother. Maggie, who had taken her in and helped her through some of the most momentous occasions of her life, was once again offering Kate a place to stay.

"Hi Grandma!" Kate opened her arms.

"Hi sweetie! Don't you worry...everything will work out." Maggie's loving embrace served as a welcome.

Kate felt calm with her grandmother. They walked together to retrieve her bags and then headed for the car.

"We can drive out to pick up the kids early in the morning, and then spend the afternoon together," Maggie said on the drive home.

"Thank you so much, Grandma... for being here for us," she said with tears in her eyes.

Kate sat and visited, telling Maggie all about the changes her life had seen since she'd last been at the house. Kate cried tears of joy before her grandmother as she shared her excitement, thrills, and nervousness at the thought of having her children back home with her – a home that was shared with a man who would be new to them.

Kate listened for hours to Maggie's stories and ate the snacks that had been prepared especially for her arrival; Kate then adjourned to the room where she, Mia, and Casey had once slept together and would again the next evening.

The morning alarm clock startled her awake, and Kate sprang to her feet as if ready to don her fire gear. She realized what actually lay ahead of her, and was a little nervous, but more anxious to get the difficult part of this journey over with and have her children back. Kate stood in the bathroom brushing her teeth, and thought about how they were going to react to the move – wondered if they were disappointed to leave the home they'd known for the past year. That thought saddened Kate and dampened her spirits, and she brushed it aside, trying to assure herself that she would give them every reason to be more than happy with the change of atmosphere.

Maggie and Kate ate blueberry muffins and each enjoyed a cup of coffee. Wound up already, Kate wasn't sure she needed the caffeine. It was early, but Kate had told Avery she would be there at 9:00 AM, and she certainly wasn't going to be late. Maggie drove for the hour ride to Avery's house. The mix of emotion – excitement at seeing her children and nervousness at how it would go down – had Kate dancing in her seat. Maggie placed a comforting hand, for just a moment, on her knee. Kate smiled to her grandmother, extremely happy to have her companionship.

When they arrived at the house, there was no vehicle in the driveway. Kate turned to Maggie with fear in her eyes. "He's not here. Avery's not going to let me take them." Kate had come all this way and now felt sure he had disappeared with them. She was a muddled mess of emotion and did not know what to do.

Maggie, not really sure what the proper solution was, suggested, "Maybe they went out to get some breakfast or something of that nature. We are a bit early." Maggie shifted the car back into gear and proceeded to drive away.

They did not go far before swinging a number of rights and ending up in front of the same driveway again. The two of them drove around for nearly an hour, checking in on the status of the house every few minutes. Again, it was empty, so Maggie repeated the process as if they were on a merry-go-round. Kate became more apprehensive with each pass of the empty driveway.

Finally, their persistence paid off. Just as they looped back around for the umpteenth time, Kate saw her children being unloaded from the back seat of the van that was now parked in the driveway. First a smile tugged at her lips, then anger boiled up inside her toward the man she once loved, as she watched Avery's new wife holding Casey. Kate tried to push it away with the thought of reuniting with her children.

"Mia…Casey!" She let out, swiftly walking up the driveway.

"Momma, Momma!" Mia jumped from the van running to Kate.

"Momma!" Casey started crying, squirming to get down from Mary's arms.

"Hi, sweetie! I missed you guys so much!" Kate said, practically being knocked over by Casey while she hugged Mia, then Casey joined in on the hug.

Being forced to stand in the company of Mary, who had been a large player in the demise of her marriage, was nearly unbearable for Kate. Every hair on her arms stood in defiance, like a cat met with its foe. "Where is Avery?" Kate blurted out.

"He had to work and couldn't be here. I'm sorry they're not ready. I thought you would be here later. I'll run in and get their clothes. They're still wet in the washer," Mary said before she turned and walked to the house.

"We're a little early, but they still should have been ready. Just put their wet clothes in a plastic bag, and I'll dry them at Grandma's house," Kate said, expressing her irritation.

The time it took Kate to prepare her children for the journey seemed endless, and she cursed Avery for putting her in this uncomfortable position. She was upset that he had left the responsibility of having their children ready to his wife, Mary. Though Kate had to will her body not to shake as a result of the mental and emotional stress of having to be at this house, she was also thankful that neither Avery nor Mary was fighting her.

Once loaded in the car with her children, Kate immediately regained her composure. Her life felt complete once again, and she had been strong enough to withstand the mental torture it took to reclaim it. Once she'd unloaded Mia and Casey at Maggie's house, Kate hugged and held them tight and swore she'd never let them go again.

Later as she stood folding their clothes, Kate was proud and happy to be with them, to be able to care for them, and to provide them all the love they deserved, although it was not the life she had dreamed for herself years ago. Now that one awkward moment in time was over, another series of them was about to begin.

28

KATE AND HER children returned home, and there she saw her two worlds collide into one. It was not a bad experience, yet she knew that she would never forget how strange it felt to introduce the man whom she intended to marry to her seven and four-year-old children. Fortunately, Drake returned her love and was more than willing to accept all aspects of her life into his. Drake greeted the children with warmth and excitement.

Each day saw the relationship between Drake and his soon-to-be step-children grow more real and full of father-child bonds. Kate's heart swelled each time Drake agreed to play ball with Casey, or guided her daughter, Mia, while riding her bicycle. They were becoming every bit the family that Kate wished they would be.

Kate was very proud that both children found her chosen line of work extremely interesting. They asked Kate over and over again, the night before she was to go on duty, to tell them about the trucks and the turnout gear. They wanted so badly to go with Kate when she left the house and watch her put on her gear and mask, or maybe even venture high into the seat of the giant fire engine. Though it filled her with pride, it was also very difficult the first day Kate had to leave them behind to return to her job.

This turned out to be the first night of duty in a long time when Kate hadn't been called out for a fire. That night she could not sleep due to her excitement about getting back home to be with her children for the following two days.

Kate spent the next few days getting them settled into their rooms and enrolling them in school. At first, it was a bit awkward to leave her children for the night with a man who wasn't their father while she went away to work, but Drake was good to them, and they had taken fondly to him, so it quickly became just another part of their routine.

It wasn't until a few weeks later when a set of strange faces appeared at the front door that any uneasiness was truly felt in their little world. Much as was the case when Kate was first welcomed by the city, a man and a woman were at her doorstep that morning; but this time, instinctively, Kate knew the news they came bearing was not going to be pleasant. They each carried a clipboard and introduced themselves – Kate was so overwhelmed at hearing the first part of the introduction that she completely missed their names – as being from Child Protective Services. They were at her home to do an investigation. Though Kate knew she was required to allow these people into her home, she was upset that they were standing at her door.

"An investigation of what?" she asked. *Who in their right mind would turn her into CPS?* Then all at once, as Kate was asking the question in her head, she realized the answer. *Avery! Ah Ha!* He had willingly given her the children that day, but that did not mean he was going to make things easy for her.

As it turned out, Avery had called in a complaint with the agency, actually reported the new man in her life – accused him of molesting the children. Avery was not happy to hear of her new love and the good relationship Drake had with the children. For the next two hours of that morning – and for much of the next couple weeks – questions were asked of her, of Drake, of his family, and of his friends. Their house was inspected, Drake was interrogated further, and the children were interviewed at school away from Drake and Kate, and inspected for signs of harm. The neighbors looked on, and Kate felt herself playing a war within − half of her wanted to crawl under the nearest piece of furniture to hide until the whole ordeal was over, while the other half was angry − more than angry. She was downright furious at this situation and wanted to drive to Dallas and give Avery a piece of her mind. Neither side of her emotions won. In the end, Kate elected to remain stoic in the face of torment − brought on, once again, by a man she'd once promised her life and love to − and stood by Drake and her children.

When the initial investigation was completed, and, of course, had turned up nothing, Kate allowed herself just a few moments in the privacy of a warm shower to shed tears over the unfairness Avery had once again treated her with. When she stepped from the shower, she vowed to be done shedding tears over him and went to the other room to be with Drake − the one who loved her and her children despite everything that had transpired.

The tears ended that day, but the investigations did not. The man so many miles away was bound and determined to wreak havoc on her life. It not only affected her, but her children, Drake, and their relationship with him. They lived for more than four months in embarrassment as more and more of the people around her found out about what was happening. Two more times Kate and her family were forced to endure the mental torture of having their lives turned upside down by a federal agency. Though each time the results were the same, the effects were lasting. Her family was finding it more difficult to cope. The children were not receiving the same amount of attention or affection from Drake because he feared that it would lead to more false accusations. The entire dynamic of her home was changing due to an evil force that was hundreds of miles away. For the first time in her life, Kate actually felt true, unbridled hatred for someone, for the man that she had once loved, wondering if her family would ever get back to that happy place she'd so longed for.

The stress of her home life was beginning to have an effect at work as well. Though her performance was never something to be questioned, Kate was finding herself having more doubts than ever. This job was forcing Kate to leave Drake at home to care for two children who were not his own and in a situation where he was being put through mental and emotional torture. The guilt associated with that, coupled with knowing she was working in a highly dangerous profession that could result in physical injury or worse, was beginning to take its toll on her.

Kate worried about what would happen to her children if something were to go wrong at work. *What if I were seriously injured? What if I died in a fire?* If those worries and the harassment she was facing at home were not enough, Kate was also putting up with a lot more men who were suddenly finding it "threatening" to work alongside a woman. Kate had always known there would be those men and had met her fair share of them in her short time with the force, who simply did not feel she belonged there. At first, though, most had been kind and welcoming, but as she became more comfortable, was assigned to more tasks and was proving herself capable, more of these same men began to show their resentment.

With all the stress she was dealing with, Kate finally couldn't take it any longer. All she could think about was the hell her kids were going through. She picked up the phone and called Avery.

"Hello." Avery answered as if not surprised.

"I'm calling to tell you that I know it's you calling the CPS and making false accusations and I want it to stop," Kate said through clenched teeth, and then, unable to hold back her anger, she added a forceful, "NOW!" Her hands were shaking so badly that she held the receiver with both to keep it still.

"I don't know what you are talking about. I didn't call anyone," he said unconvincingly.

"I don't want to hear anything you have to say. They told me it was you, and that it is all unfounded. Nothing is going on and you are hurting Mia and Casey by subjecting them to these accusations and investigations. I called to say if you do not stop calling the CPS, I'll take them to Mexico and you will never see them again…EVER!" At that Kate slammed down the phone. Though she knew that her threats would never be followed through on, all she could think about was what he was doing to the kids' stability. She was furious that he could be so vindictive and selfish and that he did not care about what he was doing to their children.

A couple weeks had passed when Kate received a call from the case worker. "Ms. Matthews, I called to let you know I will be closing the file on your case. We have found no validation to the accusations made, and there have been no further phone calls. I'm truly sorry your family had to go through this, but we are required to investigate situations reported to our office." The woman spoke sympathetically.

"Thank you for calling, and I am sorry that my ex put everyone through this, and wasted yours and the department's time," Kate said, trying to remain calm and sincere.

"I will be sending you the forms stating that the case is closed and our results. You take care. Bye now!"

"Thank you!" Kate hung up thinking that her call to Avery had been successful, and wished she'd done it sooner, but was glad the ordeal was over.

Kate arrived at the station fifteen minutes early so she would have time to grab a cup of coffee and unload her belongings before starting the day's chores. She found herself on duty with a couple of the men, Frank and Tim, who she knew didn't want her there. It was Friday, and Kate had been excited to find herself scheduled for duty this day, knowing it would mean she'd have both Saturday and Sunday off to spend with the kids. It also meant, though, that it was "truck" day, and she'd be getting grimy while cleaning and doing the maintenance on the truck and its equipment. It would be a physically demanding day, but she was feeling up to it. Given the fact that she was working alongside Frank and Tim, who found her such a nuisance, Kate thought it best to prove herself worthy. As soon as she finished her cup of coffee, Kate set to work with her day's chores.

By the time Kate climbed the stairs for lunch she was more than two-thirds finished with what she had to accomplish for the day. Kate had lugged the heavy hoses and laid them on the drying rack, scrubbed away the toughest grime from the tire rims, and made sure to check each and every compartment to ensure that all equipment was accounted for and in working order.

When lunch was over, Kate was the first back to work, and she quickly finished all she had left to do. Her reflection in the chrome plate on the engine's side was one of a very beat up and exhausted woman. Kate took just a second to look at herself and laughed about the hair falling loose from her ponytail. She'd truly worked at a pace worthy of the strongest and fittest man and felt proud as she walked inside the office messy and physically tired to report her status to her superiors. These men were not impressed by Kate's ability to keep up and do the same work as they did. If anything, it seemed to only irritate them further.

Kate fought to hide her horror as Frank belted out another list of chores for her to complete. She felt the burn in her arms when Tim handed her a coiled hose to put away. Kate knew they were trying to break her, and a small part of her felt it was working. Her body was worn out, and that piece of her wanted nothing more than to run home to be held and comforted by her family, but she wouldn't give up. She couldn't. For her family and for herself – she knew that.

At twenty-four years old, Kate was learning a valuable lesson – though it was not one she liked. If she wanted to make it here, if she wanted to have the energy and strength to respond to fire calls, she couldn't be the best; she had to pretend to be mediocre. For the rest of the day, the week, and for many months to come, Kate paced her work, ensuring that she was done just in time for the arms to tick five o'clock just as all the other men did. Then, she would retire upstairs and live with the men who resented her for being there.

It was time for Kate to begin the journey to the station after a relaxing fun weekend with Drake, Mia, and Casey. She wanted to love the job, and there were aspects of it that made her proud, but she still worried that she'd never be fully welcome. Today, she was sent to cover at another substation. It was Kate's turn in the rotation, and until Station Two found a replacement for their vacancy, all would be having a turn doing so.

Station Two was much smaller than Central Station and located in a quiet suburb; Kate figured it may turn out be a low key day. *Hopefully!* By the time Kate reached her car, she felt sticky under her uniform shirt and wished she were at a pool in her bikini instead. The heat was unbearable, and it wasn't even eight o'clock yet when she glanced at the thermometer on her way out the door, wondering if it could be right. *Eighty-two! Thank God it's not yard day!*

Kate jumped in the small car and pulled away from the curb. The music blared from her speakers as she drove, waking her from the morning grogginess and bettering her mood while she moved in the direction of the smaller station. As Kate pulled into the station parking lot, the beat sounded a bit off; she turned the knob to lower the volume, hoping there was nothing wrong with her car. *That's all I need,* she thought, saying a silent prayer.

SHRIIIIEEEKKKK!... "Grass fire at..."

Kate could barely make out the words as she stepped out of her car. "Shit! Not today!" She wasn't even inside the station and already she was being called out.

Kate grabbed her bunker gear and raced to the station. It was chaos as men came running from every direction during shift change. Kate donned her gear and headed to the truck. *So much for an easy day.*

Kate held tight as the truck barreled out of the garage in the direction of the fire. As they approached, she could see the billows of grey and white smoke, dancing in midair as it climbed high into the morning sky. In the center of the billows came the occasional high climbing flames that surged upward as if trying to escape the earth. This was no ordinary grass fire.

When they arrived at the scene, there was a resounding, "Holy shit!" from all members of the crew. Large trees once filled with delicious orange fruit intended for morning beverages now bore flames, smoke, and ash. The forgotten trees nearest the road were wilted from the heat, and farther back, Kate could make out tiny black leaves hanging on for dear life before succumbing to the inevitable fate and fluttering to the ground. However, it was not these crispy little leaves that attracted the attention of her crew. It was the giant, ferocious flames they were headed toward that took the spotlight.

Just shy of the wall of fire, the truck came to a stop, and Kate moved as one with her coworkers, jumping from the truck and pulling the hoses from the reel. Kate grabbed the nozzle of the red line and pulled on it, moving forward until she could feel the burning effects through her suit. The hoses came to life, and the team pushed the flames back. The smoke was heavy, but they were making progress. It might not be the day she was hoping for, but even Kate could feel the effects of the adrenaline that began to flow freely as thoughts of conquering the blaze became a near reality.

With Lieutenant Patterson just behind her, Kate pushed forward. Suddenly a gust of wind surged through the field of burning trees. The heat grew to a nearly unbearable level, and Kate couldn't imagine standing there without her gear. Kate held fast to the hose, and fought to control the section of flames in front of her. Without warning, the hose jerked backward, pulling her with it and spinning her around as if in slow motion; she saw the helmet that had once rested on her head fall and bounce off the ground before landing solidly. Kate turned back to retrieve it, but all at once the flames were rushing toward her.

"Run!"

The single command from Lieutenant Patterson was all she needed. Kate's legs could not cover the ground fast enough. The truck, which had seemed so close before, now seemed to be a football field away; her legs ached under the weight and heat of her gear despite the adrenaline that kept Kate pumping her legs. Kate wondered if she was about to be burned alive from the flames snapping at her heels. She could see the truck and wanted so badly to touch it. Without thinking, Kate reached out for it as she ran. Closing the gap, she was filled with renewed hope that came from somewhere deep within and found another burst of speed -- now sprinting, as if in a race against the fastest runners in the world. One of the men grabbed her still outstretched arms and, in a single motion, pulled Kate into the truck. Her heart was thumping nearly out of her chest, sweat was cascading from her face and back, but Kate was alive. She looked at the men beside her, and they wore an expression of mixed fear and relief. When eye contact was made, they broke out in laughter. No one was sure why, but it felt so good that Kate gave in too, as the truck sped out of the literal line of fire.

When the truck had reached a point where it was considered safe, Kate and the men climbed from their seats and placed their feet on solid ground once again. The flames were obviously not going to be put out as long as the winds were fueling it.

"We're going to do our best to keep it contained," Lieutenant Patterson said, climbing from the truck.

Once again, Kate was armed with a hose, minus her helmet, but this time her mission was to secure the perimeter rather than to eradicate the fire monster that had been devouring the orchard. They wet a perimeter around the fire and watched as it turned gorgeous trees into an eerie field of blackened stubble. The air smelled of burning wood and orange, and Kate marveled, once again, at the sheer force and unwavering fury of fire.

Before they left that evening, they went back to their starting point in search of her helmet.

29

I GOT IT," SHOUTED Pete. The short, dark, mustached, older man held the smoldering lump up for all to see. There was little of the original coloring left. It was now mostly black with burn marks and soot. "I think you'll want a new one," he chuckled.

Kate noticed that he didn't discard the helmet and shot him a curious look.

"I'm keeping it as a souvenir," Pete said, waving it the air.

She laughed, though in her mind, Kate wondered what she would have looked like if she had been left behind with the headpiece.

Another few days passed, and Kate was back at Central Station. She pulled up, parked the car and, with a sigh, opened the door. Swinging her legs out, Kate longed to be walking into the small station with the men who had treated her so kindly during and after the raging orchard fire. Instead, Kate knew, she was walking in to greet several men who would rather see her waiting on their table rather than working alongside them. Kate grimaced and entered the station.

"Captain Carter wants to see you." Without greeting her or awaiting a response, the man strode away. Kate rolled her eyes and headed for the office.

The man who sat before her was not a large man. The dark hair that had covered his head in his youth had grayed and repositioned itself much farther from his eyebrows, which had remained full and bushy, but were also mixed with streaks of white. When Captain Carter stood to greet her, Kate noted a rounding paunch riding just above his belt. His dark brown eyes were hard to read, but something about his stance, tone, and look made her waiver a bit. He addressed Kate by her last name and thanked her for coming straight to his office – as if she really had a choice. He wasted no further time with acts of kindness or small talk.

"We have received news from the Chief that a firefighter from Station Six was injured and will be out on indeterminable leave." He took a breath – the first since he had started his little speech – and allowed her a moment to take in what he was saying. "You will no longer be assigned to this station and will report to Station Six on your next working shift."

Kate was a bit taken aback by the news but wasn't really sure whether to be excited or upset. Was she chosen for the transfer for doing too well, because she wasn't fitting in here, or was this really just a random reassignment? Kate was about to ask how long she'd be placed at that station when he answered the question for her.

"You'll be serving there until further notice," Captain Carter said and continued filling out the paperwork.

Kate had no time to hide her reaction and knew the shock was showing on her face. The station she'd been at was quiet and calm compared to the one he'd just mentioned, which was – by far – the busiest in the city. Kate had once met the commanding officer of Station Six at a fire they'd been taken to during training, and she knew he was not overly thrilled to see a woman joining the ranks of firefighters.

When Kate left the office, she was still in a state of confusion over the information that had been presented to her. She went to work, but the day did not go smoothly. It seemed as though at every pass she was meeting trouble, and Kate felt curious, gossiping eyes looking her way. While rolling up hoses from the hose rack, Kate caught her finger and grazed the tip of it on the edge of the rack, causing it to bleed all over her uniformed red jumpsuit, which camouflaged it well. While carrying the broom to the walk she was meant to sweep, Kate turned too quickly and caught one of her coworkers in the arm.

"Hey...hey! Watch what you're doing, Matthews." He jumped back glaring at her.

"I'm so sorry," Kate said. He walked into the garage as if he'd not heard her apology. *It seems I can't do anything right today,* Kate thought as she started sweeping.

By the time her head met her pillow that evening, Kate was mentally exhausted. She didn't remember falling asleep, but the next morning, when she awoke, she was relieved that there had not been a call that night.

Kate arrived home to a message on her answering machine. She couldn't believe her ears when she played the message. It was Avery letting her know that he'd moved back from Dallas and was living a few towns over. He wanted to pick up Mia and Casey for the weekend.

Kate reluctantly agreed to let Mia and Casey visit Avery over the weekend since the children had not seen their "father" for awhile – even though Casey was still sick with a cold.

Kate's first day at Station Six felt like her first day all over again. She was once again concerned about being accepted, realizing there would always be men who wouldn't ever accept that a petite woman like herself could perform as well, or better, than they could.

As Kate walked into the truck bay, Robert walked toward her and said, "Hi, Kate!"

"Good morning, Robert." Kate returned a shared smile.

"The captain is expecting you. Put your gear on the truck and then report to him in the office. I'll show you around when you're done."

"Alright...thanks!" Kate felt more comfortable after being greeted by Robert.

The substation was large and laid out in a completely different manner than the one she'd been assigned to originally. Kate walked in with an air of satisfaction and with a purpose. She didn't want to cause any greater disruption than would already come from her simply being present there.

Kate tugged hard to open the heavy metal door to the captain's office. It had a thick glass window filled with uncountable crossing wires and certainly served as intimidation to all who entered. The captain was sitting behind his desk, eyes averted, talking on the phone. His hair was grey and silver, except for a small patch that had disappeared in his later years. It was only visible to her each time he bent forward to take a note about what the caller was saying – which he did two or three times. Kate stood patiently awaiting his glance of recognition, but he did not look up. Kate was not sure how to handle the situation. She stood back and waited a good amount of time, and then cleared her throat, hoping the captain would end his call and welcome her to the station and her new assignment. It was past the time when she was supposed to have reported for duty, and Kate was concerned that the other men would be upset she'd not started performing her assignments. Her nerves were fighting against her, but Kate refused to back down, and announced herself. "Excuse me, Captain. I wasn't sure you heard me."

"I heard you," the captain said, and continued his phone call without giving her any further direction. Kate stood planted in her spot and waited for him to finish. He obviously didn't care that she heard his conversation, for if he had, he would have asked Kate to wait outside.

He stood, and Kate could now see his name tag – Captain Gordon. He set the phone down on its cradle and for the first time, looked her in the eyes. "Matthews. I'd appreciate if in the future you'd be kind enough to wait outside when I'm on the phone."

Well, this is starting out great, she thought.

"I apologize, sir." Kate made no further excuse.

Captain Gordon did not appear to be as concerned about Kate being there for his phone call as he was bothered by her just being there. Each time Captain Gordon addressed Kate, he used her last name, which would dribble from his lips as if it were pure torture for him to speak it. Everything about the man was harsh. Captain Gordon only overlooked Kate by three inches, and he was not large around at all, but he was intimidating in every sense of the word. His nose was bulbous and red, but his lips, which spewed the undertones of absolute annoyance with each syllable, were thin and made his every expression seem somehow cold. Typically, it was easier to deal – mentally – with men who despised her role when they were small and inconsequential, but Captain Gordon had served with the department for many years and was a senior officer.

The last thing Captain Gordon said to Kate before leaving her to find her own way around was, "You are expected to act, dress, and perform as well as any of the men here." His tone was harsh, and he emphasized the word "men" as he spat the words in her direction.

30

KATE TURNED TO the truck bay door thinking, *this did not start out as well as I had hoped.* Her shoulders sagged for a moment as the notion crossed her mind.

The men, Lacey and Joe, showed her around and explained to her the day's tasks as they each grabbed a broom.

"Kate, get that huge mop in the supply cage. The faucet is around back," Lacey shouted across the bay.

Kate did as she was told, and they had the morning work of cleaning the truck bay done and in no time headed in for coffee. It was an off day, so there were no tasks other than their routine cleaning to do.

Kate grabbed a map and began studying the new district to familiarize herself with the streets and hydrant locations. As the day passed, the crew became friendlier than upon her arrival. She felt a little sigh of relief except when Captain Gordon shot a look of disgust her way to indicate he was unhappy with her presence.

Finally, morning arrived without any fire calls and Kate was excited to go home. She was looking forward to a weekend with her family and away from critical eyes.

It was only a few weeks into her new placement when Captain

Gordon told Kate that she would be accompanying the crew for a fire safety presentation at the local elementary school. Her new station was known for doing a great deal to educate the community, which was the one thing Kate was truly excited about when she heard she'd be reassigned here.

She was fitted, like the men around her, in her turnout gear and equipment, then took her seat as if going on an actual call. The day was gorgeous, and Kate felt great on the drive over to the school. As they pulled into the school's entrance, Lacey, the driver, turned on the sirens. Out the small side window, Kate could see a large group of children and adults assembled on the front steps spilling over into the parking lot. It was a large school, and the children created a truly massive crowd when all were brought together like this.

The truck pulled into position in the parking lot in front of the huge crowd of children and faculty; a tingling of excitement filled the air. Cheers and clapping were almost deafening. Kate and her colleagues climbed from their seats as if they were celebrities. Together, in front of the bubbling mass of exuberance, they each took a place, assembling in front of the large truck.

Captain Gordon began his speech. He was surprisingly eloquent and made the children giggle with a couple of remarks.

This was her first fire presentation, and Kate was thoroughly enjoying it. The sun was bright and high in the striking blue sky where just a couple clouds drifted freely above her.

"...so on with the show...to tell you all about what we do..."

Kate thought she heard her name. In fact, she swore that was exactly what Captain Gordon said. Kate looked at the man who was now waving her toward him. Captain Gordon wore a smirk on his face. She had not been told at any time that she was expected to speak. She felt the need to bend over so she could pick her chin up off the ground, but Kate wasn't sure her arms, which shook visibly, would be strong enough to put it back in place. Her heart was beating so hard that the words she uttered were not audible to her own ears as she began to address the crowd.

Kate introduced herself and moved directly into the information she knew – backward, forward, and upside down – Kate spoke from experience: trucks to hoses, smoke detectors to 9-1-1 – somehow she managed to give a worthwhile presentation that even the kids seemed to enjoy. Kate had a few children come up in front to practice the stop, drop, and roll procedure. She even had Lacey fill the red hose line and spray the hose so all could see how powerful the water really was. Then Kate let a selection of children come up to try wearing her helmet to feel its weight. Kate looked back, with a winning smile on her face, at Captain Gordon who had set out to embarrass her, and then back to the crowd. She concluded with a sharp, "...and now, I am living proof that – boy or girl – if you want to do something badly enough, you can make it happen."

The assembly applauded wildly.

31

KATE ARRIVED HOME to find that Avery had dropped off Mia and Casey with Drake. After giving Kate a hug, Drake held out his hand which held a Ziploc bag and said, "Avery left this for you."

"What is that?" Kate said as she took the bag with a puzzled look.

"Just open it...you'll see!" Drake said shaking his head side to side.

Kate opened the Ziploc bag to find a hand written letter and vitamin C tablets cut in half. She read the letter addressed to her from Mary. It was a detailed explanation to Kate no how to take care of Casey and his cold. She had cut up the vitamin C tablets and went on to state when they should be given to Casey.

"Are you kidding me?" Kate said with disbelief.

"Nope!" Drake let out.

"I can't believe the gaul of this woman. She is writing ME a letter? Telling me how to take care of my own child. A woman who had her own children taken away from her by the courts and given to their single father...an airplane pilot who is away from home a lot." Kate said with disgust.

Kate crumpled up the letter and threw it and the vitamins in the garbage and went to take a shower to calm down.

Her life was now consumed with work at the station and raising a family at home, and she had no time for the drama Mary was trying to invoke. Kate began to find her place at the new station despite clear and continued disapproval from several of the men. The level of practice was a definite step up from what Kate had experienced at the other stations before this. Though there were calls that she would care to forget, Kate found herself becoming a stronger, smarter, and a better all-around firefighter after being assigned here.

Kate arrived fully awake and ready for any challenges these men decided to throw at her. She had become accustomed to their torturous ways now, even their incessant need to tell her the most horrid details of each and every call they had ever responded to in an effort to turn her stomach. Thus far they had been unsuccessful, and Kate made a point, in return, to continue eating – even using her finger to pick up the last of the crumbs – as they recounted the vile particulars. In a way she welcomed their taunts, for it made her feel somewhat accepted, versus the silent treatment she had received during her first week on assignment there. Kate laughed at their silly wager regarding the amount of time she would last before vomiting at her first body retrieval. Though secretly, Kate was happy she had yet to be called out for such a horrible thing, she had no doubt that she could handle it as well as any of them. Kate had proven to herself – if to no one else – that she was meant to be exactly where she was.

It was "yard" day, and Kate was thrilled that she would be outside – even if it meant doing arduous, physically demanding tasks. Station Six sat just outside the center of town and was seen by a large number of local residents and tourists every day. Therefore, it was expected to be kept in the nicest condition possible. It also meant that Kate, along with the others, was on yard duty, which was different considering that her previous workplace, Central Station, was surrounded by pavement. This was something she knew a little about and she was excited to use a gas powered lawn mower instead of a reel push mower like the one Avery had bought for her to use on their yard. The station did not have much in the way of actual flowers, but the few floral arrangements that had been placed around the grounds were full and beautiful – mostly due to her own influence. Kate was finding that she had quite a green thumb. Today, with the weather being so beautiful, she was happy to be put in charge of such things.

After working a fire call at a trailer park on her last shift day and fighting alongside Lacey and Robert for nearly three hours to get the blaze under control, Kate had spied some small baby palm trees near the trash at the rear of the property. On her way back to the truck, Kate had snatched up the discarded trees, kept them in buckets of water while off-duty and today, intended to put them to good use.

Just as she suspected, the rest of the crew were also in high spirits. The sun was warm, but not overly brutal; the breeze was mild and refreshing. Before she realized it, dinner time was upon them. Lacey suggested an outdoor meal, then went to the kitchen to put together some sandwiches and sides while Kate laid out the plates and utensils on the picnic tables. A warm funny feeling came over Kate; she thought she'd never have imagined herself sitting around a picnic table with a group of men eating dinner, but she certainly wasn't going to complain. The group of firefighters talked and laughed as they ate and enjoyed the light breeze. Kate finally felt that she was beginning to fit in with this crew.

After an hour or so, Kate, Captain Gordon, Lacey, and Robert moved their assembly inside. Kate took a cool shower to wash away the grime of landscaping, and then stretched out on one of the couches along with the others to take in some television before bed. It was still fairly early in the evening, and the sun streamed in through the single window in the large room, making visible the dust particles floating in the air. The room was fairly quiet as each of the men and Kate decided upon a calming activity to wind down – the TV was turned on; books were open; newspapers were unfurled. All was pleasant and peaceful until…

SHHHHRIIIIEEEEEEEKKKKKKKKKKK! No matter how long Kate remained in the department, the loud sound of the alarm was something she figured would always startle her; she jumped to her feet with the rest of the men and ran out to the smell of diesel, lights flashing, and the growling of the awaiting engine.

It was not until she boarded the giant truck and Lacey and Robert began smirking and elbowing each other that Kate realized where they were headed. This would be her first body retrieval. Though Kate did her best not to show it, her stomach knotted, and beads of sweat lined up about the nape of her neck. The men around her did not help Kate's unease – joking about the rancid smell, and the horrible images that came with these types of calls. She tried to block out their voices as they went on and on about how sick she would feel at the sight and smell of dead bodies. Kate yearned for the peace and quiet of the barracks moments before, but all her wishing was for naught. They were still en route and would be arriving in a moment's time.

The body was reported to have been seen in the Resaca – the tributaries that led to the main body of the Rio Grande. Once on the scene, Captain Gordon, Robert, and Kate exited the truck. Though she felt anxious, Kate acted in exactly the manner she was expected to, grabbing the pike pole from the truck that would be used to pull the body ashore, and moving in step with Captain Gordon and Robert to the water's edge. Twenty feet offshore, in the dark murky water, a corpse floated face down. The once live person's hair spread over the water as it fell over and around the head. Kate wondered – if she hadn't been reporting to the scene as a firefighter – if she would have known that this was not someone foolishly swimming or snorkeling in the unwelcoming waters.

Kate worked with Robert to hook the pole into the clothing. As they pulled with the pole, the body would slightly submerge, causing a great deal of drag, and the hook would become dislodged, requiring them to begin the process again. This happened twice before the lifeless figure was finally resting at Kate's feet. Any relief that came with getting it out of the water was quickly erased at the smell and sight before her.

The odor, though rancid, was not as bad as her mind had imagined it to be. However, Kate did find herself feeling a bit queasy, but mostly due to the disturbing sight.

This body, once a beautiful, live and breathing young girl, was now unbelievably disfigured. The skin was white and pasty, almost like a mannequin, and the black hair was matted and mussed. A portion of the scalp was exposed, filling Kate's mind with images of it snagging on a rock or a branch or some other obstacle before breaking free.

Kate wanted to look away, but in order to do her job, she had to stay focused. She wanted to turn off her thoughts, but Kate's brain continued in overdrive, conjuring up stories of this girl and how someone once so youthful and pretty had become this grotesque thing that lay before her feet.

Just then, Lacey gave her the greatest gift Kate could have asked for in that moment – a snide comment. "Oh look! I think Matthews is going to hurl!"

Though his words were meant to tease, perhaps belittle, instead they served as the perfect distraction. Kate's thoughts returned to the task at hand, proving to herself and these men that she could not be brought down by any aspect of the job. Presented with the opportunity to show them that she could conquer this or anything else, Kate puffed up her chest, stood tall and turned to the group.

"This…is it?" Kate shrugged. "I've smelled worse!"

When Kate saw the men's jaws drop, in unison, it was her turn to smirk.

Less than one month after pulling the body from the Resaca – an experience occurred that would remain permanently ingrained in her mind for as long as she lived – Kate was informed that her training was going to progress. Kate was to learn how to drive and operate the large truck that, until now, she had always taken a back seat in.

The day she first took the driver's seat, Kate chuckled on the inside at how small the large padded seat and steering wheel made her feel. Kate imagined being an onlooker, seeing the tremendous truck *en route* to a call but barely able to make out the top half of a woman's head behind the wheel. A smile pulled at the corners of her lips at the thought. Unfortunately, it was taken as cockiness by Lacey, who was training her, so he was not about to go easy on her. Lacey had Kate drive the huge truck out onto the busiest city roads and even wanted her to back it into a parking spot in an empty parking lot on her very first day. Kate was taken aback by what was being asked of her, but as usual, she refused to let it show. She was determined to be the very best at everything she tried, and that included driving around in a vehicle four times the size of anything she'd ever driven before.

For weeks Kate practiced and, to her surprise, she found that she was getting quite good at maneuvering the gigantic piece of machinery. Before long, she had secured her license to operate it on a regular basis.

"Hey, Matthews," came a morning 'greeting' from the captain. "You're taking the wheel today. Lacey's out sick."

The Captain's words filled Kate with joy. Though she was nervous about receiving a fire call, and hoped she could remember everything Lacey had taught her, she was also ecstatic for the opportunity. Kate had not only learned to drive the truck, but she could also operate the truck's pump to supply water at fire scenes.

Just as Kate had completed a radio check, performed her routine check of the truck and was about to head inside for coffee, the alarm sounded. As soon as Kate heard the call was for her station, she immediately felt butterflies in her stomach. She ran to the truck, and just as she was about to climb up in the back, she remembered that she was driving this time. Embarrassed at having forgot, Kate corrected herself and climbed into the driver's seat, started the engine and turned on the lights just in time to see Captain Gordon climbing aboard. He radioed headquarters that they were responding as Kate drove out of the bay.

It was a short distance to the car fire. Kate positioned the truck so that Robert and Captain Gordon could easily pull down the red hose lines and attack the fire that was devouring the small blue pickup truck as a crowd of people gathered.

Robert was holding the hose and waiting as Kate turned the throttle to raise the pressure. She then pulled the lever to supply water to the hoses. *Success!* was the single word circling her head. She had performed exactly as she'd been trained; the fire was out in no time, and she felt bigger than life as she took to her new seat once more. As Kate drove the truck back to the station, Captain Gordon begrudgingly let out, "Good job, Matthews!"

Just as things were beginning to look great, news came that the Department of Public Safety was mandating a company-wide test for all personnel who would be driving the fire trucks. Passing it was the only way to keep the license Kate had just received.

Her heart sank for a moment, *Stop it, Kate,* she scolded herself. *You can do this!* With the mental pep talk complete, Kate felt a renewed sense of calm.

The day of the obstacle course found many very brave men shaking in their boots. The course was nothing to sneeze at. The cones, which were meant to serve as a sort of slalom street course, appeared ridiculously close to one another and provided very little time for cranking the large wheel in the opposite direction. The part of the test that was far more intimidating was the parallel parking section, which most drivers never had to do at a fire scene. The first of her colleagues to take the wheel was Bob, a very large man. Bob had been on the force for several years and was a sort of the alpha male within the group. Though Bob was not always the one to drive this large engine to the calls, he had been known to on occasion, and showed no signs of concern about this test.

Kate watched, nervous for her comrade, as the engine roared to life and Bob started on his way. He brought it up to speed smoothly and started through the slalom cones as if they were going to present no trouble at all. For a brief moment, Kate thought that maybe the course looked harder than it actually was, then...*boom, boom, and boom.* Three cones in a row were crushed or sent flying by the large tires. Bob's certitude was obviously down at this point, for the rest of the course went anything but smoothly for him, and he walked back to the group slumped and semi-defeated.

Several of the other men went before Kate had her turn. One after another they returned less animated than when they had left the group. Of the dozen or so who had gone before her, just a few had managed to do well and finish without any major mistakes. When they announced her name, the anxiety Kate had been feeling about the course ramped up a notch.

Kate refused to be defeated before even trying. She reminded herself, *these men expect nothing of me. If I fail, no one will be surprised or shocked. I've only been driving for a very short period of time compared to the rest of them. But, when I pass… well, then, they will take notice!* Whenever presented with a challenge, Kate would always rise to the occasion.

Kate jumped up into the large seat, smiling yet nervous, and again marveled at how tiny it made her feel, but she wasted no time in turning on the ignition and bringing the truck to life. She carefully and steadily brought the machine to speed; then, approaching the forward serpentine portion, Kate sat as tall as she could and focused all of her attention on the task ahead of her. One by one, she weaved the monstrous truck through the cones, without misplacing a single one.

Next, Kate was told to do the same course, only in reverse – a task no one had been able to do successfully. With a deep breath, Kate put the truck in reverse, checked her side mirrors, and began to push on the gas pedal. While constantly rechecking the reflected views of what lay behind her, Kate turned the steering wheel to the left and then back to the right, then left, then right again. It seemed to take forever, and she found that she couldn't take the time to breathe, but when it was over, Kate had again successfully completed a task no other had. Finally, Kate was required to bring the truck's bumper as close to a set of cones as possible without touching them. Unable to see the cone, she did it – bringing it within just three inches. After a tiny celebration in her head, Kate reminded herself that it was not over. The hardest part still awaited her. The spot allotted for parallel parking could not have been more than two feet longer than the truck itself. Kate looked at it as she approached and gripped the wheel a bit tighter, revealing a row of white across her knuckles. It took her several minutes, but slowly and methodically, Kate placed the truck exactly as it was meant to be parked, between the cones.

"Woo-hoo!" Kate unintentionally cheered aloud, then caught herself and put the truck into gear to move it out of the spot and back to the starting place.

When Kate climbed down from the truck, the men looked at her in stunned silence. One among them managed a "nice job" half under his breath, and her heart filled with pride and joy.

The officer who administered the test approached her quietly and gave her the figurative slap on the back: "I don't know how you managed it, but you were undoubtedly the best out there today." He shook his head and gave her a smile before walking away.

32

KATE AND DRAKE began to discuss marriage and having a baby one night over dinner. Filled with excitement about making their relationship more permanent, Kate couldn't wait to show Drake just how much she loved him.

Drake slipped the key into the lock, turning the knob, and as soon as they were in, Kate began kissing him as she shed the clothing from her body. Passion heated up as they wrapped their arms around each other. Drake unhooked her bra, and then raised his hand to cup her face and bring it closer to him for another soft kiss. They turned to go upstairs to the bedroom where they continued to satiate their mutual lust for each other in a night of unguarded passion.

The following day, Kate was thinking about their future plans while working side-by-side with Drake to prepare dinner while the kids played upstairs. It was a rare occasion that things were so peaceful – so quietly romantic – in their home. She tried not to let the ringing phone alter her peaceful state, and she did not argue when Drake went to pick up the receiver.

Kate listened to his end of the conversation while she cut up the vegetables for their salad, able to determine that it was his brother,

Dean, on the other end. Kate quietly waited for Drake to finish the conversation, hoping, secretly, that it would be a short-lived one. Much to her dismay, Kate heard Drake offer a dinner invitation to Dean, and then heard the words, "Sure...bring Ellen too."

There was a pause, and Kate hoped her future brother-in-law was formulating an excuse for not taking Drake up on the offer; then, "Yes, I'm sure. We have plenty of food. Just come on over," and the receiver was placed back on the hook.

Without realizing it, her knife had stopped midair. *What has he just done?* Their quiet, romantic Sunday afternoon was not only ruined, but the kids would be home soon, and now she was supposed to somehow miraculously throw together a meal for four adults and two children. Kate had only purchased enough to feed her own family.

Drake apparently felt her discomfort – how could he not; when the knife froze, Kate was staring with a look of disbelief – because he reached over and touched her shoulder as a form of consolation. Kate unconsciously moved away from his touch.

"What is your problem?" Drake said in a harsh tone, "it is just my brother."

Angry heat filled Kate's face, and she wanted to scream back. Instead, with a concerned calmness she said, "We don't have enough food here for two more people."

Drake shook his head and rolled his eyes and moved back to the stove. "There is plenty here. We will be fine. Stop being ridiculous!"

"Ridiculous?" Kate was bubbling over inside. "You asked them here without saying a word to me! You told them to come and not to bring anything! We don't...have...enough...food! I'm not a magician who can whip up more food at the snap of my fingers. I'm going to feel like an idiot!"

"Well, you're acting like one!" Drake said. "It's just my brother. He won't..." He couldn't finish the statement; his last words had pushed Kate to her brink.

She shouted back, "I AM NOT AN IDIOT!"

"I DIDN'T SAY YOU WERE! I SAID you were ACTING like one!" With this, Drake started to walk off.

"Where do you think you are going?"

"To let you cool off! I'm going to get changed!"

"Oh...no...you...are...not!" Each word was enunciated as clearly as Kate could make it. "You asked your brother to dinner! Now, you can help me finish it!"

"I would have, if you weren't acting like an IDIOT!" Drake shouted in her face.

Without thinking, Kate saw her hand slap Drake across the face.

He recoiled only a moment before raising his own hand. *WHAMM!* Her face stung and her eyes poured tears; a look of disbelief vividly shown on her face. Drake glared at her and said, "You have no right to hit me," then turned and walked out the front door slamming it behind him.

What were you thinking? she asked herself. *What made you think that it was okay to do that?* Kate dropped to the floor.

Dean and Ellen never showed up. Kate sadly realized she'd gone from not having enough food to having way too much, given Drake's disappearance and her own loss of appetite.

For the next couple of weeks, Kate did not hear from Drake. She figured he must be staying at his mother's house, but when she finally broke down and called there, she was told that Drake had not been seen.

Late one night, Drake called. He sounded remote and cold. "I need time, Kate." he said. "Right now, I don't know if marriage is the best thing for me...or us." He hung up the phone to the sound of her sobs on the other end.

Kate spent that night crying. In fact, tears seemed to be ever-looming and ready to fall at a moment's notice. Kate, feeling depressed, tired, and unable to focus at work, decided to make an appointment with her family doctor. She needed help to get herself out of her funk given the fact that the man who she was supposed to marry was showing no signs of returning.

At the doctor's office, Kate was immediately asked to provide a urine sample. She did as the nurse directed and then was led to a small room at the back of the office suite, where she was weighed, and her vitals were taken. When her doctor joined her, Kate had the feeling that he knew something she didn't. Kate sat up straighter and waited for him to begin.

"Normally, I would ask you several questions regarding your current emotional state that might lead me to a conclusion as to why you are seeking help," Dr. Mason said tentatively, "but I don't really think that is necessary."

Kate gave Dr. Mason a baffled look.

"I feel that I can provide a pretty conclusive reason as to why your emotions are a little less controllable than usual...also the reason for your sleepiness, and lack of appetite." Dr. Mason paused just a moment, then, "Kate...you're pregnant."

The room began to spin around her, and Kate bent forward until she could make sense of what he had just said.

"Are you alright? You look faint. Lie down for a few minutes, and I'll have the nurse go over your prenatal package."

"Uhhh...yeah! Okay... thank you... Dr. Mason..." Her voice trailed off as she said his name and he exited the small, suffocating room.

Another baby would not have been such bad news had her fiancé been living at home with her, and had she not found herself with a job that was so physically demanding. As it was, she was in no situation to deal well with this news. During her drive home, Kate knew that she had to take responsibility and that meant addressing her superior at work.

At least I have a job that provides good health care, Kate thought at first, but upon reading the department manual, there was nothing in the book that mentioned pregnancy. Kate made an appointment to meet with the fire chief hoping he would let her continue working at a desk job or some kind of light duty. After all, she had seen other men given special accommodations when they were injured off duty and did not have enough sick-leave. *Maybe they will do the same for me?*

33

THE DAY KATE was to meet with the fire chief, she found herself unexpectedly nervous. *I shouldn't be,* she told herself on the drive over. *This is a normal part of life, and I am a young woman in a new relationship, and it should be somewhat expected as a possibility. Surely they had considered this when they thought to hire women to work as firefighters?* Yet, Kate could not shake the uneasy feeling of not knowing what lay ahead.

Chief Gibbons seemed cold when Kate entered his office. She fought back a shiver; goose bumps covered her arms and legs as she waited by the chair for him to give instruction for her to sit. Kate's mind spun trying to determine how to best start this conversation.

She didn't like that he greeted her by her last name. "Take a seat, Matthews. What can I do for you?" Chief Gibbons walked past her, pointing to the chair as he shut the door behind her. He returned to his desk, not quite to his chair when he started speaking. "I assume there is a matter of great importance that you want to discuss if you have requested a private meeting with me." Chief Gibbons did not wait for her to respond before continuing. "I hope there's not a problem with one of the men." His tone almost dared her to complain about one of her colleagues.

Kate immediately shook her head from side to side, and then found words in the back of her throat. "No, sir. So far there are no problems with any of the men that would be cause for this meeting. This has to do with me."

His face contorted in confusion, and Kate knew he was wondering if she was about to resign.

"I recently had a visit to the doctor's office," she started, easing herself in, "I was informed that... I am pregnant," the words spilled awkwardly from her mouth. She waited for his reply with her stomach in knots. Her superior looked dumbfounded by her announcement.

When, at last, Chief Gibbons regained composure, his tone had cooled. "We have no protocol on the matter, as you might have guessed." He seemed to be waiting for her to resolve the issue for him. When Kate didn't respond, his eyes flared with frustration. "We cannot have you working active duty while you are pregnant. You will have to go on leave immediately."

The color drained from her face, and Kate felt she might fall from her chair as he continued. "You can use your sick and annual leave to collect pay, but unfortunately, when that runs out, you will be put on leave without pay until you are cleared by your doctor to return to full duty."

Panic rapidly overtook her. The thought of her two young children at home, the one now growing within her, mixed with no man, no income, and no way to provide for them made Kate want to scream at this man for not having a policy in place for this type of circumstance. *How can he not be understanding?*

Kate knew she had to remain calm and tried to reason with him. "Can't you put me here, in the office, helping the inspectors...or the secretaries? I don't have enough leave to cover the amount of time I'll need to be out...and I have two children at home to take care of."

Chief Gibbons appeared to be moved by the desperation in her voice. He let out a sigh and said, "I'll check with the city attorney and discuss the situation, since no policy has been put into place."

After three sleepless nights and having heard nothing from Fire Chief Gibbons, Kate called and made an appointment with a prominent attorney who a friend had recommended. She prayed that this man could offer her some help, could make some sense of this situation, which seemed discriminatory toward women. Mr. Anthony was able to see Kate the next day, and as she steered her car to his office, it was as if she was operating on auto-pilot – exhausted and emotionally strung out. The skies poured fury down onto her small car. The deep grey of the storm-ridden skies was perfectly in line with her mood, but not a good omen for what she hoped this meeting held in store.

The weatherman had gotten it right this time. The rain was still coming down in heavy sheets when she left the small remodeled house that served as Mr. Anthony's office, but Kate didn't bother with the umbrella. She let it soak her hair, clothing, even her shoes. She was officially an unemployed single mom with two children, pregnant, and according to the attorney, there was nothing the law could do for her. Kate terribly missed the companionship she had shared with the man she loved. Her tears mixed with the rain drops that ran down her face. Her arms felt too weak to dry them. So, Kate drove, half blinded by her sorrow, back to the home she shared with her children, the very same children she felt she was, once again, failing to support in the way she so desperately longed to.

Although she was stressed out and unhappy with the cards that life had dealt her, Kate determined to deal with the fact that she was pregnant head on. Unfortunately, she could not say the same for the man who had planted the seed.

"Hey, it's Kate. Is Drake there?"

"No, Kate. I'm sorry." The instant that Drake's mother said the words, Kate knew the woman was covering for him. She turned to the pile that was forming on the bed. Kate had gone through every photo album and pulled the pictures of her and Drake from them. Now, they lay in a heap covering her bed.

"All right, please have him call me. It is important." The receiver went dead, and Kate knew that she would not hear from Drake. Anger boiled the blood in her veins; she took a picture from the top of the pile and tore it into bits. Then, another and another until all the pictures in the pile were shredded along with her hopes.

When the adrenaline faded, Kate looked at the mess she'd created. Her eyes filled with tears of frustration, as she swept all the pieces into a bag. She looked at herself in the mirror, put a hand to her belly and picked up the phone.

A few minutes later, her friend Melissa was at the door to watch the kids, and Kate was headed out. She climbed into the car with the bag in hand and headed in the direction of the home of Drake's mother. Kate knew he would be there.

When she arrived, Kate heard a commotion in the back. She instantly recognized his voice and headed around the side of the house to find him. "Drake! We need to talk. Why won't you answer my calls?"

In a drunken stammer, he found his way over to her and told her to go away. Her first thought was to shove him, but she figured he would only topple in his inebriated state. "We NEED to talk," Kate said in an exaggerated whisper.

"No. I'm busy." He laughed and then turned to his brother who was standing beside him. That was all it took. Once again, Kate felt rage exploding within her. In one swift motion, she lifted the bag in her hands, opened it and emptied it all over the ground.

34

O F COURSE YOU are! This WAS us! Now there is nothing. I never want
to speak to you ever again!" With that, Kate turned her back on him
and walked away, determined to keep her word.

Two days later, Kate realized that giving in to her depression would
not be productive. She woke with the determination to make things
right. Kate had to make the best of this forced time off and that meant
finding the help she'd need to ensure her children were fed, clothed,
and sheltered. Neither pride nor ignorance could be a barrier to these
things, and she was running out of time. It wouldn't be long before
she'd receive her last paycheck, and she had to find a way to provide
for her family.

The day that Kate was to meet with the representative at the Welfare
Office, her nerves were so far on edge that she twice missed her eye
lashes when attempting to apply mascara. She finally decided that it was
best not to tempt the tears; she opted against the makeup and moved
her attention to readying the kids – now eight and six years old -- for
school. Her level of attachment to her children was always intense, but
in this moment, Kate could barely hold herself back from hugging them
tight and not letting them go. Some mothers might have felt resentment

toward their kids in a situation like this, but for Kate, there was none, just absolute love and the fear that she might lose them to Avery once again. She hated the thought that she had put herself into this position of uncertainty.

The Welfare Office was simple and small, unlike many of the other federal buildings she had been in, but still it seemed overwhelming. It had been two weeks since she had scheduled the appointment, and the money was getting tight. Kate was able to stretch the food and supplies thus far, but she walked in with the fear that she would be turned down and sent home, unable to care for herself, Mia and Casey, and the one yet to come.

Kate checked in, and after waiting for two hours, found that her anxiety was not completely unfounded.

"Kate Matthews?"

Kate reacted to her name, and moved across the large, chair-filled room to the front window.

"Ms. Matthews...Uh, Ms. Peterson will not be able to see you this morning. She was called out of the office due to an emergency. We will have to reschedule..." The small, graying woman behind the window tapped noisily at the keyboard with long fingernails as she spoke. The sound was beginning to grate on Kate's nerves, as she imagined herself going home without money, without food, and without the promise of any to come.

"No, that's not right," she cried, interrupting the woman's typing. "I waited two weeks for this appointment. I cannot wait any longer." Kate tried to maintain composure as her heart pounded. She made the decision to speak up. She did not scream the words, nor whisper them. Instead, they rolled off her tongue in a calm, but serious fashion. "I need to speak to a supervisor...Now!"

The woman behind the window sized up Kate for a moment, and then made a decision. She picked up the phone handset and punched in a couple numbers. "Ms. Watters," she said evenly, "you're needed at the front desk, please." The receptionist then gave the woman on the other end of the phone a quick rundown of what had taken place.

Kate was feeling like an unwelcome and unwanted guest, but the panic of having nothing to feed her children was consuming her. She forced herself to stand tall and wait for the supervisor to arrive.

Five minutes later, a tall, slender woman arrived, who appeared as stressed as Kate felt. "Ms. Matthews!"

Kate walked toward the woman, and without exchanging another word she was led to the back of the building to an office. The other woman pointed to the vacant chair. "Take a seat." When the door was closed, the woman sat behind the desk with an ungraceful plump. "My name is Shelly Watters. What can I do for you, ma'am?"

Kate had no time to think before words fell like a waterfall from her mouth. "This is all new to me, but I waited the two weeks for my appointment, and two hours since arriving, only to be told that it had to be rescheduled, and that I'd have to wait two more weeks because my case worker had an emergency. I only have enough food to last a few more days. How am I supposed to feed my children? I'm a single, pregnant mother of two young children. My last paycheck from the fire department is already spent, and now they want me to reschedule my..." Kate was set to continue, but Ms. Watters stopped her just as her voice had become unsteady from the sobbing and tears.

"I understand, and I'm sorry for the inconvenience. This will get you through till you return for your next appointment." Ms. Waters pulled out a large booklet and began filling out some sort of form. The next thing Kate knew, she was leaving the office with food stamps in hand. The woman also gave her information about applying for unemployment benefits and special programs for women in her situation.

Though it was not how she had expected the time to go, Kate left unashamed of what had taken place. The paper she held, which she had once believed would make her feel inferior, did exactly the opposite. Kate felt full of pride that she had stood up for herself, for her family, and received the help she needed, the help her hard earned tax dollars were meant to provide.

Kate immediately drove over and met with a woman from the unemployment office. After some time in her office, it was decided she could still work but not in the position the city had hired her for. As a result, by being placed on forced leave, it was deemed the equivalent of a layoff, and Kate was awarded full unemployment benefits along with food stamps. It was one less hurdle she had to jump over, and it meant that her children would have what they needed until they would allow her to return to work.

35

LTHOUGH THE ASSISTANCE from the state was much less than what she'd been making at the fire department, Kate was able to relax somewhat, take care of herself, and enjoy her children. She was still overwhelmed with what was ahead, and she missed the companionship she'd had with Drake. For many nights, she lay awake worrying about how she would raise three children on her own.

The next evening, Kate was sitting in her chair longing for a good night's sleep when the phone rang. When Kate heard his voice, she had to fight the urge to hang up; instead, she sat quietly and listened as Drake said he missed her. Kate's heart longed for him, despite what he had put her through. At last she returned his sentiments and even apologized for that night so many months before.

Now five months pregnant, Kate was thankful to have Drake back in her life and found it easier than she had imagined forgiving and forgetting all that had taken place before. The first night he stayed with her was filled with relief and happiness. Kate felt comforted and loved as he held her that night. Though her belly bulged, she was more than willing to be his blushing bride when Drake suggested once again that they move forward with their original plans to marry. Kate immediately got to work hunting for a gown that would fit over the growing bump at her midsection.

The day started out just like any other. Kate climbed out of bed in the wee hours, and showered before making breakfast for her family, running a warm bath for the children and laying out their clothes. It was not, however, typical for Kate to pull out the dress she'd chosen for this special occasion. It was a gorgeous peach satin and lace wedding dress that tickled her skin as she pulled it on. It hugged her belly tightly, but pulled away beyond that point, flowing gently around her hips and legs. Kate stood in front of the mirror and saw a happy woman staring back. But sadness slowly crept in for a brief moment when Kate realized that her parents and family would not be a part of this happy day. They did not approve of her marriage because Drake was not of the same religious faith, so they would not be attending.

A group of their closest friends and several members of Drake's family gathered in the apartment's club house. She could not see him in that moment, but Kate knew that Drake, too, was nearby. He would be dressed in the light grey suit he had chosen. Around her hung flowers, and folding chairs were lined up to accommodate their guests. It was a simple but beautiful setting and perfect for the woman who was to wed here. Once her arrival was noted, the children were ushered away from her, a long scroll of white paper was unrolled dividing the two, sections of chairs and music began to play. Kate was led out of sight by her new father-in-law Joe; then the children were directed to begin their walk down the aisle. When it was her turn, the excitement filled her, and Kate found it difficult to keep her stride in time to the music.

Drake stood at the end of the short aisle. His eyes sparkled with his own excitement at seeing her; his hair looked mussed as if he had been running his hands through it nervously, but he remained handsome in the grey apparel. Kate smiled at him, and his eyes smiled back at her. Together, they stood in front of a tall, lanky man dressed in a black suit with a white tie. He began to speak, and his voice was full and loud – not really a match for the thin frame. His words to them were sweet and filled with love more profound than she had heard at any other wedding. By the time Drake was kissing his bride, she was bubbling with joy, warmth, and renewed confidence that all would work out.

The reception was simple, filled with good friends and new family. The cake – a simple ivory for her and a German chocolate cake for him – and the drinks were enjoyed by all. After two hours of talking, laughing, dancing, and fantasizing about her new life, the pregnant bride slipped away with Mia and Casey to her apartment to put them to bed. Kate felt happy and content as she lay on the bed, expecting that her new husband would be there very soon to wake her once again.

Her expectations were soon deflated. Instead of returning home after the guests had left, Drake's brothers took him out on the town to celebrate, and caught up in the fun, he failed to watch the clock. Hours passed before Drake returned to their home where his bride was fast asleep. He climbed quietly into the bed and passed out. Four hours later, Kate awoke to find Drake fully dressed on top of the covers, reeking of booze. This was not exactly how she imagined her wedding night would go, and she hoped it was not an omen.

36

THE FIRST MONTH of their marriage passed by quickly and comfortably and not much had changed in their small home. The day-to-day rituals continued as they had before, with the exception of her being home and not reporting to the station every third day. The children enjoyed her being there when they arrived home from school and on the weekends. She played games, sang, danced, baked, and crafted with them. Though she missed work as an outlet, Kate did enjoy and appreciate the extra time she was sharing with Mia and Casey.

At six months pregnant, however, Kate found herself speaking with the doctor nearly every day. The pregnancy had become very difficult, and finally, Dr. Mason instructed her to be on bed rest for the remainder of her pregnancy. The thought terrified her. Three months on her back with nothing to do was pure agony to a woman that had spent years moving at a pace unmatched by most competitive sprinters.

The frustration, discomfort, and boredom that she faced made her miserable. It became more difficult for Kate to tolerate portions of Drake's personality that she typically overlooked. In this state, Kate was overly irritated by the littlest things and was not shy to say so. Hardly a day went by that did not see the two of them in a heated dispute, and she would only grow more angry when he simply walked away, leaving her to the bed rest she was assigned. Kate knew she was intentionally picking fights, but she was feeling so out of sorts she just couldn't bring herself to refrain. She wasn't sure if it was frustration over her situation or her condition that caused her to be so irritated by him. Yet Drake was so patient, understanding how difficult this pregnancy was for her.

Three agonizing months later, Kate recognized the pangs of labor. The contractions came sporadically and far apart at first, but it was not long before she realized this was the real thing. She called Drake to drive her to the hospital. Dr. Mason was already there and expecting her. Kate could not overlook the fact that this was a highly different process than what had happened with her first two pregnancies. The room was perfectly sterile and filled with pastel hues of mauve and blue, as well as stainless steel, a far cry from the dark room with the orange lace curtains during the birth of Mia.

Dr. Mason was a tall attractive dark haired man, much older than her. Grey streaked the sides of his head, and wrinkles were beginning to show around his eyes. Dr. Mason looked at her with concern as he finished his examination; he explained that there was a slight problem. Due to the size of the baby, the umbilical cord had been pinched, and the amniotic fluid surrounding the child was meconium stained. The only way to safely deliver this baby would be through a cesarean section.

Anxiety flooded her body. Kate begged to speak with her mother. Though hundreds of miles away, hearing Leah's voice on the phone provided tremendous comfort. But the thought of being put under anesthesia, cut open, and not able to see the face of her child immediately after birth tormented her.

The voice on the line changed as her father spoke lovingly, but firmly to her. "Kate, you are a strong woman. You can do this. There's no need to be afraid." She was going to disagree, but he did not provide her the opportunity. "Dry your tears and remember that your grandmother just went through a quadruple bypass, and if she got through that then certainly you can handle this."

In a childlike voice she whimpered, "OK, Daddy! I love you, and I'll call you when I'm able to let you know how it went."

"Okay, sweetie! Your mother and I will be waiting for the good news. We love you!" Brad said endearingly before he hung up the phone.

The nurses moved quickly around her, checking vital signs and watching monitors, then quickly departed, leaving Kate alone with her thoughts and the beeping of the monitor, but not for long. Just as quickly as it had gone quiet, the room became a beehive of activity. Dr. Mason was back with a discontented face. "We are taking you to the OR now. The baby's heart rate is dropping, and we need to get him out as soon as possible. The nurses will get you ready and take you down to the OR."

The baby's in distress! She's worried. The nurse unlocked the wheels on her bed and rolled her out into the cold and sterile halls of the hospital. Soon Kate lost sight of Drake, who had been by her side holding her hand.

Three nurses worked together to quickly move her from her bed to a hard metal table, which was covered with padding and lined with sheets and absorbent pads. The room was freezing cold, and her body began to shake. They covered her legs with warmed blankets but left her belly bare, and began to prep her for the procedure ahead.

Cold, mucky brown iodine was poured in a large quantity over her belly as the nurse worked to scrub every square inch, then pulled a razor and began to shave the surface. Kate watched in horror as these women methodically worked on her like she was anything but human. She was not able to concentrate on what they did next; the large door was swung open behind her and another man – this time much shorter with a round belly – came to stand at her side. He introduced himself as the anesthesiologist, then turned his attention to the monitors beside her, asking her questions about what she had had to eat, if she had ever had surgery before, and other equally personal matters. All the while, he was smiling and making her laugh with his jokes. He was distracting her from everything else going on in the room, kindly explaining each step and all that she would feel. He took one of her arms and strapped it down to an outstretched portion of the table, then moved to the other side and did the same.

Kate lay as though on a cross, knowing that she must have looked something like a deer in the headlights. She watched him adjust the Velcro straps to make room for the IV already attached to her arm. He then hooked up a line leading to some sort of liquid hanging just to her right. Kate longed to rip her arms free and jump from the table when anesthesiologist placed a mask over her face and instructed her to begin counting backwards as he continued with his jokes.

Enough with the humor! She wanted to scream, and then all went black...

When Kate awoke, she found herself in a dark room, surrounded by curtains; no one else was there. She instinctively moved her hand to her belly, to find it flat and wrapped snuggly in bandages. Kate would go in and out of consciousness, and each time she came to, it was as though she had awakened from a nightmare. At last, she began to feel like she could hold her heavy eyelids open. The curtain pulled back to reveal the most glorious sight she could have imagined in that moment. Drake was standing over her and reached down to caress her face, pushed her hair back, and kissed her on her forehead.

The next morning, Kate was in a regular room that even let some light shine, thanks to the large window at one side. She was beginning to feel better, though each time the drugs began to wear off, her belly ached with a tremendous pain. Every time a nurse entered, her mouth opened, almost subconsciously, and Kate would ask once again about the baby that was taken from her. She knew, by this point, that he was alive, but still she had not held, nor even seen her new child. Too weak to move on her own, Kate was told that she was not able to get up and visit the intensive care unit where baby Drew was being cared for. Kate lay in the bed – alone, sore, and depressed – waiting for Drake to visit and not only bring her news about their son, but to bring her a breast pump. Her breasts were now becoming engorged with milk, and in need of relief. She couldn't decide which she would be more excited to see – her husband or the pump.

At five o'clock the next morning, and for the third time since ten o'clock the night before, she was awakened to the sound of the nurse checking her vitals on the monitor. Kate was exhausted and wanted nothing more than to pack up and go home. Frustration began to take hold. Thus far, she knew little of Drew's condition.

Now, after three days in the hospital maintaining a brave face, she could hold her emotions back no longer. The moisture was soon too much for her eyes to handle, and small rivers formed down her cheeks. The nurse, having just noticed her being awake, looked at Kate with sympathy. Kate felt as if on the brink of a complete breakdown. The nurse moved to her side and lightly touched her arm. "It's all right, hon. Your son is doing wonderfully. You'll be able to see him this morning."

That was all Kate needed to calm her and bring a smile to her face. She wiped the tears from her eyes and thanked the woman.

As promised, a few hours later, two nurses came to her room and helped Kate from the bed and into a wheelchair. One of the nurses wheeled her out of the room and in the direction of the Neonatal Intensive Care Unit where Drew had been since birth. The other nurse stood not far behind her, pushing the IV bag that was still attached and dripping into her arm. They entered the large room, and Kate felt her heart beating faster and was not sure if it was the excitement of seeing her baby for the first time, or the agony of seeing him so fragile. This area was highly sterilized and smelled of chemicals. The room was drab in whites, grays, stainless steel, and beeping monitors with wires attached to babies. Kate felt horrible that her child had been living here, without her, for three days. They wheeled her close to a small glass enclosed bed. This was when the tears really began to fall. In fact, they poured harder than they had that morning.

This can't be my child, she thought, but she had no way of knowing for sure because she was not awake during the delivery and had never seen him. This child had a head full of thick black hair and was already in need of a hair cut. Drew had monitor wires attached to his tiny body and tubes in his nose as he fought to breathe. He had aspirated the meconium, and now his lungs fought to clear it. His face and body were tinged a yellow hue from jaundice. She looked at the nurse with confusion as she tried to stand up to be closer to her son. Her body was still so weak that Kate collapsed onto the floor. The nurses rushed to help, waiving ammonia under her nose to revive her, and then lifted her back into the wheel chair. Once she regained consciousness, the nurse rubbing Kate's shoulder, assured her, "This beautiful little boy is yours, Kate, and though he still looks sick, he's doing much better, and you should be able to take him home in a few days."

Kate was unbelievably worn out after her ordeal. At the start of the fourth day, she was beginning to feel a bit like a zombie. Her body ached and her mind was weary from worry over her newborn son. Kate also spent many of the nighttime hours thinking of Mia and Casey, who were at home without her. She missed them; she missed her own bed, and she wanted to escape this place and go home. Yet, when the nurse came in that morning and delivered the news that she would be going home today, she did not feel joy. Instead, Kate felt distressed when told she would not be taking Drew home with her. He was not ready to leave the intensive care unit. Her heart ached for him, and when Kate was rolled out of the hospital that day in a wheelchair, it was all she could do not to turn around and run back to the small boy covered by protective glass.

Mia and Casey greeted Kate at the door, ecstatic that she was home. Though her stomach still ached from the incision that had functioned as a substitute birth canal, she tried to go on with the day almost as if it were the same as any other. She remained very weak and in pain from the surgery. But Kate willed herself to be strong, resisting the doctor-ordered bed rest, and made daily visits to the hospital to see Drew. On the morning of her third day home, she rose before five o'clock. Like a child excited about a trip to the amusement park, Kate was far too overjoyed to sleep. Her baby was coming home at last. Kate went to wake Mia and Casey, but what she found there replaced the excitement with terror. Mia looked up at her with a face full of swollen red spots. Casey complained of a stomach ache, and when she leaned over to calm him, she saw the same red spots covering his shoulders and chest. In total disbelief and ready to lose what sanity she had left, Kate paced the kitchen.

"What are we going to do, Drake? He's been in a sterile environment since birth and now we're going to bring him to a home infested with chicken pox." Kate continued pacing back and forth.

"Call the doctor and ask him what to do, and I'll call my mother to come over to watch Mia and Casey," Drake said as he picked up the phone.

Two hours later, her mother-in-law, Teri, was standing outside the front door. "Thanks for coming over to stay with the kids. I don't know what we would have done without you. Please come in." Kate had to fight the urge to collapse from the stress. Kate quarantined the children in their rooms with coloring books, crayons, story books, and toys. When Kate felt that they had ample entertainment, she left Teri to care for them, while Drake drove her to pick up the fragile infant who was entrusting her with his health.

When they arrived at the hospital, Kate was required to fill out an enormous amount of paperwork. She felt, momentarily, like an adoptive parent. Although she had birthed this child, the days since his birth had dragged; Kate had spent very little of that time with him. This would be the first chance she'd have to hold him for any real length of time. When they finally brought the baby to her, Kate was surprised to see how healthy he looked. The yellow had faded so that his skin was almost a normal shade of pink. His big brown eyes were open and staring into her own. Kate nuzzled his hair covered head, pulled him close, breathed him in, and somehow knew that everything would be okay.

37

OR THE NEXT three days, Mia and Casey were confined to their bedrooms, except when they needed to use the bathroom. They were unable to hold or touch their new baby brother, and this brought with it a whole lot of disappointment. Her small house echoed with frustration and the cries of an infant at night. Once the chicken pox was no longer a threat, Kate invited Mia and Casey into the living room, where she let each take a turn holding their new baby brother. In that moment, as she and Drake looked on, and the three siblings sat together on the couch, Kate felt the closeness of her little family.

The thought crossed her mind, a few weeks after things had settled out, that this pregnancy had taken a toll on her body. Life was almost back to normal with the addition of one more person to share her love, and now it was time to face the fact that soon she would have to return to work. Yet, looking at herself in the mirror in that moment, Kate wondered how much of a possibility that would really be. Though she had not gained an excessive amount of weight, the surgery had left a large scar on her belly, and she was lacking muscle definition from the months of bed rest. She was also missing the endurance and stamina that she'd had nine months prior. If she was going to be a firefighter once again, she would have to do some serious training. Just the thought of it made her muscles ache, but Kate was determined to give her family and herself a stable comfortable life, and that meant returning to work.

The next morning, Kate rose before the sun, a bit anxious and still very tired, yet knowing that if she was going to find time for running, it needed to be before the kids awoke. While the older two slept – as did their step-father – Kate set off on her first post-pregnancy run. The sun, as soon as it began to peek over the horizon, was hot and her body, which was no longer used to this sort of demanding activity, fought her urge to move onward. Kate hated that she could feel areas of her body shake as she ran.

In the beginning, for a couple of weeks, Kate found it difficult to pull herself from bed at the early hour. The new routine soon gave Kate the energy and strength she'd forgotten about over the past seven months at home. Time passed quickly, and Kate reported to the administration office to fill out the necessary paperwork for her return to work. Afterwards, she was directed next door to Central Station to get her assignment location.

She had been a bit nervous about returning and leaving the children behind, but Kate found that seeing some familiar faces, the surroundings that had served as her second home, and the well organized equipment, made her happy to be back.

Her reintroduction to work, assigned to Station Three and a new crew of men went unbelievably well. Kate found herself right at home in the barracks and didn't even think twice when the men dropped their pants at the end of each evening before climbing into bed. This was her life, and even though she had left it for a short time, it had not left her. In fact, the only difficulty Kate faced was the awkwardness that came with her decision to breast feed. This, of course, had not been an issue for the first six weeks while she was home with the baby, but now, back at work – in a man's world – it created several obstacles. Every couple of hours, Kate would sneak into the only restroom, move all the way to the back of the room to unbutton her grey uniformed shirt and expose her breasts. The pumping did not take long; still the fifteen minutes seemed an eternity. She knew that the men were outside working hard at their assigned tasks and grumbling about the fact that she was allowed to slip away so often.

Kate went to the kitchen to put the milk in the refrigerator so that it could be stored and given to her baby during her next shift. She then went outside and continued her work alongside her coworkers.

38

KATE'S SECOND SHIFT back went well, during the day, but just after dusk that familiar shriek of the alarm filled the station. As always, the initial shock caused her to jump, but like riding a bike, she had not forgotten procedure.

"Are you ready, rookie?" one of the men looked right at her and chuckled.

"I'm no rookie! I can outperform you any day," she laughed while donning her gear.

In no time at all, Kate climbed aboard the truck, keeping perfect pace with the men around her. The call was for a house fire just inside their assigned territory. When they arrived on scene, the building was burning with red and orange flames spiking out from almost every window. Their attention turned to the police vehicle parked unattended in front of the house and the officer nowhere in sight. Lacey was irritated that he was unable to position the fire truck in the best place for the firefighters to gain access.

With quick thinking, Kate jumped from the truck. "Watch this Lacey!" She headed for the driver's side door of the police car. The keys were in the ignition and the motor was still running. Kate jumped in, put it in gear, and drove it around the corner onto the next street and out of the way. She returned to the truck, already positioned in front of the house, turned to Lacey and said, laughing, "Who's the rookie?"

Kate began pulling out the hoses. She turned her attention back to the house which had all of the windows open. She assumed this was the tenant's way of letting in the cooler night air. She noticed a few windows with box fans that spun as smoke rushed through them. The plastic was melting and they sagged and drooped much like the famous painting by Salvador Dali, in which clocks melted into the landscape. As was expected, the police officer finally came walking from behind the house. The look of shear panic on his face was priceless when he began to look around realizing his vehicle was missing. Kate approached him, restraining the smile that was about to explode on her face. "Are you looking for your cruiser?"

"Oh my God! Where is it?" The officer's head spun left and right. Kate looked him in the eye and said, "I moved it around the corner, onto the adjacent street. Next time you respond to a fire call, make sure you park your cruiser so that it does not obstruct the fire department from doing their job." She then turned her attention to the crowd of onlookers, looked back at him and said, "Now how about keeping that crowd of people away so no one gets injured?" Kate tossed her thumb in the air as a signal to her comrades, and finally let go of her laughter before returning to battle the blaze.

An hour or so had passed. Kate held one of the hoses aimed at the building, still burning at a rather rapid rate, and felt a familiar tingling in her chest. When she looked down, the front of her shirt was starting to develop two strategically placed wet spots. Not long after this, her breasts began to ache with pressure, and her shirt was beginning to look as if it were crying. When the blaze had been successfully extinguished, Kate stood amongst the men, arms folded across her chest and cheeks burning with embarrassment. Not a word was said, but she knew they all had noticed. How could they not? The entire front of her shirt was as wet as if she'd turned the hose on herself.

For the next few shifts Kate was fortunate in that she did not have to go out on a call and experience the humiliation of a drenched uniform again. For that she was grateful, and she continued to hide away in the bathroom for short periods of time so that she could ensure her baby was getting everything he needed to grow healthy and strong. However, after six months, the breast pumping ritual was becoming more of a burden than she could handle, especially when she was called to work overtime one Thursday – a rather laid back day – at another station with a different crew. She excused herself to the bathroom yet again and emerged a little later with the bottle of milk and placed it in the refrigerator.

An hour later, Lieutenant Neilson walked into the TV room holding a cup of coffee. "Kate, I forgot to bring cream for the coffee so I used the milk you brought. Hope you don't mind?"

She stopped dead in her tracks and busted out laughing harder than she had in weeks. "Why are you laughing?" a puzzled look on his face. "Did I miss out on an inside joke?"

"That issssss…my breast milk, silly!" She tried to contain her laughter.

"Whaaaat?" He managed to say as he spit the coffee from his mouth.

"You heard me! Breast milk. I just finished pumping it and put it in the refrigerator. You didn't notice that it was in a baby bottle?" unable to quell her laughter

"No. I just thought you used it as a container for REGULAR milk. It's actually not that bad!" He joined everyone in laughing at his own expense.

"Well, it is for the baby, so keep your paws off of my milk," Kate grimed.

Kate reported back to Station Six on her next work day. This happened to be the Fourth of July, and though she was disappointed she wouldn't be celebrating with her family, she was more concerned she'd be on duty during the busiest day of the year. Drinking and celebration combined with the use of fireworks by those who were not qualified made for a night full of fire calls.

Kate sauntered into Station Six, head hanging and coffee in hand. She was not happy to be there, and from the looks of it, most of the other men were dreading it as much as she was. Each knew that the chances they would make it through the evening without a call were slim to none.

The day slowly began to feel like any other, and the group went about completing the work assigned them. It wasn't until they were free to move about the station that there was a renewed sense of impending trouble. Each of them walked slowly and quietly as if one wrong move would set off the alarm. The only noise that could be heard in the large room was the opening and closing of the fridge, the occasional smack of a pan as it hit the stove or sink, and the fire radio traffic, which was busy. Fire stations all over the area were being called out, one after another, but Station Six remained inactive.

Day turned to night, and all dishes were cleaned and put away, Kate joined the men in the sitting area. Though she had a book in front of her, like many of the men, she was unable to comprehend anything she read, thanks to the continual sound of the fireworks going off outside.

Could it be? Are we really going to make it through this night without a call? Kate thought, moving to set the book down, thinking that maybe a glass of water would calm her overactive nerves; but before she could reach the kitchen...*SHHHHHRRRIEEEEEEKKK!* Her heart nearly jumped out of her chest. *Damn!* Station Six was being called out.

Kate geared up and headed for the garage where the trucks' engines were rumbling with lights flashing. She stepped out into the bay and heard the scanner squawking wildly through the intercom. "...warehouse fire..." which took her by surprise. They weren't being called out for a fireworks-related grass fire; they were headed for the Port of Brownsville. The nerves and adrenaline pooled within her, pushing her to move faster than normal. Within seconds they were in the truck, en route to the fire.

The port was a good distance from the station, making the ride longer than usual. This combined with the fact that it was a warehouse, caused questions to circle through her head about how bad the fire would be, and their safety in a situation like this. As far as she could tell, the other station within the district was out on a minor call, but would provide backup as soon as they refilled their tanks.

The sky turned to an eerie color as they approached. There was an unnatural orange glow in the black night sky that made the hairs on her neck stand up. The truck came to a stop, and Kate saw a building that seemed to be crafted of fire rather than brick or metal. The whole structure was engulfed, and the flames flew high into the sky above them. The smoke was thick, and when the door of the truck opened, it was almost as if it had to push the black-grey swirls out of the way. The warehouse was burning rapidly, and the building that stood to its right was in danger of being involved; the flames were stroking it vigorously.

"The neighboring building is housing a fuel tanker truck, so let's get a move on." At these words from Captain Gordon, the crew quickly sprang to action. Kate was in the first engine to arrive at the scene, and got busy pulling hoses from the truck. Lacey readied the pump and charged the lines as soon as Kate positioned the hose, aiming it at the large mass of yellow, blue, and orange, and doing her best to calm the fury. Meanwhile, another crew arrived and moved quickly to the neighboring building, prying the door open. Flames were rushing in violent waves, burning the walls of the second building and teasing the truck like tiny feelers growing from the main structure.

Kate heard her name and swung her head around to see Captain Gordon standing behind her.

"You're needed over there!" He pointed to the building with the tanker, and her heart sank a little. "Take your hose! Aim it at the back of the tanker to keep it cool while they work to get it out of the warehouse." Though he screamed, his words were barely audible through the noise of the burning building, the rush of water, and the padding of her helmet. "Keep those flames down! We don't need that damn thing exploding on us!"

Terror flooded her veins, and she felt like she was running on Jello.

"...close highway...tanker might explode..." Kate vaguely heard someone say into a walkie-talkie behind her, and what was mild fear turned to full-fledged panic within her. She fought to keep calm, but her mind was screaming, *"RUN! Who will take care of my kids?* She could almost see tomorrow's headline: *"Female Firefighter Blown to Bits in Explosion." My body in a million pieces and unrecognizable?* Kate could not keep the ugliness from her thoughts as she stood there directing the water to the tanker truck.

"Just do your job," said Captain Gordon, behind her, as if reading her thoughts. He placed his hand on her shoulder. "Ignore everything else around you." His words were strong and in control, yet calming.

"We're all going to die!" The voice of a coworker and ex-Marine could be heard above all else, as his panic took hold, and he began climbing the chain-link fence nearby in an effort to get away. The words cut through the muddle in her brain.

I have to...have to hold my ground and protect my coworkers, so we can all be with our families! Kate took three steps toward the large truck, just twenty feet away, planted herself and held tight as the flames emerged through the walls of the warehouse and climbed the sides of the building, shooting over the back of the tanker.

A few moments later another hand touched her shoulder. "I got it! Go! Go take a break." A fighter from Station Three took her spot and pointed Kate in the direction of the ambulance stationed nearby where she would be immediately fed oxygen. She reluctantly surrendered the hose, then did what she was told.

With a giant step she climbed into the ambulance. There on the floor in front of her was a man, at least six inches taller and forty pounds heavier than her, with a paper bag to his mouth. He was the one who had, moments before, been climbing the fence. Now he was curled in a ball on the floor of an ambulance fighting a bout of hyperventilation. A smile fought at the corner of Kate's lips, and inside she desperately wanted to laugh as she watched the bag inflate and deflate with each breath he took, but her pride and sense of comradeship wouldn't allow her to do it. Kate put a mask to her face and breathed until her lungs filled with the sweet, clean oxygen – giving her a bit of renewed energy.

39

KATE, STILL IN shock at how close she came to losing her life that night, stood there in the station after seeing the news broadcast. The reporter stated that the highway to the port was closed for a mile in each direction to protect the public in case the tanker truck – the one Kate helped to keep cool – exploded. The next morning, when she returned home, Kate went straight to the kids and gave each of them a good long hug, followed by Drake.

The days of endless waiting for the next big event were long gone. With three children and her career, there was no time to be bored or to contemplate how long it would be until the next birthday, holiday, or other family affair. Some would have seen her home as hectic or overwhelming, but Kate always enjoyed the chaos of children running and laughing, the baby blabbing away, and music playing in the background.

Kate felt accomplished at work but had growing animosity for the man she'd married. While Drake's temperament at home was easygoing, whenever he was faced with troubles or confrontation at work, he would flip his lid. While she was in the kitchen putting together a meal for the family, the front door opened with a *CRASH!* The baby, once resting peacefully, now began to scream out, but Kate could not get to Drew because the pan threatened to sear the food should she walk away from it in that moment. Her heart tugged at her, pulling her to the infant, but her head instructed her to finish what she was doing first.

Drake walked right past his crying son, straight to the fridge and pulled a can of beer from the door. Drake was clearly nearing his breaking point. He looked right through her as the can popped, and he took a large swallow. Her own expression of confusion quickly turned to anger.

"What are you doing?" Kate tried to control her volume while removing the finished food from the stove, and then moved to the playpen. Once the baby was peaceful again and resting on her hip, it suddenly dawned on her. "Why are you home?" Drake was early by well over an hour. Usually she had time to get the whole meal put together, on the table, and the children seated and served before he came through the door.

Kate watched him take the can of beer, still a third full, and finish it in one large chug. He lowered it, took a deep breath and told Kate the story of his day and the reprimand his boss gave him over a difficult customer who would not back down until he refunded her money.

Kate understood Drake's frustration; it would be difficult to handle a situation like that without upsetting someone, but she was completely caught off guard when he said, "Then the bastard fired me!"

"You got fired again?" The question spilled angrily out of her mouth, still hanging open from shock. This was the second job he'd lost since they'd reunited, just six months before.

Drake recoiled as if he'd been hit. He spat his words at her. "I thought you'd give me some support, but obviously..." He never finished the statement. Drake headed for the front door, threw it open, and slammed it behind him.

Two months later, Drake still had not found a job; he continued to sit around the house as if waiting for a knock at the door with a job delivered to him on a silver platter. It was becoming difficult to pay the bills on just her income; Kate decided it was time for her to do something about their predicament. She still worked every third day at the station, but Kate applied for a second job with the nearby Sheraton Hotel. The position for an indoor cocktail waitress and part-time poolside bartender sounded perfect for her personality, and apparently management thought so as well. Three days after her first interview, Kate reported to the hotel to start working. Clad in the short black tuxedo wrap dress they provided her as a uniform, Kate followed after a veteran waitress to learn the ins and outs of the position. She moved easily on her feet due to her firefighter physique. It took her just two days of training to be given the go-ahead. Not long after that she had won over a number of the staff members and regular guests. The company was fun and exciting. Kate found it exhilarating when top executives who came from out of town requested her to wait on their table.

Her job was refreshingly low-key as compared to the one she called her career. Kate quickly learned that being a gracious server with more than a hint of playful flirting led to bigger tips than she'd ever imagined.

One night in particular, a group of top executives from General Motors entered the lounge and upon looking around opted to sit in her section of assigned tables. She'd been waiting on the men for about an hour when she approached the table once more to ask about refills. One of the men turned and pulled an empty chair from a nearby table.

"Have a seat," he said, with a warm smile. Though she was not supposed to sit among the guests, she obliged. She had seen other waitresses there do so on occasion.

"So, what is a woman like you doing working at a place like this?" Though his words were a bit obnoxious, Kate found the man to be cute, and knew that the sudden presumptuousness was likely a result of the four scotch and sodas since his arrival. She flashed a smile in response and fluttered her eyelids, not feeling it necessary to explain herself. The men found this very amusing and shared a hearty laugh.

"Can I get you anything else to drink...gentlemen?" Kate gave them a wink and popped out of her seat. They laughed again.

"What time do ya get outta here?" A different man sitting across the table asked.

"Not for another couple hours," Kate smiled knowing what would come next.

"Well then, we'll jus' have ta endure another couple rounds."

This banter continued, and as suggested, they stayed until just before her shift ended. The man, who seemed to be the alpha male of the group, smiled as he handed her a large wad of cash folded inside the thin paper bill. "Keep the change." He winked at the group and they left. When Kate was in the back, away from the curious eyes of fellow employees and customers, she counted the money to find that they had left her a hundred dollar tip. She chuckled to herself before slipping it into her pocket book.

In the few weeks since Kate began working at the hotel lounge, she realized she was receiving way more attention from the male customers than any of the other waitresses. A tall man walked outside to the patio and pulled a stool up tight to the small Tiki bar where Kate was working, and leaned his face in his hands, which were propped by elbows on the bar revealing his gold Rolex watch, making it obvious that he was financially well off.

"Hello, beautiful."

Kate just laughed and inquired as to what he would like to drink that evening. After the awkward moment of a not-so-classy, "I'd love to drink you up," she busied herself making him the gin and tonic he requested. For over an hour the man kept her company. He told her stories of work, of places he had traveled, and, of course, kept up a constant stream of flirty banter, concluding with, "So, what time do you get off this evening?"

Kate was beginning to wonder why everyone was so interested in her work schedule.

"Umm...not for a few hours still," she answered in a noncommittal tone.

"Well, I do believe I can stick around for 'another couple hours'," he attempted to mimic her soft voice. "I'd love to take you to dinner." He gave Kate no time to respond before starting in again, "I could fly you to New Orleans for dinner," and then with a very conceited air, "I own a plane and I could have you back in the morning."

194

Kate gave him a gracious grin and refilled his drink before answering, "Thank you, but I can't accept your offer. I have a family at home waiting for me." She left it at that, and he laughed heartily before taking a big sip of his drink.

Kate continued to spend the evenings of each weekend attending to customers in the lounge, or bartending by the pool, on the days she wasn't fighting fires. In the lounge, Kate enjoyed the live music. At the pool, she was able to wear her bathing suit and enjoy the sun and the water while she worked. She moved effortlessly about the patio and poolside, greeting all with smiles, waves, and pleasant words.

One evening as the crowds began to die down, she sat on a stool talking to her coworker, Angie, about her life. The two had become close and shared many of their stories. Both had children and needed this job as a source of extra income. Angie, who was five years older than Kate, was telling her an unbelievable story about what had happened during her day job as a teacher. Kate loved these tales, filled with childhood antics. Just as Angie was reaching the end of her account, laughing so hard she could barely speak, her tiny voice went silent. Kate felt nervous as Angie stared directly at her, another thought having obviously taken precedence over the initial story.

"We need substitute teachers right now...and you'd be good at it," Angie said, as if it were the most thrilling observation ever made. When Kate didn't answer, Angie said it again, only this time it was more like a question. "We need substitute teachers right now?"

As if life wasn't hectic enough with three children, a demanding career, and a part-time job, she was now being offered a potential third job. Although it was enough to cause her great stress, she knew they needed the income, and she did enjoy being with and teaching children.

Kate applied for a substitute teaching position and was accepted. Two weeks later, dressed in a long skirt and a button-down blouse, Kate entered the school building prepared to work with third graders all day. *How bad could it be?* Kate thought. *They are the same age as my children.*

Three jobs and a family — with almost no help from her husband who couldn't hold down a job and did little to help with the cleaning and kids — proved to be a bit too much. After a few weeks of the balancing act, Kate decided, per the suggestion of a friend, that it was time to get some help, and began to interview potential candidates for the position of live-in nanny.

A week and a half after she had started her hunt, a young girl strode up to her door. The short black cropped 'do' worked perfectly with her young, adorable face, and the sunglasses that were lifted from the brim of her nose uncovered stunning brown eyes. There was nervousness written all over the way the girl approached, yet something told Kate that this girl would be the perfect fit.

Kate instantly liked Marie, after only a few minutes of speaking with her, and was happy that her friend had made the recommendation. Marie spoke very little English and Kate could tell that this had been an issue in the past. Thinking back on her own struggles, due to a language barrier, Kate felt for Marie, who was five years younger than herself and had two children of her own. *This is going to work out*, Kate thought opening the door and thanking her for coming.

40

T HAT NIGHT, AFTER hanging up the phone with her friend who knew Marie, Kate smiled and let out a deep sigh. This was going to be good. She could continue with her jobs and make the money they needed to survive with the security of knowing that her children were being well cared for.

It took very little time for the household to adjust to the new member. Marie was wonderful with the children and was efficient with the laundry, dishes and other household chores that had suffered as a result of Kate taking a third job. Kate was ecstatic that she had made the decision to hire some help, especially during this time of year. It was hurricane season, and she knew there was a good chance she would be needed at the station at a moments notice if a storm hit the area. Thus far, since starting with the department, she had managed to avoid working in one of the tremendous storms as one after another had navigated out of the way of their small city. This year, however, Kate had the eerie feeling that things might not go so well.

Just as hurricane season was winding down and Kate thought they had escaped another year of Mother Nature's wrath, the local news plotted Hurricane Gilbert – headed straight toward them. Warnings flashed on all radio and television stations alerting the public to begin preparing for the inevitable blow that would be taken, if and when the storm tore through. This storm was reported to be the most intense Atlantic hurricane on record, to date. When it hit Jamaica as a category 3, everyone thought it would be the end, but it kept moving like a freight train, gaining strength, reaching a category 5 by the time it hit Cozumel. The land mass slowed it slightly, but still it continued on toward Brownsville and the mouth of the Rio Grande, carrying the power, once again, of a category 3 hurricane.

Kate felt unnerved and out of her element as she rushed to the grocery store, where she was met by everyone else in the neighborhood. Kate bought the essentials and rushed back to assist Drake with boarding up the windows. With the first window covered to the point that they felt safe, they moved on to the second. Kate held the board tight as the nerves within her tingled. Drake fussed with it a moment longer before he raised the hammer.

"Dammit!" he swore when the ringing phone startled him and caused him to miss the nail completely.

"I got it…" Kate let the board down easily and begrudgingly headed to the phone, knowing exactly what would be coming from the other end. From that point on, everything seemed to be moving too quickly. She couldn't slow it down. Kate listened to Captain Edwards on the phone saying that she was to report for duty. The next words he spoke sent a shiver down her spine.

"You are welcome to bring your family here to wait out the storm," he added with genuine concern.

"Thanks! I'll get there as soon as possible," Kate said, looking at Drake with concern.

It was very rarely permitted that non-firefighters enter the barracks, and in that moment, Kate knew that the fire department was expecting the worst. She returned the phone to the hook and then pulled her husband aside. She wanted him to hold her, to tell her everything would be all right, but Drake seemed to be as fearful as she was in the moment.

Kate grabbed his hand. "Captain Edwards said I have to report to

Central Station, and you and the kids are welcome to come along and stay until the storm passes. What do you think?"

"I need to call my brother to come over and help me finish boarding up the windows. This house has been here for decades, so I think we will be alright. No sense dragging all the kids and packing up everything. We will manage just fine here. You get ready and take off. I'm more worried about you than us." Drake took her in his arms and held her tight.

Kate agreed, somewhat reluctantly, that the house, which had withstood other storms for more than twenty years, was the perfect place for them to stay. Kate gathered the stuff she would need and tightly hugged Mia and Casey and told them not to worry. Then she picked up baby Drew, held him close and breathed him in. "I will miss you, sweetie…be good for your daddy," she whispered in his ear.

Kate walked to the car, her hair blowing violently behind her in the increasing winds. Though she was the one who would likely be out in the storm that night, Kate could think only of the little ones she had just left behind, and hoped they did not know enough to be scared. Her heart was breaking, feelings of mixed emotions ran through her at the thought of leaving them there, even though she believed they would be safe.

The sky grew darker as Kate drove the short distance to the station. The scene overhead when she arrived was ominous and made the hairs on her body stand at attention. Kate fought off a shiver, grabbed her duffel bag, and headed for the station's large bay doors where the fire trucks rested. As always, she strode confidently up the stairs to the barracks, but when she reached the top, the same feeling of anxiety washed over her once again. There before her were the families of several of her coworkers. All were huddled in the sitting area, speaking quietly about the night that lay ahead of them. Kate thought of her own family, imagining what would happen if the storm was worse than she expected, and wondered if she would be able to speak with them that night – or ever again. The thought made her knees weak, wondering if she had done the right thing leaving them home with Drake. Richard, her colleague, came to her side to make sure she was all right, and his hand on her shoulder brought her back to present time.

Kate pushed the hair from her face and assured him, "I'm fine. I'm just psyching myself up for what's coming our way." Once her bag was safely stowed away, Kate made quick work of tying her hair back in a tight braid that was unlikely to feel the wrath should she have to go out in the winds again.

While the families waited out the storm, they talked, and even managed some lighthearted jokes. Kate sat off to the side watching through the window as the storm rolled in, listening for details faintly coming from the TV room where most of the men were gathered. The plate glass window rattled with each gust of wind. The rain that was now pouring down from the charcoal grey sky seemed to be traveling horizontally as the wind pushed it off course. Kate knew she was now sitting right in the middle of her very first hurricane. The scanner was abuzz with unusually stressed voices; she clung to the stool under her waiting to hear which stations would be called out. When hers was not listed, she hung her head in relief, only to find that she was white-knuckling the stool. Kate released her grip and took a deep breath to regain her composure.

Over the next hour, calls continued to sound, and each time it would take Kate several minutes to recover from the fear that gripped her. The storm was still swirling violently, and she was praying not to be called out in the midst of it. The tops of the trees were forced sideways by the wind until they threatened to break under the pressure; objects flew past with no site of landing. Kate could only watch in horror as the town was overtaken by the storm's fury.

SHRRRRRRRRRIEEEEK! SHRRRRRRRRRIEEEEK! Nearby family members, who were not used to the unusually loud alarm, gasped, screamed, and jumped in surprise. She felt her heart drop. For half a second, her body locked up, and she felt that she might not be able to make it move; then she saw the men rushing to grab their gear, and she instinctively did the same. Kate moved so quickly, as if robotic, that she was dressed and sliding down the pole before the majority of her fellow fighters.

Kate climbed up, took her seat within the gigantic truck, and listened as Captain Edwards told them that a house just two blocks away had caught fire. The winds whipped as they rolled out of Central Station, and she felt the truck fighting to stay on course. Kate wondered how they could possibly control a blaze while working against the gale force winds. The rain hit the roof of the truck hard, making a threatening sound as they drove, siren blaring and lights flashing against the pitch black sky.

The fire, which had ignited from a spark in the laundry room, was small and easily contained. Much to her relief, it was only a short time before they had it extinguished. They stood in the yard outside the house, rain hammering on their helmets and the winds threatening to rip them off the ground. At last Captain Edwards was certain there was no possibility of reigniting, and ordered the team back to the truck. It was so dark that it was difficult to make out the faces of the men until they were lit by the lights of the truck. Every one of them, including herself, looked like drowned rats. Water dripped from Kate's helmet, and her bunker gear felt heavier than usual as she pushed herself up the steps and into her seat. Kate removed the helmet that had protected her face from the violent wind blown rain, pushed a tendril of hair back from her face, and breathed a sigh of relief. The men followed suit. All were happy the call was over, and now prayed that nothing more would happen till the storm had passed.

Just as they were turning back into the station, a loud announcement came over the radio. Her unit was being called out again. They all exchanged looks of frustration. The truck quickly circled the block and headed back in the direction from which it had originally come. The lights flashed to life again. Kate returned her helmet to her head and said a silent prayer as they made their way to a call outside their normal district.

The truck felt as if it were dragging an anchor along behind it as it made its way through the roads that were more like riverbeds now — water rushing quickly down as the ground swelled with more than it could absorb.

When, at last, they arrived on the scene, Kate peered out the small window to see sparks of light jumping off the ground, flying this way and that. It looked surreal against the black sky beyond. Kate climbed down and followed the men's gaze up to the house, where a power line had freed itself. It jumped, hissed, and sparked with tremendous fury as the electricity surged through it.

Kate, as well as the stray onlookers who were willing to tempt the weather for a peek at the action, were mesmerized by the sparks. Aware of the imminent danger that the electricity could pass current through the water, she worked with the men to move everyone back from the area and rope off the yard. They stood in the downpour once more, their jackets hung from the weight of the water and their helmets became miniature waterfalls; still they waited for the electric company to arrive.

41

KATE HAD SPOKEN to her family just once that night after arriving at the station from the second call. The hurricane had hit just south of the city in Mexico, and the storm's outer bands were creating the high winds and rain. Everything had been relatively calm after returning to the station, and each of her coworkers had time to shower and warm themselves after a night of misery.

Next morning, Kate threw her bag together and prepared to make the journey home. The streets were filled with debris, making the commute much longer than it normally would have been, but she was not concerned with that. Kate was just thankful that the town was mostly intact, especially the small house that had managed to withstand yet another storm and to continue its twenty plus years of existence. When she saw it, her eyes became wet with joy and relief. She rushed inside and hugged everyone – including Marie. Kate was so happy to be home, so happy to have this family, so happy that life could go on as before.

The first couple of days after the storm, she lived on cloud nine with a renewed hope, but slowly Drake lowered her feet back to the ground. The realization hit her a few weeks after that horrible night.

She was married to a man who cared very little about himself, but still more than he did for his family. On the weekends, while she was working at the hotel and Marie was caring for their children, Drake was off gallivanting with friends and coming home reeking of alcohol.

Drake spent more time unemployed and at home than he did at work. His efforts to hold down a job began to seem ridiculously weak as time and time again he came home filled with rage over an argument with his employer. After a few more months, Kate realized that she could no longer handle caring for a man who was not committed to being a responsible husband and father. Kate watched as his anger took control of him following her asking him to leave.

"You don't know what it's like to work all day with complaining customers for the money they pay me," he shouted while packing his clothes.

"I know that when you have a family that depends on you, you don't fly off the handle and quit every time you don't like how you're talked to. You have never tried to find a way to either accept it or make your situation better, and I can't keep supporting you and the kids. It's just not fair and I resent you for putting us in this mess." Kate tried explaining her view.

"You think you know everything and have all the answers. Fine, do it on your own! I'm outta here!" he shouted at her, closing up his bag.

"What the hell are you talking about? I *have* been doing it all on my own with no help from you." her voice rose in anger. The last thing she heard was the slamming of the door as he stormed out of the house.

Though her professional life was going strong, Kate spent the next few months feeling ashamed and disheartened at the fact that her personal life was continually in shambles. Mia and Casey were with Avery for summer vacation, so she picked up the phone and called her friend, Angie, looking for an excuse to get out of the house that had once held so much happiness for her. A short time later, Angie was outside honking.

Kate followed her friend through the doors of the club. A ball hanging from the ceiling shot colored lights in every direction as the DJ yelled something into the mic, then another top twenty hit began.

Unlike before, Kate now felt comfortable in this type of setting, perhaps because of her experiences at the hotel. She confidently strode to the bar, ordered her favorite drink and bent at the waist, propped her elbows on the bar and laid her chin in her hands while she spoke sweetly to the cute bartender.

Kate was done feeling sorry for herself, and for another marriage gone wrong, a marriage she had given more to than should be required of anyone. She was bound and determined to have some fun tonight. That included some innocent flirting with the bartender. As the man took her money for the drink, smiled, and turned to help the next customer, she started to step backward, but a hand stopped her. Kate turned to find herself staring at the very same man she had met in a bar years before. Though he was not playing with the band that night, Fabian still had the same handsome, chiseled features she remembered. His black hair was slicked back, revealing gorgeous chocolate brown eyes that danced with amusement at seeing her again. When Kate realized her jaw was still resting on the floor, she flashed a quick smile in correction. This made him laugh out loud. Fabian coolly reached a hand out and moved a stray hair away from her face, staring into her eyes. She was spellbound and hardly noticed when he took her hand and led her to the dance floor.

For the next few hours Kate didn't see her friend; she didn't notice when the DJ changed songs; she didn't even care when a drunken idiot behind her sloshed beer on her foot. Kate was totally engrossed in the man before her. They talked about all that had happened since they'd last made contact. He too had moved on and found a wife, but they had separated not long before Kate had asked her own husband to leave. This brought up other topics of conversation about marriage, commitment, broken promises, and loneliness.

42

KATE WAS FORCED to leave earlier than she wanted to that night, not wanting to be rude to her friend who needed to get up early the next morning and was ready to go. He too seemed reluctant to say goodbye. Fabian finally leaned forward and gently brushed her lips with his all the while whispering his promise to call her very soon. Her heart fluttered, goose bumps formed on her arms and legs, and she felt a slight weakness in her knees when he turned to walk away.

Kate felt happier at home now that she didn't have the constant worry about Drake losing his job, or getting drunk. She actually looked forward to coming home for a change to a clean and peaceful home. She was also seeing Fabian, but only occasionally, since neither of them was officially divorced. Everything was moving very slowly; nevertheless, she loved the attention, his sense of humor, and of course, his good looks, and he continued to enchant her. Kate could not believe there was a man she could talk to for hours without losing interest.

The morning came with a call from Avery asking if she could pick up Mia and Casey. He had to work, and Mary was ill and couldn't drive them home.

Kate drove the hour to Avery's house to pick up the kids. She was buckling Casey into the back seat when she noticed he was protecting his finger. Kate took hold of it, and Casey whined and pulled it back. "What happened to your finger?"

"I got a thorn under my fingernail and it hurts," Casey started crying.

"Didn't your dad take you to the doctor?" Kate said with concern.

"No. He said you'd take him since you have the insurance." Mia blurted out matter-of-factly.

"When did you hurt your finger?" Kate asked Casey, now noticing the green puss under the fingernail.

"The day we got here!" Casey said sniffing.

"That was almost a week ago." Kate explained, trying to stay calm while inwardly raging at Avery and Mary's lack of concern for Casey's injury. "I'll call the doctor when we get home."

After taking Casey to the doctor and having his fingernail drilled to release the puss and soliciting prescribed antibiotics for the infection, Kate called Avery and gave him a piece of her mind about the lack of care he showed their son.

"He could've lost his finger if I hadn't taken him to the doctor. What the hell is wrong with you? If this is the kind of care you're going to give our kids, then don't bother picking them up." With fury, Kate slammed the phone down on the receiver.

At work the next day, Kate learned that a position she sought had become available. The force needed a new "chauffeur." This meant Kate could use the skills she had learned behind the wheel of the large trucks in a very meaningful way. Not only would she be driving the crew to fire calls and be responsible for operating the pumps to supply water, this also meant that she wouldn't be going into burning buildings anymore – a less dangerous position. She wanted it badly, and Kate went in to sign up for the exam. She could still maintain her career, and the idea of driving the large truck thrilled her, so each and every free moment she could squeeze out of the day was spent with her nose in a manual.

The process was not something simple. It required a strong understanding of math in order to do the calculations and determine the right settings to ensure proper pressure to the hoses. She also had to understand proper procedure for connecting to the fire hydrants and siphoning from large water sources to supply water to the pump. After months of studying, Kate was sure she could ace the exam. It was a lot to learn, but with the experience she already had, her brain seemed to be processing on super drive.

Three days before the exam, Kate was scheduled to work at the hotel but had the morning and most of the afternoon to spend with the kids. She helped bathe them and make them breakfast. Upon hearing the mailman, Marie volunteered to retrieve the mail so Kate could stay put and enjoy a board game with Mia and Casey. They were right in the middle of a heated game of Chutes and Ladders when Marie returned. She handed Kate the pile of mail and urged her to look at the piece on top. It was from the fire department, but not like those she had received in the past. Kate quickly tore open the envelope and pulled out a very formal looking document. As she read, Kate sank into the chair behind her.

"Dear Ms. Matthews,

This letter is meant to inform you that a petition was formally filed removing you from contention for the position of Chauffeur. Due to your extended leave of absence, you do not meet the time of service requirement, which would qualify you for taking the exam. You have the right to file an appeal with the Civil Service Commission if you disagree with this decision."

Kate let out a bitter laugh at the irony. This paper that weighed no more than an ounce was crushing the dreams she'd been working so hard to achieve over the past few weeks. Her children, sensing her distress, came to her side offering hugs, and "It's okay, Mommy," as comfort. She hugged them and tried to wipe away the tears that began to fall from her face so they wouldn't see.

It's not fair, Kate thought, deciding she would not give up. The feeling of her children in her arms amplified her fortitude, and she made a resolution to read the company manuals at every free moment over the next two days, in order to find the loophole that undoubtedly hid there.

The next day, Kate arrived at Central Station early for her

shift. She used that time to locate the manuals and begin digging for information. She found nothing to help her situation and became slightly discouraged but was still not ready to throw in the towel. Kate went downstairs to begin her work without an answer to her problem. At lunch, while the men ate their meals and talked together, she retreated to the corner of the barracks, books in hand, searching once again. The men had to pull her from her own world when the lunch break drew to a close. Kate threw the books on the table with a thump and growled to herself, "This is not over." She trudged away from her reading material and finished the last bite of sandwich that was being crushed in her fist.

Not long after lunch, the alarm sounded, and she and the men grabbed their gear and were on their way. The call was for an apartment complex. Three units were already reporting flames, and she knew she would not be back to the manuals anytime soon. Kate stood, holding the hose that doused one side of the building for hours that evening. Her sleeves were soaking wet, the smoke stung her eyes, and frustration flooded her body. Kate could think of nothing else but how badly she wanted that promotion.

It was after nine o'clock when they arrived back at the station, wet, covered in ash and soot. Kate was exhausted but waited her turn at the showers. Once the men were all in bed, sleeping soundly, she quietly slipped off to the kitchen with manuals in hand and started in again.

She didn't know what time it was, nor did she care. Kate silently sprang from her chair and cheered to herself. She had to respect the men, but this was the loophole she'd been seeking all day. There she stood, in the middle of the night, with the best piece of news she could have wished for, and Kate could share it with no one. She memorized the page numbers, made a mental note about which paragraph applied, then headed to her bed. The night moved slowly, and she tossed and turned from the excitement of the newfound information she needed. She couldn't quiet her mind, but it didn't matter. The next morning, Kate rushed home to share her news with Marie and her children, and together they all cheered and had a celebratory breakfast together.

Kate stood in front of the mirror mouthing the words just loud enough for her own ears. Her makeup was perfect, her hair was perfect, her uniform was perfect, but her insides were a mess. Tonight, the night before the exam, she was going to be standing in front of the Civil Service Commission, her fellow firefighters, the fire chief, and the press, to fight her case as to why she was qualified to take that exam.

Kate sat in the front row of the large auditorium, waiting for the rest of the proceedings to take place. She placed her hand on her knee that was nervously bouncing up and down as if she could make it stop. When at last her time had come, Kate took a deep breath and stood. She made a short introduction of herself and her history with the department then summarized all that had taken place over the two weeks prior. At last she picked up the manual from her seat, flipped to the earmarked page, and read, verbatim, the statement that she hoped and prayed would save her chances of a possible promotion.

"A break in service is when an employee quits, is fired from, or leaves the department and then returns." Kate looked up making eye contact with the members of the commission sitting behind the raised curved desk with microphones. She continued, "I did not quit nor was I fired. I was placed on involuntary leave, and remained an employee with full benefits."

Much to the dismay of many of her coworkers, after discussing the situation, the commission agreed with a unanimous vote and determined she would be able to take the exam scheduled for the following day. Though she thanked them politely, her insides were screaming with joy! Kate had stood up and defended herself without the representation of a union lawyer, which should have been provided to her as a union member.

The press obviously loved the decision as well. Each member snapped a few pictures of the first and only female firefighter who chose to stand up for her rights, and against the barrage of men who wanted to see her fail. The first female firefighter now had a chance of becoming the first female firetruck driver. All Kate had to do now was pass the exam.

The next morning, Kate awoke extra early, before the children were up, and did an hour of last minute studying. Kate believed she would do well on the exam, and the thought excited her to no end. As the sun rose and lit the room, she closed her notebook, stood and stretched, and prepared for the big day ahead of her.

She walked outside into the bright, warm, and sunny weather, hoping it was an omen for what the day held in store for her.

Kate parked the car at the Civic Center, and jumped from her seat. She anxiously headed to the entrance, not knowing what to expect, not only from the test but also from the men who would be there taking the test with her. There were thirty other firefighters prepared to take the same exam, and only one position was available to the firefighter who had the highest test score.

Along with those men sitting for the test, there was also the Civil Service Commissioner who was the exam administrator, and close beside him stood Fire Chief Sanders. He was not typically seen at such an event, nor was he required to be there. Nevertheless, apprehension regarding the fact that she was taking the exam had all the men up in arms.

Kate felt the first twinge of nerves as she walked into the full room. It wouldn't be an easy task, but Kate was sure she was the most determined person there and joined the men, who all studied her with interest – some with animosity. The Civil Service Commissioner welcomed everyone before covering the general rules of the exam. Meanwhile, another individual was asked to pass out the test papers. The palms of her hands felt moist. Kate reached down and rubbed her legs to relieve the sensation, feeling the on her from every direction, but she did her best to block them out. Butterflies in her stomach kept her company she stared down at the blank back page of the exam.

"When you have finished the exam, please bring it to the front to be graded immediately," the commissioner announced.

Kate's blood was pumping and the excitement of knowing she was well prepared for this flooded her thoughts. As soon as the Commissioner gave the word, she frantically flipped the paper as did all in attendance, and started to work through the questions one-by-one. Kate quickly noticed a trend. She was flying through this test without even second guessing an answer. The feeling that came with knowing this was almost too much excitement to bear. Kate wanted nothing more than to cheer, but bit down and continued on.

With more than an hour of time left, she was finished. Kate headed up to the table as the second to finish the exam and anxiously stood while the test was graded, right there, on the spot. Chief Sanders gave her a puzzled look, but she knew she had done well – really well. She could feel the anxiety coming off of him, but there was just something about seeing him pacing the floor while he waited for the results of her exam that made her feel more at ease – even amused.

PART 3

FLAMES TAKE HOLD

"Discipline is the refining fire by which talent becomes ability."
- Roy L. Smith

44

KATE ANXIOUSLY WAITED to see her grade, but she knew that if she didn't get the position, it wasn't because she was under qualified; it was simply because another had out tested her.

At last, it was her turn to be graded. Kate handed her test to the commissioner and the crowd about her moved in closer. The man grading her test slowly and methodically compared each answer to a master copy. With each line, his pen moved lower without the red slash that signified a wrong answer. Each time it descended, leaving no mark in its wake, the men moved slightly closer. By the last page, Kate was beginning to feel slightly claustrophobic but also terribly excited. When he reached the final question, Kate knew she had the highest score so far. Each applicant was now looking at her in amazement. She had correctly answered more than ninety-five percent of the questions on the test.

Though it was apparent that Chief Sanders was not overjoyed with the results, as soon as the last paper was graded, he walked up to Kate.

"Congratulations. I can't believe you scored the highest on the exam," he let a breath out, "but you did. You will receive an official letter notifying you of the results and of the promotion. Then you will need to go for your physical. Come by my office to fill out the necessary paperwork."

Nothing more was said. Chief Sanders turned and walked out of the room. Others stood nearby, staring at her, as if she were a miracle of science. Kate held her head high, leaving them to ponder how it was that a beautiful young *woman* had just kicked their collective ass at their own game.

A couple weeks later, Chief Sanders informed Kate that she was needed at Station Three. Normally, being assigned to another station wouldn't have bothered her at all, but this station was in the roughest neighborhood of any in the department. Kate was to be there for two weeks to cover for the regular driver who was on vacation. The mere thought of working in that district made her head spin with worry. Nevertheless, given they were direct orders from her superior, Kate did not question his decision. She would show up at the station two days later, ready to do her part.

Kate pulled into the station parking lot and immediately noticed that the station itself was not very large. It was, however, well kept, unlike the rest of the neighborhood. It looked new and out of place amid the attendant squalor. There was something about the area that plainly stated, "Beware!" Just inside the entrance there were a few men who greeted her warmly. It was a house day, so they'd be spending the vast majority of their time indoors cleaning.

Maybe this won't be too bad, she figured. After all, there was little anyone could do to hurt her inside the station with her coworkers by her side. Just as she would on any other shift, Kate took her orders from a senior officer, in the case, Lieutenant Norse and got to work hoping the day would go smoothly. She listened calmly as the men told of their experiences working at this station, even if some did scare her a bit more than she let on.

"No, seriously. There are some strange people around here. They've thrown rocks at the truck while we were at a call," one of the firefighters said, shaking his head in bewilderment.

Kate was happy that her assignment there would only be two weeks after all the wild stories.

"Go bring down the flag before it gets dark outside," Lieutenant Norse passed on the order before heading back inside his office. Kate headed out to the flag pole; the sky was still bright, but the sun was fading behind the surrounding houses, and the air was warm. It felt good to be outside for a few minutes after working inside all day. The rope used to lower the flag was looking a bit frayed, and she hoped the flag would come down easily. With a few pulls of the rope, it labored down the large pole.

"Bitch, go home!"

Kate flinched, and turned to see a black car with tinted windows to match, speed by. Her heart was racing as she fought to get the flag down faster. With each tug, Kate looked around to ensure that the car wasn't going to return. By the time the flag reached the bottom, her nerves were wound so tight that the sound of a pin dropping would have sent her sky high. Kate unclipped the flag, tied off the rope and then, with flag in hand, sprinted for the door of the station, hoping none of her coworkers had noticed her. Kate let out a huge sigh of relief once she got inside and closed the door. She folded the flag, her hands shaking as she looked out the window, then replaced it in its rightful spot; she said a silent prayer in hopes she would get to remain inside for the rest of the night.

Kate went to the bathroom to wash her face and just stood there in a daze looking into the mirror. A knock at the door brought her out of the trance. She unlocked the door, stepped out of the bathroom, and began unbuttoning her dress shirt, remaining in her t-shirt and pants. Kate went to lay on her bunk with her book and settled in.

SHHHHHHREEEIKKK! SHHHHHHHREEEEEIKKK! Though she had gotten slightly more used to the sound of the alarm in the middle of the night, this time it rocketed her straight to her feet. Her heart was pounding so hard she thought it might burst from her chest.

Kate ran to the garage, and hopped up, this time, into the *driver's* seat as Lieutenant Norse filled them in on the facts of the call. The only thing that could have made Kate even less anxious to leave the station that night was a car accident, and she was now about to face just that.

So far, no rocks had been thrown on this call, but the sight they came upon was no more inviting for all that: two cars mangled so badly it was almost unclear where one started and the other ended. Kate parked the truck to the side and out of the way, then jumped from the truck, acting more out of habit than anything else. The paramedics, already treating a girl in the back of the only ambulance on site, pointed to the blue car. Kate ran to the car, along with her crew, to assess the situation. A young woman lay in the backseat with a young man draped on top of her like a heavy blanket, and with each breath, she cried out for help.

"Get me out of here! Pleeeease!" The girl's screams tore at her heart, and Kate knew she had to act fast.

According to the paramedics, three teenagers, a male driver and two female passengers, were in the first car. The young man was already deceased. The force of the head on collision had thrown him from the driver's seat to the back where he landed on top of the second female passenger, pinning her where she sat.

Kate fought to enter the car with the help of her coworkers and could hear that the young woman's breathing had become labored. "I can't breeeeeathe! I'm going to die!"

They carefully removed the young woman from the car and brought her to a flat spot near the fire truck. It was obvious her ribs were broken in several places and had likely punctured a lung. The young girl fought hard to breathe yet found the strength to scream when she saw her sister lying in the back of the ambulance, "Sooooophie!"

"Shhh. You're going to be okay. It'll be alright." Kate did her best to calm the girl, placing a blanket around her shoulders, hoping that she wouldn't go into complete shock; then rubbed the girl's arm gently to comfort her.

Kate continued to observe the girl and could see the effort she made just to maintain her normal breathing. The young girl was looking at her with large, terrified eyes. Nothing was said, but Kate understood that look. It was the look of someone who knows you will be the last person they'll ever see.

"Thank you. We can take her from here." The paramedics made

quick work of loading the young woman onto a stretcher and moving her to a second ambulance that had just arrived.

The emotionally charged situation combined with heavy diesel fumes from the rescue vehicles had her head spinning and her stomach feeling queasy. Kate felt weak as she ran to the truck. Her feet were heavy; her head felt like it might fall from her shoulders. As soon as she was out of sight, Kate gave into the urge to crumble. She pressed her hand against the truck, holding her weak body in place, falling forward and losing everything she'd eaten for dinner that night. It was the first time that the job had affected her so badly.

On the way back to the station, Kate overheard the men discussing the accident.

"The teenagers were racing home to meet curfew. A drunk driver had swerved off the road, and when he maneuvered his car back onto the road crossing the center line…BOOM!" Lieutenant Norse described the fate of these young people.

Her mind raced back to the dead limp body that had been lying on top of the girl. The thought of her own children leapt into her head. *Curfews are a guideline*, she imagined herself saying to her children when they were older, but now Kate saw that it was more important they just get home safely and decided it would be better to have them call if they were going to be late instead of speeding to get home to meet a curfew.

"So…you think you can stomach this job, Kate?" The comment from one of the men had the others chuckling. The laughter brought Kate back from her reverie. She rolled her eyes and glared at the man who had dared to poke fun.

"I wouldn't be human if it didn't affect me – and yes I did do my job tonight and plan on sticking around for a long time to come." Her eyes dared him to joke about it again and at the same time she thought, *Are you human?*

That night, she lay awake in bed thinking of the poor injured girl and her sister's boyfriend who had died while trying to get them home on time.

Kate found herself more motivated than ever now to help others.

Though there was a moment in the rush of that evening when she had wondered if, in fact, she was prepared to deal with the catastrophes and high emotional drama that came with the job.

Her next four duties came and went without a single call. It was her fifth day, and upon arrival, Kate noticed how unusually cool the air outside was. She walked inside and saw the men were already bustling about. Kate looked at her watch wondering if she was late, but as usual, she was actually early.

"Get to work." One of the men shot her a smile and a list of chores to be completed. "If we finish early, we might be able to catch the game."

The Cowboys were doing well that year and the men were eager to watch the game. She was not one to interfere with such displays of testosterone; plus she actually wanted to watch the game as well. Kate quickly tossed her bag on her bunk and got right to work on her list of chores.

About an hour later, as she sped along at the same pace as the men, Lieutenant Norse opened his office door and shouted out to them. "We need to make a run to Central Station to pick up some supplies and refill the SCBAs." (Self-contained breathing apparatus) The groan from the men was deafening. This would undoubtedly hold them up and lessen their chances of finishing in time to see the start of the game.

Though they were likely to miss their so-called deadline, the men were chipper at the opportunity to be out of the station. They'd loaded their supplies and were headed back when a call came over the radio. Kate flicked on the siren as she turned the truck to circle the block, heading in the direction of the address given by the dispatcher.

This is not a call any of us want to go to, she thought.

According to the dispatcher, a tree had fallen, and there were injured children at the scene. She hoped for the best, but something inside her cried out, *this is not going to be good.* Then she thought, *Perhaps a prank call,* when there was nothing to be seen. They scoured the area beside the highway where the given address had placed them, yet there was nothing.

Lieutenant Norse picked up the microphone and called dispatch. "Nothing here... we will continue to search the area..."

"Let's make a U-turn and check the other side of the highway, just to be sure," Kate suggested to Lieutenant Norse after hearing that EMS was returning to their station.

"Can you check the address again? We're going to check on the other side of the highway," Lieutenant Norse addressed dispatch with the microphone pressed into his chin.

The truck sprang to life once more, and before long they were coming upon a crowd of people gathered on the opposite side of the road. Just off the highway was a small housing section and not far from it a fallen palm tree was visible in the courtyard. The diameter of the trunk had to be at least twenty-four inches. She tore her eyes away long enough to park the truck, while Lieutenant Norse reported their location to dispatch.

"Victims located at the housing development at the end of the highway. Send EMS back to this location."

They approached to find a small boy lying in the shade of the small white duplex. He was placed in a manner that made him look as if he had simply been discarded -- an unwanted possession. The second child, a small girl, was already en route to the hospital, accompanied by the parents, while the boy lying misshapen on the ground had been left there to suffer on his own with helpless onlookers. Her heart sank as she glanced over at the boy.

Minutes later, a paramedic prepared the monitors and began hooking the child up to the EKG. He instructed her to begin CPR. The body was lifeless under her. "1,2,3,4,5" *breathe* "1,2,3,4,5" *breathe*, "damn it...1,2,3,4,5..." *nothing*? Come on sweetie, breathe!"

The paramedic touched her shoulder. "You're doing great! Okay, I'll take over now."

Kate hid her eyes, not wanting him to see the sadness in them. For a few moments, Kate watched the paramedic work, hoping he would get a response from the child. When the other paramedic arrived to assist, she walked away from the child on the stretcher and reported back to the men, who were now forming a group around the truck.

How could the parents have left him behind, alone? She couldn't help thinking, standing with her colleagues watching the paramedics load the boy into the ambulance. Sometimes it was disheartening the way the world worked. Two children had simply been lying in a hammock tied to two large trees, and one dead tree fell, in a freak accident, crushing them.

Back at the station, the men turned on the game and Kate sat alongside them watching what was left. She later found out that the young boy died shortly after his arrival at the hospital. The fallen tree had been dead for quite some time but had never been properly disposed of. Again, she thought of her own kids and wondered if she would ever feel right about the things she witnessed, especially when they involved children.

45

KATE WAS ECSTATIC to receive another call from Fabian, the handsome teacher/musician she enjoyed spending time with. The days since the exam had been the best she could remember, in all senses. The warm temperature that day was matched perfectly with a steady cool breeze and clear skies overhead. It was the perfect weather for spending all day outdoors, and that was just what Fabian had in mind. He'd invited her to meet him at his place where they could share a picnic and some time together, and within an hour she was pulling her car into the driveway of his house.

The house was small, not at all what she had pictured, but adorable. Yet, she knew it was the right one. There on the small porch stood the gorgeous man; black pants hung loosely from his hips and a lightweight linen button-down clung to his shoulders and chest.

When she reached the porch, he took her hand and led her into the house, the entry through the kitchen, and out the back door. Fabian's yard was surrounded by a nice wood fence that was recently installed. In the center of the quaint yard was a table covered with a red and white checked tablecloth and all the makings of a wonderful picnic. Kate was stunned and could only smile in appreciation of his efforts.

The day was perfect — the best date she could recall with the romantic simplicity of it all. Though both discussed their spouses, who they had yet to officially part with, neither seemed to be longing for anyone except the person sitting opposite each of them.

Before she knew it, the sun was setting on their day. Fabian outstretched his arm and took her hand. Together they walked the short distance back to the door. Kate figured that very soon she'd be making the equally short trek to her car, and the magic of the day would end. At that thought, her chest felt tight and her heart heavy.

Just inside the door, Fabian turned around quickly. In a single motion, he shut the door and clasped her face in his hands. He slowly moved his lips toward hers, as if asking permission. Kate's eyes fluttered closed, and her lips parted just slightly in acceptance of what he was offering. The kiss was long and full of passion that left her unsteady on her feet. Her back hit the door behind her and the startling impact caused Kate to cling to him. As she did, Fabian's lips moved from her lips to her ear.

"Tell me if I'm moving too quickly..." His voice trailed off, and he planted tender kisses along her neck and the underside of her jaw before picking her up and heading down the hall.

It might be too quickly, it occurred to her, but the thought didn't linger, and their mouths met once more. Before Kate had time to answer him, they were standing just millimeters apart in his bedroom.

Fabian's hands caressed her arms then moved slowly up to her face. Kate raised herself up on her toes so she could reach his mouth with hers. What was passionate was now also heated and demanding. The two moved as if dancing about the room as one piece of clothing after another hit the floor, and finally they crashed, one on top of the other, onto of his soft bedding.

Before Kate drove away that evening, Fabian invited her to join him again the following weekend. Earlier, she had encouraged him to take an interest in making his yard an even more inviting and relaxing place. When Kate then suggested he call her for some help, he immediately took her up on the offer. Kate was more than happy to oblige since it meant spending more time with him.

Over the next few months, Kate spent several weekends helping him with his renovations, plus picnicking in the small backyard, and studying his physique while lying atop his bed. All the while the two discussed the happiness and troubles of their past, spoke of their careers and their homes as they were, but never made mention of what the future might hold. One evening, while sitting across from him at the small kitchen table, the phone rang. Fabian made no move to answer it; he was enjoying the moment with her far too much to jump up for what was likely someone trying to sell him something he didn't want or need.

They sat, laughing about how difficult it was to ignore a ringing telephone; the answering machine picked up, and a woman's voice was heard.

"Hi. It's me. I know you said you didn't want to talk, but I'd really like a chance to see you. Please, call me back when you get this..." the voice faded and a sigh was heard before the line went dead.

Fabian shot his dinner guest a look of apology, and Kate returned one of curiosity.

"It's my wife," he offered. "She's been trying to talk with me lately, but I'm not sure I have anything to say to her." His mouth said one thing, but a faint look in his eyes told Kate that he was not at all certain about what he was saying.

"Maybe you should. Maybe it's important." Similarly, the look in her eyes contradicted her statement as Kate pulled her hand back from his.

They sat in an uncomfortable silence for some time before he could find anything to say. "I like you a lot."

Kate could feel the "but" in Fabian's statement before it even left his mouth.

"But... I still have feelings for her. I can't tell if they are feelings for the old her, or for the woman she has become, but nevertheless, I don't want to lie to you about the situation." His words flowed more quickly; Kate struggled to take them in. "I haven't seen her yet, but I feel guilty turning her down time and time again. I feel I owe her the opportunity to say her piece."

Kate nodded her head, in understanding, even though she didn't want to.

Kate stood at her car that evening looking at Fabian with many questions running wildly through her brain. He bent down and kissed Kate softly, and under his lips, she muttered, "Does this mean that we won't be seeing each other any longer?"

The kiss stopped suddenly, and he held her face, looking into her eyes. "I want to see you, but I need to resolve things with my wife first."

Kate nodded, gave a half smile, and received another of his delectable kisses before taking her place behind the steering wheel.

A few days later, having not seen or heard from Fabian, the phone rang. Kate, on her way out the door, was forced to turn back to answer it. The voice on the other end caught her off guard, but she tried to remain calm, mindlessly wrapping herself in the extra long phone cord and then twisting back out of the tangles of curled cord.

"I'm sorry to just call, but I really wanted to talk to you today and could find no good reason not to dial the number."

Kate held back her anger and said nothing.

"Are you busy?"

Well, she thought, *of course I am. I'm raising three children and working three jobs...and seeing someone...maybe...*"Yes, actually. I have to be at work in fifteen minutes."

Kate could hear his frown. "Oh. That's right. You have to be at the hotel?"

She nodded and then, realizing that he couldn't see her, "Yes."

Drake was silent for a few moments, and then the two said goodbye, and Kate headed for the door, feeling slightly less put together than she had been.

Kate could not get the conversation – albeit a very short one – out of her head. Drake had barely spoken to her in the months since they'd separated, and now, out of the blue, he wanted to talk. The thought half frightened her and half intrigued her. She couldn't shake the thought of it all evening.

Near the end of her shift, Kate walked into the back to take a moment for herself as the crowd finally started to die down. There were just five couples scattered about the large lounge area, and most had opted for one of the secluded leather-upholstered half-round booths where they sat sipping their drinks very slowly. This gave Kate a few minutes to think, breathe, and consider what the call meant.

"Hey, there's someone here asking for you as a server." The news, delivered by a young coworker, did not come as any surprise. There were often groups of regulars who would come in and request a specific server. Kate was well liked, so she took a deep breath, rounded the corner and grabbed her order pad; but when she looked up to see the table in question, she was knocked off kilter. Sitting there was just one man, and although she was looking at him from the back, she knew exactly who it was.

"Hey...what are you doing here?" Kate tried to hide her shock, and made every effort to remain as professional as she would be with any other table. She really didn't need everyone in the place realizing that her husband — who she was no longer living with — was now asking her to wait on him.

"Hi." He looked at her with a mix of sadness and longing, "I knew you wouldn't call me back, and I knew that you'd be getting outta here fairly soon, so I just drove over to wait for you."

Part of her was flattered; the other -- larger -- part of her was annoyed at Drake's persistence and that he'd willingly make her uncomfortable at her work place. "Did you want something? A beer?" the last word came out of her mouth ice cold. Kate hadn't intended to sound bitter, but even to her own ear, that is exactly how it came off.

"No, I'm not drinking anymore." Drake said, ignoring the stunned look on her face. "How about a Coke?"

"Yes, of course." Kate moved back to the bar and poured the soda into a glass. Her hand was shaking fiercely, and she had to concentrate in order to get it back to the table without spilling it. Drake did not hide the fact that he noticed.

Kate was unsure of what was about to happen, but knew she had to escape the interrogating eyes of her coworkers. The moment the clock struck ten, Kate untied her apron, grabbed her belongings and wished everyone a pleasant evening. She walked out of the lounge with Drake following, straight through the main entrance of the hotel and out the front doors before turning on him. "How could you? I was at work! Do you know how upsetting that was?" Her hands were shaking.

Drake reached out, took her small fingers in his, and looked into her eyes. "I've really missed you. I know its been a long time since we really talked, but I wanted to make sure I was done with the drinking and the weed, for good, before I saw you again." He paused, smiling at her face as if seeing an angel. "I've been sober for six weeks."

Kate looked at him with amazement, but said nothing. Without a word, he leaned forward and kissed her squarely on the mouth; and despite her better judgment, she melted into him.

Kate felt guilty about essentially seeing two men at the same time. The next day, she dialed the number of the man she could never quite connect with. Kate was very attracted to Fabian, but at the same time felt slightly drawn to try and fix what was left of her marriage.

The phone rang... and as she sat in the chair, it rang again...she stood back up, it rang again....and she leaned against the wall. Just as it was starting a fourth ring, the buzzer to her apartment rang. She stared at the phone, wondering if it was worth waiting another ring and ultimately set it down on the hook and moved to the door.

"Who is it?" she spoke through the building intercom, and the response that came back made her giggle. There was nothing funny about what the man said, but it was terribly ironic that Fabian was buzzing her just as she was dialing him. She invited him up, turned around, and she found herself horribly embarrassed. The kids had been having a free-for-all in the living room, and toys were spread from one end of the small room to the other. It looked as if a toy-loaded bomb had gone off. She went to work, hurriedly picking up the toys and tossing them into the toy box without any concern for how they landed.

Maria, seeing her sudden regard for the state of the room, also went to work, shuffling toys from the floor to the box as quickly as her arms could work. By the time Fabian arrived at the door, and gave a small knock, the floor was clear, and both women were panting frantically.

"Thank you," Kate whispered with a smile.

Maria nodded and ushered the children in the direction of the kitchen.

Kate's stomach was fluttering with butterflies when she reached for the door knob, allowing the very handsome man who stood on the other side into her home.

"Hi." Kate's voice sounded like a teen with a crush, which made the blood rush to her cheeks.

Fabian smiled warmly, "Hello. You look beautiful today."

Kate returned the smile with one of her own, and longed for him to offer a kiss. But Fabian now seemed a bit preoccupied – even uncomfortable; and Kate began to feel unsettled herself.

"I'm sorry to just drop in..."

"I was calling you just as you buzzed."

They both laughed for a second.

"There is something I have to tell you," he opened.

Nothing good ever came of that statement, and her face gave away her sense of worry.

"I, uh...I have been seeing my wife."

Kate sighed deeply, relieved. "I know."

"And well...she's pregnant."

The words spilled from his mouth as if rushing over a gigantic waterfall and flooded over her, making it difficult for Kate to breathe.

"Oh." It was a stupid response. She knew it was, but at the moment, it was all she could muster.

"I just found out last night, and I wanted you to know right away." Fabian paused, expecting her to protest or yell, but Kate said nothing. "We're going to get back together and try to make it work. It seems like the right thing to do...considering."

Kate nodded, fighting back her tears. She didn't know why she was getting so worked up since she wasn't even sure where things stood in her own marriage. Nevertheless, when Fabian reached out to offer the comfort of a hug, the floodgates opened, and tears fell in never ending streams, silently down her cheeks. Kate clung to him even as it hit her that Fabian was not hers to be hugging.

Kate walked him to the door once their embrace had ended, and neither found it comfortable in the other's presence.

"I'm sorry."

Fabian said the words and she knew he meant them, but she wasn't entirely sure if he was apologizing for ending whatever happened between them or for getting involved with her in the first place.

Once he was a safe distance from the door, Kate shut it softly and moved to the couch where she sat sobbing. When the phone rang, she let it. When it rang again, she yelled at it. When it rang a third time, she stood, picked it up and yelled, "Yes?!"

"I hope that anger is not really directed at me."

The voice was not one she wished to hear at the moment, but he was right, Kate was not mad at Drake, nor would she have been right in directing her anger at anyone who happened to call at the moment.

"No." Her voice was low and apologetic, but at the same time did not suggest that she was looking for conversation.

"You sound like you need company." Drake said it in a flirty tone.

No I don't! Kate thought. She felt anything but in the need of company, especially his, which would only further confuse her emotions in the moment.

"Not really," Kate said in a depressed tone, though with the assurance that she meant it, and left it at that.

"Bad day?"

"You might say that." Despite her attempts, Drake seemed intent on keeping the conversation going. Kate had no intention of maintaining her end, but if he was inclined to continue, she was not going to discourage him. She sat back in the recliner that stood in the corner of the room and put up her legs. The exasperated sigh that escaped her lips was not intentional, but Kate didn't try to disguise it either.

"Are you busy?"

"No."

Drake still didn't understand that Kate was not in the mood to talk and continued on, telling a full story of his feelings for her, how much he wanted to see her, how willing he was to change in order to be back in her life, and that of their kids. Kate listened, but said very little. Her mind was reeling from the news she'd received just before his call. Her heart still aching, yet somehow hearing what Drake had to say made it all seem a little less horrible. Besides, she reminded herself that she was planning to call Fabian that very night to tell him she was going to start seeing her husband again. She just hadn't been expecting to be told they were done for good, that the opportunity for them was nonexistent.

"Yes." Kate didn't know any better than he did what she was agreeing to. Drake had been mid sentence, not even asking a question when she said it, but she hadn't been able to stop the word from working it's way beyond the point where her lips met.

"Yes?"

"Yes..." Kate said it again and it occurred to her that she knew what she meant by it. "Yes, you can take me on a date."

Drake broke out in heartfelt laughter that made a smile form on her face.

"I'm very happy to hear you've accepted my offer."

Had he offered? She wasn't sure, but it didn't matter. Within seconds, Kate was hanging up the phone with plans for dinner twenty-four hours later.

46

"OOD LUCK," SAID one of the men, just leaving the station after a long shift he would never forget. "It's horrible down there." Bob looked like the walking dead. His eyelids were heavy and carried large purplish bags beneath them from working all night with no sleep. Kate thought back to the day before, and her heart began to pound against her chest.

Kate and her children had been navigating the streets leading to a nearby beach. The July sun was extra hot that day, and it felt as if they were stepping from the car into a sauna. All were in a hurry to hit the cool water. After a few hours of swimming, playing, and laughing, they, like many of the other beach-goers, were forced to look upward as the sky quickly filled with dark clouds. What was a bright and sunny day had suddenly turned dark and dismal. They packed up their gear and headed for the car. She didn't want to be on the beach when a heavy rain came. Kate was disappointed and felt robbed of a rare day off to enjoy time with her kids and a relaxing day at the beach. The following day she would have to report to the station for duty, and she really wanted this day to be all about fun in the sun. Instead, they were headed home and not more than a few blocks away from the beach when the rain came.

At first, Kate flipped her wipers on low and the rain fell as if a normal summer's shower, but just as she reached the highway, it began to fall so hard she could barely make out the road in front of her. The only sound was the rain beating against the car. Kate peeked behind her to see that the children were already asleep. Kate decided to turn on the radio to calm her nerves since the traffic was moving at a snail's pace, and it would be a bit of a drive before reaching home.

She sat stunned in the car, even after they arrived at the house, having just heard on the radio: The roof of Le Tienda Amigo, a clothing store downtown, had buckled and given way from the heavy rain. The building collapsed on all who were shopping, the employees, and those who were there to get out of the rain. The broadcaster attempted to describe the mess, "...just a mound of debris...chaos as firefighters and rescue teams make slow work of...two confirmed dead...twelve seriously injured."

"The building didn't stand a chance. At least that's what they were telling us. The water was coming down fast. The truck had trouble getting down the roads because they were so badly flooded," Bob said, sounding dumbfounded.

Kate looked at Bob, stunned, as he recounted all that had happened to him and the crew over the past twenty-four hours.

"We pulled at least thirty people with various injuries out of the rubble so far. Not sure if there are any others down there. Poor people! I just can't believe this happened."

Bob's face bore a sadness Kate was not accustomed to seeing. She gave a half smile and touched his shoulder to offer some comfort. He shrugged and headed for his car.

Kate, like the rest of the men, moved quickly to relieve the remaining firefighters who had been working for endless hours. Again, Kate found herself thinking back to when she first heard what had happened on the radio. The truck pulled up to the pile of rubble, and her heart sank as she gazed upon the site for the first time. It was a mess of concrete and debris. Nearby, authorities fought to keep onlookers and the families of victims back so the rescue crew could continue their work. Slowly Kate climbed down from the truck, thinking, *I hate this! I don't want to be here.* There were many aspects of her job that Kate loved, but seeing the hurt, the injured, and the dead was certainly not one of them.

"There's one woman still missing, assumed to be buried under the debris somewhere. Unfortunately, there's another woman who was located dead with her body cut in half by the impact of the collapsed roof, but we have to retrieve her," the fire captain said, going through a briefing.

Kate studied the man before her. He had been there for many hours and looked like a zombie, yet he continued to speak as if he was perfectly rested.

"One of the men thought he heard something in that vicinity," his arm stretched out pointing to a section of the wreckage, "maybe another victim, but nothing has been confirmed yet."

Kate could not imagine pulling a dismembered corpse from the rubble; the sight of a human being, cut in half, was a vision she did not want to have lodged in her head.

They went to work, clearing large areas of debris, but each time Kate looked up to take in the scene, she realized they hadn't even made a dent.

"Why don't you come down and sit for a minute?" A reverend touched her shoulder as he spoke. He was there to comfort the families and the victims who were literally buried alive. "It is so hot. We don't need more injured."

Kate smiled kindly at the man, but like her colleagues, she declined his offer. There was no way that she could walk away from this disaster while the other men continued to work, and with the possibility of someone being down there still barely alive somewhere. It scared her to think that someone could be lost beneath the maze of concrete and wondering if they would be found in time. No one could produce a list of the customers who were in the store, and they were forced to go by missing person's reports and the sobbing requests of frightened family members. Every twenty minutes or so, a refreshing mist of water would fall down on them as they worked. It came from the hose of their own engine and was a mere attempt to keep them cool in the blistering heat.

Just as Kate felt she could work no longer, she heard her name, followed by, "We're here to replace you. Time to get some rest." Kate turned and saw one of the men from her station. She mindlessly looked at her watch and discovered she'd been there for nearly sixteen hours, only stopping once to briefly grab a bite to eat and drink. Kate looked around, stunned at how much debris still filled the street and the area where the building once stood. There were people and the media everywhere. She felt sad for all who stood there.

"Let's go. Time to get some rest," he repeated, more emphatic this time.

Kate looked into the eyes of her colleague. Richard's face was bright red from working all those hours in the beaming sun, and when Kate touched her own, she realized that his was not the only one.

Kate and the men on this shift finally arrived back at their station and wearily climbed the stairs to their bunks. Most of them chose to grab a quick shower to rid their bodies of the dirt and sweat of a hard and heavy day. Kate did the same and then fell into her bunk. Her body was exhausted, but her mind was reeling.

The next morning, before she left the station, the chief let them all know that the final victim had been recovered, albeit dead. She let out a sigh. The family of that poor woman could rest a bit easier, knowing that she had, at least, been found; though a huge part of Kate wondered how much comfort it could really offer at a time like this.

47

KATE HELD TO her commitment and went out with her husband. Things heated up rapidly, and over the next month they were spending fewer nights apart. Kate was happier with the decision than she thought she'd be. It appeared as though Drake was trying to make it work this time. He was more devoted to both her and the kids than he'd ever been in the past.

Kate woke early to help prepare the kids' meals and hug them goodbye before reporting to the station. She was ahead of schedule and decided to stop in at a diner to grab a cup of coffee before work. The breeze felt good while walking up to the front entrance of the diner. Kate pulled the door open, and was hit with the aroma of bacon and eggs. The smell was delicious, so she ordered a small breakfast in addition to her coffee. It was not common practice for her, but she simply couldn't resist on this morning. Kate sat at the front counter and chatted with the short waitress; though advanced in years, her face had sweet, child-like features, and crystal clear blue eyes resembling the sky on a bright sunny day.

Kate enjoyed the woman's company and was sad to rush through her meal in order to be at the station in time for work. Kate gave the waitress the money for her check and one more smile of appreciation then turned to leave. As she did, a pain jabbed at her midsection. Kate ignored it and continued to the station.

The sun was so warm and the breeze was so pleasant making Kate grateful it was a yard day. She would be able to enjoy the weather all day while working to improve the appearance of her second home. The men she worked with that day seemed to be equally happy, greeting her with smiles and hellos before moving in the direction of their own assigned tasks.

Perhaps, Kate thought, *life is in balance once more.*

Kate could hardly believe it was already midday when they all went in for their lunch break. Kate followed the men up the stairs, not believing how exhausted she felt. Her lower back ached intensely as she climbed each step, and when Kate reached the top, the pain radiated around to the front. She cursed the fact that she was a woman and moved to the bathroom to deal with her femininity.

Grrrr! she wanted to scream. What had been a light spotting of blood that morning was now more like Niagara Falls. She bent over as the pain returned once again, and swore, "Holy shit! What is wrong with me?" Thankfully none of the men could hear her.

Once cleaned up and feeling a bit better, Kate went back to the kitchen area to join the men for a quick meal of chicken corn stew and fresh hot corn tortillas. It tasted delicious, and before she knew it, Kate had finished every bite. The break did not last quite long enough. All the energy she'd had in the morning hours was now gone, and she was now feeling completely drained.

Kate followed the men down the stairs, fighting the urge to stop as another cramp seized her midsection.

She continued with the day's chores until the evening was finally upon them. Kate moved to the barracks and said a silent prayer that there would be no fire calls that night. Though her prayers were answered, the pain she'd felt during the day continued to ravage her body throughout the night. By morning, when Kate was free to return home, the blood was drained from her face; large dark circles ringed her eyes.

Kate was worried that something was seriously wrong, and made a quick dart for her things and hurried to her car. The ride, which was actually very short, seemed to last forever as pain came in sharp waves every few minutes. She screamed out when another hit her just as she turned into the drive. *What is wrong with me?* Kate tried thinking back, but couldn't remember ever having menstrual cramps this bad before. Once inside, she said a quick hello to the kids before rushing to the bathroom. By the time Kate sat, the pain was so excruciating she was forced over, and bent in half when she heard something splash.

She called out, "Draaaaake!" as he stood there looking helpless, "Something's not right. Look! What is that?...I think I need to go to the hospital. Can you help me to the car?"

At the hospital, Kate explained the pain she'd been experiencing to the nurse to the best of her ability. She began to describe the blood clot that had passed from her, and her eyes teared up.

"It really didn't look like a blood clot. It was oval and a grayish blue tissue," Drake offered, reaching to hold her hand in comfort. Kate's level of discomfort was obvious, and the nurse hurried to retrieve the on call OB/GYN doctor.

After the nurse left, Kate's younger brother, Robert, who worked at the hospital, came running up to her. "Are you okay?"

Kate could see the concern that filled his eyes. She attempted to smile at her little brother through the tears, but his distress visually increased.

"I don't know! I haven't seen the doctor yet."

Just then a woman who was younger than Kate and surprisingly beautiful entered the room. She was a petite woman in mauve colored scrubs, whose body seemed to get lost in them. Her head was crowned with a scrub cap atop light brown hair resting just above her shoulders. More importantly, however, the woman was extraordinarily kind to her as Kate made an effort to rid her face of the endless tears.

"Hi! I'm Dr. Marsha. Let's take a look and see what's going on." A quick exam and the woman turned to Kate with a look of regret and sorrow. "I'm sorry to tell you this, but that was not a blood clot this morning. I believe you miscarried."

Kate's face registered confusion. She hadn't even been pregnant, or at least she had no idea she was.

Both Drake and Robert looked equally confused.

"But...I wasn't pregnant..." Kate thought a moment, "I...I mean I didn't know." Tears flooded her eyes again and were soon pouring out uncontrollably.

Drake leaned in and hugged her, while she sobbed into his shoulder feeling afraid, confused, exhausted, and a little sad for the baby who would never be.

"I hate to share more bad news with you," Dr. Marsha started when the tears had subsided a little, "from what you've told me, and based on my examination, it appears that you were at least six weeks pregnant. We'll need to perform a D&C to remove any remaining tissue and to prevent infection."

Kate nodded at the young woman and turned back to Drake. When Dr. Marsha left, Robert followed and she was alone with Drake. The two held each other for comfort and support while Dr. Marsha prepared to rid Kate's body of the remaining portion of the unsuccessful pregnancy.

Kate took a day off from work which allowed five days for her body to repair itself from the trauma, her mind from the mass confusion, and her heart to accept the loss of her baby.

48

KATE AND DRAKE became quite close again after sharing in the scare, disappointment, and sorrow that came with her miscarriage. They found themselves turning to each other more than they had in the past.

On the day Kate was to return to the station, Drake woke her early with a kiss. "I'm going to miss you tonight." He said the words as his lips were pressed to hers.

Kate smiled under the pressure and kissed him back.

Drake moved his head back for a minute and looked at her with concern. "Be careful, okay?"

She smiled again.

"I will be." Kate dismissed him with another kiss, but he cut it short.

"I mean it. You scared me the other day. If you need help, ask for it this time."

Kate nodded and waited for Drake to hug her. He obliged and pulled her to him so that her head fell comfortably into the nook formed by his arm and chest, and kissed her head. Kate sighed with contentment.

It was obvious, when Kate arrived at the station that day, that her husband was not the only one who was concerned for her well-being. Each of the men who greeted her that day offered an apology for her loss, and asked Kate how she was feeling. To each, she happily gave a large smile and an "I'm better, thanks." Her assigned chores were lighter than usual, but Kate said nothing, figuring it was better to take the good graces rather than rock the boat. Kate did all she was assigned by three o'clock and reported back for more. Instead, she was given a meaningless task of preparing the food, which allowed Kate to sit atop a stool for the remaining two hours leading to dinner. Kate laughed under her breath at the difference in how she was treated at the station of late versus when she'd first arrived. It felt good that the majority of the men now accepted her as one of their own.

Just as Kate was set to finish the last bite of her meal that evening, the alarm bell sounded. She moved to her gear and began to suit up, but noticed that a couple of the men were shooting her worried glances. Kate simply smiled at them and hurried to the pole. Within a minute, she was manning her seat at the front of the large engine. It didn't matter what she had been through anymore, Kate felt on top of the world behind the large wheel, in control of the big truck. Once the men were loaded, she pulled it from its bay and headed off in the direction of the address provided by dispatch.

That night Kate helped fight an enormous house fire that blazed large and hot against the black night's sky and into the wee morning when the sun just began to peek over the horizon. No one said a word to her about taking a break and for that she was grateful. Kate drove the men back to the station once the job was wrapped up, where each of them were afforded just two hours of sleep before they were free to go home. Her first day back had been eventful and enough to prove her a worthy, healthy member of the team.

For more than a month, life continued as if the miscarriage had never taken place. At home, Kate enjoyed a renewed happiness in her marriage. She soon began to find it harder though to drag herself out of bed in the morning, and she found herself dreading the physical demands of her work at the station. She felt the ache in her feet and back after a night of waitressing. The exhaustion wore on her until finally she thought it best to see a doctor. It hadn't even been six weeks since her miscarriage when Kate found herself worrying there might be an issue as a result of it. After getting the kids some breakfast and getting them settled for a day with Maria, she headed to her doctor's office. Kate had opted to see Dr. Marsha since she'd been so kind and understanding at the hospital. Her brother had spoken highly of her as well.

The doctor's office was large and stunningly decorated with large pieces of artwork in the waiting room along with a huge glass partition etched with a woman holding a baby. When Kate walked up to the reception desk, she noticed a water cooler and next to it was a stand with juice and cookies. Once she checked in, Kate went to sit in the most comfortable chairs she had ever known to exist in this type of setting. Although she would have been comfortable waiting longer, after just a few moments a nurse came out and invited her through the door and down a hallway. This area carried the same inviting atmosphere, only sterile, and yet somehow pleasant.

Kate was brought back into the reality of womanhood as soon as the nurse asked for a urine sample and pointed her in the direction of the bathroom. After that, the nurse led her into a small room in the corner of the building. She was asked a number of questions regarding her health since the miscarriage and about the reason for her visit. Kate answered honestly, but now felt a bit silly that she had scheduled an appointment just because she'd been unusually tired. After all, she had three children and three jobs, one of which called for extreme physical labor. Kate chuckled as she stated her reason for her visit. The nurse smiled but didn't seem as humored by it as Kate expected.

"The doctor will be right in." The nurse handed her a flimsy piece of material with a few strings hanging from it. Kate paused, looked at the gown, and wondered if she had overreacted about her situation.

The familiar face of the doctor made her feel a bit more at ease. "Hi, Dr. Marsha."

"Hi, Kate," The woman with a grin on her face looked like she knew something or had a secret. Suddenly, the feeling of ease vanished. "I'm starting to notice a trend with you." Her tone was joking, but there was something more hidden beneath. "I'm not sure I'm going to like it if you keep putting me in the situation of breaking big news."

At this, Kate felt her heart begin to race. *Certainly this woman wouldn't be joking if there was something wrong with me, would she?*

"It seems that you're pregnant again." Dr. Marsha didn't smile. In fact her face was expressionless, perhaps because she wasn't certain how Kate would take the news.

"I'm pregnant?" The news hit her like a ton of bricks. Kate had been sad to find she'd lost a child little more than a month before, and now she wasn't sure how she felt hearing she was pregnant yet again. She was happy that her relationship with Drake was going well and they had been getting along wonderfully, but he was still having the worst luck holding down a job for any length of time. All of this was swirling through her mind while she just stared at the doctor with a dumbfounded look.

"I take it that you weren't aware at all."

Kate shook her head in a negative response.

"I'm sorry to say that I have one other surprise for you today..."

Now Dr. Marsha sounded uneasy.

"I don't understand..." Kate started, and then a thought hit her, "Is the baby alright?"

Dr. Marsha quickly realized she'd led Kate's mind where it should not be. "No, nothing like that. I'm sorry. I didn't mean to alarm you," she smiled at Kate warmly, "it's just that your brother and I started seeing each other shortly after we first met."

This, for some reason, struck Kate as extraordinarily funny, and she let out a chuckle.

"You scared me! I thought you were going to tell me something horrible." Kate smiled at the woman who had apparently won her brother's affection. "I don't mind that at all."

"Well," Dr. Marsha started a bit uneasily, "I was concerned that you'd be uncomfortable with me as your doctor."

Kate simply shook her head and smiled, and then, realizing she was with child added,

"Oh no, not at all. I need a doctor. I'm pregnant. Why not you?"

Kate was still the only female on the force and still no initiatives had been taken to address the issue of working during pregnancy. She had accumulated very little sick leave since her last pregnancy and used part of that when she had miscarried. How could they live on the income of her husband alone, especially given his unsteady work history? She broke the news to Drake, who took it with a mix of shock, happiness, and fear, then made a resolution to work as long as she could.

Ten days after she found out about her status, Kate ran for an incoming call, and was hit with feelings of panic that she might miscarry again. Kate instinctively stopped what she was doing and put a hand to her belly for just a moment; remembering that the doctor said her work played no roll in her miscarriage, she then headed to the pole.

Kate gripped the pole just as she had a hundred times before, and let herself fall, landing confidently on the ground. *I said I was going to do this, and I will*, she thought. With that, Kate climbed up into her front seat in the giant red truck. That night, she arrived at the scene of a two-story house fire that was threatening to take the neighboring homes with it.

Kate was grateful for her new position and said a silent prayer of thanks. Though she still had to help unload and reload the heavy hoses, Kate was a good distance from the flames and wouldn't be in the midst of imminent danger.

By the time they left the property in the wee morning hours, there was little left of the house, nothing left in her energy reserves, but a whole lot more confidence in her ability to keep her secret from the men. After finally falling asleep, Kate had a terrible dream: she was driving to a fire call and while entering an intersection, she swerved to avoid colliding with a vehicle, causing the huge truck to shift onto two wheels and eventually land on its side, skidding down the road toward a building. Just before impact, she awoke, trembling, to the sound of the morning wake-up call.

Kate found herself being asked to cover at another station once again a couple of weeks later. This time it was Station Two, and she was a bit apprehensive, but Kate knew it was an expected part of her job. She climbed from the car, shut the door, and walked in with her head held high. Men were standing about, talking and sipping coffee despite the warm weather. Two of the men looked up and, seeing her, gave a look that was a mix of disgust and annoyance. *Wonderful,* she thought, *the day hasn't even started and already I have to run uphill.*

"Hello. We were told you were coming to replace our driver." Captain Sullivan, a tall man with a large belly, stood there with his hands in his pockets. He looked straight at her with a smirk on his face and said, "I assume that you know how to clean?"

The question was odd and insulting, but Kate bit her tongue and headed to the dorm to put away her bag. She felt her defenses rearing up. It seemed that the rest of the men were indifferent to her being a woman. They all trickled in after checks were over and Kate headed to her bag, as the other men did, and each changed into their red jumpsuits. It was a house day, which explained the comment regarding her ability to clean. She just pushed it from her mind and piled her hair at the back of her head, ready to tackle whatever work she was given.

Captain Sullivan strode up to her once again. This time with an expression on his face that made the hairs stand up on the back of her neck. He held out a toothbrush. Though Kate was standing at the doorway to the bathroom, she somehow doubted that he meant to imply her hygiene wasn't up to snuff. When she didn't reach for it, he said, "You're in charge of cleaning the grout," pointing to the bathroom floor, "and I want it back when you're done." He started to walk off, his arm stretched out holding the toothbrush, implying she was to take it, and she did.

"Is this your personal toothbrush?" Kate asked the question as fury rose within her.

"Yes. It is, so take care of it," he said sarcastically.

This comment pushed Kate so near the breaking point she imagined herself walking in the front door of her apartment to tell her family that she was unemployed. Instead, Kate walked just inside the door, where he was sure to see her. "Good. I'll make sure I clean it really well once

I'm done." With that, Kate took the toothbrush and swirled it around in the water of the urinal beside her. She could see that the man felt the sting, but he let out a devilish laugh before walking away. She got to work, knowing better than to test the authority of a superior, especially one who was out to get her.

The inch by inch tiles, which completely filled the ten-by-twelve foot room, were filthy from years of men coming and going. The grout was even more disgusting, and she was absolutely certain that her lack of male genitalia had just won her the first chance to clean the firehouse bathroom so intimately.

The toothbrush Kate handed back to Captain Sullivan that evening had very few bristles remaining, and even those were bent or broken, much like the vertebrae of her back felt. She said nothing to the man, and he said nothing in return. Kate skipped dinner, showered, then headed straight to her bunk and was asleep within seconds of her head touching the pillow.

A few weeks later – after Kate thought she'd completely recovered from the aggravation of her stint at Station Two – she was asked again to return to the substation led by the devil himself. Kate thought for a second about asking for someone else to cover it but decided it was better to go along with the orders.

"Hello again," the begrudging tone was filled with angst, and all of it was aimed at her.

And what the hell did I ever do to you?! The thought spun around within Kate's head as morning check was performed, and it came time to receive orders for the day.

This time, instead of a toothbrush, the huge arrogant man in the blue uniform handed her a big push broom. Kate thought for a second that she was in the clear. Sweeping was not such a bad chore. "Climb up on the roof. It needs to be swept off."

For three seconds, Kate just stared at the broom. *You have got to be kidding me! You really are an asshole!*

When she finally came out of the stunned trance, Kate looked Captain Sullivan dead in the eyes. "No." *See, it can go both ways, you jerk.* "I'm the driver and I wouldn't be able to respond quickly or safely if there is a fire call."

Captain Sullivan made a move as if he intended to disagree, but she stopped him in his tracks. "If you don't see the reasoning behind my refusal, then perhaps you should make a phone call to the Assistant Chief."

This time the man said nothing.

Kate had called his bluff and won. But he wasn't done trying, and Captain Sullivan was certain he had the power behind him to break her.

On her next duty day, Kate reported to her usual station, dropped her bag on one of the bunks and walked into the bathroom. She opened the door to the single stall that had finally been added for women at Central Station, only to find that someone had urinated all over it – the seat, the handle, the wall, and the floor. She stepped backward, but it was too late, her shoes were already wet. She felt completely disgusted by the actions of an immature man who apparently was intimidated by her presence…by a female firefighter.

Kate was in her fourth month of pregnancy and felt less confident that she could continue to hide her condition. She looked a bit like she'd just enjoyed a large Thanksgiving dinner and wasn't sure whether the men had noticed the extra weight on her normally tiny frame until one of the men she was close with came right out and asked if she was pregnant. Kate shot back defensively with, "Why is it that when a woman puts on weight, men automatically assume she's pregnant?"

Richard kindly responded, "I won't say anything if you are, and if you need to borrow one of my uniforms to be more comfortable, just ask and it's yours. It's not right that they don't have a policy in place."

Upon hearing his kind offer, Kate flashed a big smile and admitted, "I am pregnant again, but you can't tell anyone. I don't have enough sick or annual days, and I need to continue working to support my family."

"I understand, Kate," Richard said in a sympathetic voice. He reached into his locker and pulled out two uniforms, one daily grey, and one red work jumpsuit. "If you need dress blues let me know."

"Thank you so much, Richard. You're a lifesaver."

The next time when the fire bell rang, Kate didn't curse under her breath. She climbed behind the wheel of the truck without the tightness around her midsection. Kate realized that in her fifth month of pregnancy she wouldn't be able to explain her weight gain, and the time was quickly approaching when she'd soon have to speak to the new chief.

Two shifts later, as Kate was preparing to leave for work, she found it nearly impossible to button the borrowed uniform. The realization of what that meant hit her like a ton of bricks. Kate fell to the bed behind her. *What am I going to do?*

"What's wrong?" Drake walked into the room and sat on the edge of the bed beside her.

"What're we gonna do?" He didn't seem to understand, so Kate motioned to the unbuttoned pants.

"Well, I can think of something," he said with a wink and a smile.

She laughed. "That's not what I meant, and besides that is what got us here in the first place."

As she fought with the button, Drake tooled her hands and pulled them away. With a quick glance at the clock, he pulled the pants from her body and led Kate to the bathroom.

In the shower, he washed her growing belly and smiled at her, as if to say, *everything will be fine.* Drake's kindness did as it was intended to do. Kate felt better ten minutes later when, once again, she struggled to pull the pants on. As she did, hands came from behind her and fastened the clasp as she held her breath, sucking in her stomach as much as possible.

By the time Kate reached the station, she had worked up the nerve she needed to get through with the day's tasks. Kate thought of the men who'd been given light duty until they recovered from an injury. This was not the same chief she'd spoken with the last time around. She thought, *maybe, just maybe, he'll give me light duty this time so I can continue working.*

The next morning her eyes were heavy and red-rimmed from the crying she'd done on the whole way home. When Drake saw her, he gave Kate a look of sympathy.

"I'm done." The sobbing made her words sound funny even in her own head. "No changes have been made." Kate wiped her face, took a deep breath and sat on the couch, looking up at Drake. "They aren't going to give me light duty. I can't work any longer and I'm in the same boat as last time. I guess I'll be making a trip to the unemployment and welfare offices again." Kate lowered her head into her palms, letting out a huge sigh.

He nodded. "It'll be alright. We'll find a way to make it through like we did before."

"Drake, you need to stay working this time. You need to bite your tongue if anything comes up at work you don't like. We won't make ends meet if you lose your job."

"I will! You can count on me this time, honey." He pulled her up from the sofa and into his arms.

Kate went to the administration office on payday to receive the rest of her annual and sick leave pay. While she was there waiting on the secretary to finish up, Fire Chief Sanders walked in.

"Hey Kate. What're you doing here?" he said good-naturedly.

"I'm here to pick up my last paycheck. Then I'm going home to rest," she said with a sigh.

"Just where a woman should be...home barefoot and pregnant!" He let out a snarky laugh.

"WHAT? Are you kidding me?" Kate gasped along with the other women in the room.

He just laughed, spun around, and walked out.

Kate turned to the secretaries and the Personnel Director who happened to be in the room and said, "I cannot believe he just said that! A man in his position? That was so unprofessional."

"I can't believe he said that either. Wow!" the Personnel Director said with a look of disbelief on her face. But she clearly had no intention of doing anything about it.

Kate left with her last paycheck and felt sick that they had to depend on help from the state again. She hated having to ask for assistance when she had worked so hard to be in a position to provide for her family. It wasn't the way she was raised.

The unemployment office was exactly how she remembered it to be, complete with the uncomfortable air about it. Kate gave herself the silent lecture on why this was necessary; she climbed out of the car and made her way in. It was a difficult walk that would be made significantly easier on the way out, once she had the information in hand that would make life a bit more bearable in the months to come. Her belly bulged beneath the standard t-shirt she opted to wear rather than maternity garb.

Although Kate was back in her car headed to the house, she called home; her mind was racing in numerous directions. Finally landing on the thought of her lease, she felt a sense of relief knowing that it would soon run out and they could find something more affordable, which was actually a blessing. Life's pace would be slowing, and Kate wasn't entirely sure she was happy about it. The time with her kids was always appreciated, but going into first gear was a bit much to swallow for a woman accustomed to driving in fifth gear.

"Hey!" Kate yelled, pushing the door open; her children immediately came over running and screaming. She hugged each and then asked where Drake was. She found him in the kitchen making peanut butter and jelly sandwiches. Kate looked at him with a smile and let out, "I got it."

"That's great." Drake wiped his hands and looked up at her. "I have some good news as well. You know my grandmother who is in the nursing home?"

She nodded.

"She still owns her house. It's not far from here and she said we could stay there till we're able to get on our feet again, and we'd be helping her out by maintaining the house while she's gone. It needs some work, but I think we can make it livable."

In a fraction of a second Kate crossed the room and hugged Drake. The problem of a place to live was no longer a source of such stress, and for that she was ready to stand and cheer. Kate took little Drew and did a few spins around the kitchen, dipping him low at the end. Squeals of laughter filled the room. *Maybe this won't be so bad after all?* she thought.

Kate wasn't sure what to expect. Drake hadn't seen the house in years and could not provide her an accurate description, other than that he remembered it being on the small side and it may need a few things repaired. Kate worried about the condition and the neighborhood after she and Drake drove by the house, but she knew as soon as she was able to return to work, they could move into something better again.

The day came for the big move, and with boxes loaded in the car, they made the trek to the small house they'd temporarily call home. There was a certain level of excitement among all passengers as they navigated the streets leading to the house. When the car stopped, the only sound to be heard was the screams and cries of protest behind her.

"NO, MOM! We don't wanna stay here. Let's go back home!" Mia begged with tears running down her face.

49

T'LL BE ALRIGHT. We'll fix it up and make it our home," she said
confidently, even though she had huge doubts herself as she sat staring
at the house.

Kate looked in amazement, exiting the car and walking down
a pavement sidewalk with grass growing through it. It had cracked
and heaved so badly that she turned to pick up Drew, fearing that
it would be too rough for his little legs to navigate. The yard was
overgrown, and the grass tickled Kate's bare ankles each time she
stepped off the walkway. The porch directly before her was sitting
cockeyed and teetering as if it might fall free from the main structure at
any moment. Behind that was the main house, which, as promised, was
very small. The paint was chipped and cracked on nearly every square
inch of the exterior, and the plate glass windows rattled each time the
wind blew past them. Kate felt as if someone had picked her up from
her happy life and dropped her in a horror film. Nevertheless, realizing
the financial boon of owing no rent, Kate continued forward with an
open mind and entered the home through the front entrance, careful
to walk lightly on the rickety porch.

Small room after small room, they navigated the house until they came to a slightly larger room which was meant to be a kitchen. It had bare cupboards hanging from the walls with doors missing, exposing all that was placed within. The faucet dripped, leaving a large ring of reddish-orange and brown circling the drain, which was simply a black hole. The stove and refrigerator stood on either side of the ancient sink, and both seemed to have been made for someone tiny. Kate, as small as she was, could easily see the top of the "large" refrigerator, which had collected countless months of dust, webs, and grime.

She stood dumbfounded as Drake kept moving. Only when he had motioned to her did Kate continue forward. The room, which jutted out from the kitchen, was in horrible disrepair. Paint flaked from the walls; the ceiling appeared to be caving in and wore the light brown rings that suggested water damage. In the back, beyond the rusting sink and filthy toilet, was cement covering the floor and walls; protruding was an arbitrary pipe that simply hung there. *A shower?* The thought terrified her. *What did I do to deserve this? How did I manage to let my life sink to this low point?* It was at this moment that Kate realized she had not seen a hot water heater. *Cold showers?* The thought made her want to dig a hole to sit in and cry, but she vowed to remain composed for the children who were crying enough tears for her already.

"It'll only be for a few months." *I hope.* "Come on guys, we can do this. It just needs our love and a little paint. You'll see!"

The first month or so was spent painting and repairing the walls to make the house livable. Once Kate put her touch to the house, it became more of a home. Mia and Casey were enrolled in new schools and slowly adapted to the changes. Maria even helped out and felt right at home.

"Ahhhgh!" the noise slipped from her mouth before she was fully awake. At once Kate recognized the pain, and within a very short time it was retching at her midsection once again. The second and third times it tore around her back, and she wasn't sure if she should cradle her stomach or support her back.

Kate climbed from the bed awkwardly with one hand on her belly and the other as leverage behind her. Once standing, she hurried to the phone to make the call.

Ronnie, who was now living with Dr. Marsha, answered the phone with a very excited, "Yes, of course!" He then handed the phone to Dr. Marsha, who instructed her to get to the hospital. Kate hung up and took a deep breath. She headed back to the bedroom to wake Drake and alert Maria that the time had come.

As always, the look, feel and smell of the hospital made her cringe. Muted colors met endless hallways and chemical smells, yet the staff was kind when they saw her coming.

Kate entered the birthing room and was surprised to see that it was quite large and actually very relaxing. The walls were painted in softer hues of mauve and blue, with a television, and even a reclining chair for guests. Her husband moved immediately to it and sat down. It also had a portion of the room for the baby once delivered. Kate, wondering why men looked to be in worse condition than a woman in labor, smiled at Drake to ease his worries slightly, and then a contraction bent her forward. He tried to smile back at Kate once she felt the relief and loosening in her stomach, but it looked more like a pallid grimace.

Kate was laying in the bed feeling like a beached whale, when in walked her neighbor, John, who was a nurse at the hospital. When John saw that she was his patient, he said in a reluctant voice, "Hi, Kate. I'll be your nurse, but if you're uncomfortable having me here, I'll let Dr. Marsha know, and she can send in someone else."

"What is one more person in the room? My husband and brother are here, and now you, John. This is my fourth child, and I have no modesty left, so why not!" Kate said with a sarcastic laugh. "I trust you."

Every five minutes, her body felt as if it was going into convulsions. *Shiiiit* she said under her breath. The nurses did their best to keep her comfortable, offering blankets, pillows, ice chips, and even a hand to grasp when the pain consumed her; but despite the violent contractions, she had not progressed or dilated past 3 centimeters. Given that she had opted for a vaginal delivery after a cesarean birth, Dr. Marsha ordered a dose of pitocin to speed up the process.

"Would you like an epidural for the pain?" Dr. Marsha's question prompted another spin on the dizzying roller coaster she was riding.

Kate clenched her teeth and fought the urge to fill the room with a deafening scream.

At last, when the tension released, Kate turned back to the tiny woman who was now talking to Robert. In a breathless voice, she answered, "I did this twice without drugs. I think I can do it again."

The woman smiled at her and patted her hand as if to say, *sure you can.*

"Oh my God!" After fours hours of contractions, the pain was beginning to take hold of her, and suddenly the epidural didn't sound like such a bad idea. Kate held tight to the rail as another wave of pain crashed over her body. "I don't remember this! I don't remember it hurting this much! This is horrible! This HURRRTS!"

Kate, finally tired of being the strong one, called for the doctor. "This hurts way more than I remember. Please give me the epidural!" What started as a simple request turned into a desperate plea.

"It's the pitocin. It's speeding up your labor and making it more painful, but I'm sorry, it's too late." Dr. Marsha's voice was soft and filled with sympathy. Kate felt pride that this kind woman was Robert's girlfriend. Kate wanted to scream at someone with each painful contraction, but could not yell at those she knew so well.

Dr. Marsha checked her dilation and then walked out of the room, leaving the nurse to finish prepping her.

"Ahhh!" This time the contraction was so strong and painful she could not hold back the screams. Kate gripped the handle of the bed so hard her knuckles turned bright white. She felt the baby's head move into the birth canal and knew it was time. "Get the doctor! The baby is coming!" Kate screamed the command to whoever was willing to listen to her and all three men started for the door, but a female nurse who had entered the room earlier kept them at bay.

"She just checked you. I'm afraid you aren't quite ready..."

"Get the Doctor," and then in the throws of pain, "THE BABY IS COMING NOW!"

The nurse, taken aback by Kate's insistence, lifted the sheet while saying, "The doctor just checked you and you are not....." but immediately took off running for the door.

"Get the doctor back in here!" she yelled, but then ran down the hall herself. From a distance, they could hear her yelling, "The head is crowning!"

When the baby girl was finally born, the doctor laid the precious little bundle atop her stomach, while Drake cut the cord and Robert took pictures. Kate reluctantly handed the baby to John, so he and the pediatrician could clean and examine her. The tiny package was then handed to Robert who simply stood in amazement as his niece, Lucy, looked around the room with her bright eyes wide open.

"You were a lot stronger than I thought. I think you picked Drake and me up off the floor while you were pushing," John said laughing while Drake nodded his head in agreement.

Later that evening, Kate and baby Lucy were whisked away to a room that was less like a hospital room and more like a hotel. She noticed a large bed for her, a crib for the baby, a big puffy chair for her husband, and even a nice dinning table with flowers where she and Drake were served a steak dinner. Less than twenty-four hours later, in that same room, Kate was surrounded by family, including all four of her children.

The next couple months at home with the children kept her very busy. Though there were moments when she wondered about her own sanity in having four children, for the most part the time was filled with love, laughs, and happy memories. When it came time to return to work, Kate was both ready and reluctant. Nevertheless, the promise of a better place to live and no more state assistance motivated her.

When she reported back to work, she was asked to report to the main office. When Kate arrived, she found that she would no longer be the only woman in the department, and a newspaper reporter was there waiting to do a story. Christine had just been hired and was about to start her training.

Kate and Christine met for the first time before the newspaper interview. They stood side by side in front of the fire truck that Kate would now be driving, to pose for a front page photo to go with the story in the local newspaper.

Kate felt a small amount of relief that all eyes would not be focused solely on her now that another female had joined, but she still had doubts about how they would treat her after the escalation in harassment she went through, and taking another pregnancy leave.

Several months after meeting her new female coworker, Kate went about her usual business cleaning up in the fire house kitchen.

"Sounds like Christine is intimidated by you," stated Tom, walking past her to find something in the fridge.

"What do you mean?" Kate looked at him, intrigued.

"Oh nothing, really. I just heard that she's been saying some stuff about you." He shrugged his shoulders and walked off with a cold beverage in hand.

50

KATE SAT AND thought about what the woman would possibly have to say about her and soon decided it wasn't worth dwelling on.

There looked to be a pattern forming. Over the months that passed, the men continually dropped hints about what Christine was doing or saying that would be offensive to Kate, until she was approached by Christine one day, while on duty at Central Station, and had difficulty being civil.

"Kate, can I ask you a question?" Christine began.

"Yeah...sure," Kate answered, biting her tongue as thoughts of what had been said passed through her mind.

Christine was obviously too preoccupied to notice Kate's hesitation and continued in a whisper, "When you were pregnant, did you get paid leave?"

Kate shook her head. "No. I was always told there was no policy in place to allow us to work or maternity leave with pay." Now Kate found herself fascinated, washing away the implanted doubts.

"That's what they told me," Christine said in frustration. "I'm not going to take it. It's not fair. I can't go through this without pay."

Kate didn't respond, but knew that feeling very well.

"I'm going to talk to a lawyer."

"I tried that and got nowhere," Kate said in a frustrated tone.

"Really? Okay I have to get going."

Christine's disappointed look as she headed to her truck that was about to leave made Kate feel sympathetic, and immediately, she blurted out, "Good luck!"

Nearly a month passed, and Kate had heard nothing about Christine going to see a lawyer. She assumed Christine had found another way to navigate the difficult situation. When the phone rang, Kate was trying to balance Lucy on her hip while struggling to hold the receiver between her chin and shoulder, and she wasn't expecting the voice on the other end.

"Kate? This is Christine...from the fire department."

"Oh. Hi," Kate responded, placing Lucy in a highchair and giving her a few raisins to keep her preoccupied while she turned her attention to Christine. "How are you?"

"Oh, I'm okay. I really wanted to call to tell you that I spoke to an attorney. She thinks she can help us."

Kate stopped and sat on a chair next to the phone. "Really?"

"Yeah, Kate, it's not fair. We work as hard as anyone in the department, and we should be treated as equal members." Christine's words teemed with resentment. "Anyway, her name is Ellen Larson, and she said she'd help file a claim with the EEOC."

Kate was excited, but didn't want to get her hopes up too high. She knew the Equal Employment Opportunity Commission heard thousands of cases each year. *Is this really going to lead to anything worthwhile?* Kate's mind was in overdrive. *Or, is it going to be a complete waste of time?*

When Kate hung up that day, she was committed to work with Christine to fight for equal treatment at the department. She also determined that much of what the men had said about Christine was obviously made up. She rolled her eyes and shook her head, thinking about how the men had stooped so low to entertain themselves by keeping her and Christine divided. Nevertheless, there was reason to be happy. This case couldn't have come at a better time. Since the birth of Lucy and returning to work, Kate was finding herself financially strapped. Arrangements had been made to meet with Christine and her attorney, so they could discuss more of the details about what had to happen in order to get their case heard.

Two weeks had passed, and on her day off, Kate drove the short distance to Ellen Larson's office. Kate was asked to testify about what she had been told and undergone during her pregnancies while working for the fire department. She related the stories to Ms. Larson in great detail.

"Kate, that is horrible. You shouldn't have had to endure all of that just to have children and keep them safe. The men never had to go through anything like you women have." The attorney's eyes looked genuinely shocked. "Listen, we'll make sure that there is a second claim filed in your name."

Kate and Christine met again with Ms. Larsen weeks later at her office once the received communication from the EEOC, as well as the fire department. It was suggested that the department change their policies. The EEOC was siding entirely in the women's favor, citing that the City had intentionally violated the rights of each and failed to offer equal treatment in times of need.

The fire department, however, did not take kindly to the recommendations. Not only did they refuse to make the suggested modifications to the policy at the time, but the city attorney essentially stated that the department would treat each case as it came up.

"That makes me sooooo angry," Christine stood clenching her teeth.

"This is ridiculous," Kate huffed.

"Ladies, remember there are still options. You have a choice to make. Do you want to follow through and file a lawsuit?" Ms. Larson looked back and forth between both women.

Kate and Christine were unanimous in their answer, both shaking their heads in agreement.

"I think that's a wise decision."

And with that the three women started on a journey to fight the City against practicing gender discrimination.

Kate arrived at Station Two as directed by the Assistant Chief only to find that the lieutenant on duty, Francis, was only leading in acting capacity. He was a driver like herself, but she had previously worked with him and held no confidence in his ability to perform in a position of authority.

Lieutenant Francis informed her that a group of children from the local elementary school, just down the street, would be visiting for a tour of the station and a presentation. Kate got busy and pulled the truck out of the station garage to prepare it for the arrival of the children.

It was an hour into the visit when Lieutenant Francis said, "Okay, kids, that's the end of the station tour, but here's something else you might be interested in…" He pointed to the large engine parked just behind Kate. "And this is Kate Matthews. She'll tell you all about the truck."

Kate finished her presentation, and Lieutenant Francis instructed her to start up the engine and attach a small section of hose with a nozzle to show the children the power of the water stream. Once Kate had connected the hose and nozzle, she began to increase the pressure while Lieutenant Francis held and opened the flow to the nozzle. As the stream of water stretched out toward the street, Lieutenant Francis turned back to her and said, "Increase the pressure!"

Kate shot him a puzzled look, and could not bite her tongue. "What? I don't think it's safe."

He insisted, "Increase the pressure!"

"No. I won't." Kate looked at him as if he were insane and spoke just loud enough so only he could hear her. "It's not safe with all the children around and the cars passing on the street. It's not safe!" she said with pronounced irritation.

"Are you questioning my order?" Lieutenant Francis turned back and glared at Kate.

"Yes! When it involves the safety of others in a non-emergency situation...YES!" Kate said in defiance. "If you have an issue with me refusing, then take it up with the Chief, but I will not endanger these children."

Lieutenant Francis backed off and turned to the children and onlookers. "This is the end of our presentation. Thank you for coming to visit our station."

There was dead silence, and the children didn't know what to do until a teacher began clapping and told the children to thank the firefighters. They let out a big "THANK YOU!" and began their walk back to the school.

After the children left, Kate unhooked the hose and put the equipment away and pulled the truck back into the station.

She walked back inside the station, and Lieutenant Francis growled, "Don't ever undermine my authority again, especially in front of outsiders, or I'll write you up for insubordination."

Kate looked directly at him. "I will say this again, if you have an issue with what I did, then call the Chief right now. I do my job well, but I won't follow an order that endangers lives when there is no emergency."

He plopped down in a chair and turned his back to her, knowing she was right.

At 2:08 AM, the deafening sound of the alarm filled the station, and Kate jumped to her feet. In just moments, the men were loaded in the truck and she wheeled the giant engine out of the station en route to the scene with full lights and sirens.

They were almost at the address given when the dispatcher canceled the call: "False alarm. Return to station." Kate reached down and turned off the lights and siren and pulled into a large parking lot to turn around. None were happy to be awakened in the middle of the night for nothing. All seemed to be letting out yawns when Kate pulled up to a red light and stopped.

"Go through the light. There's no traffic." The words came from the same man who had battled with her just hours before.

Kate shot him a look of disbelief. "I'm not running a red light. That is an unlawful order. Are you kidding?"

He rolled his eyes in frustration. "Traffic lights are to control the traffic and there's no traffic, so go ahead and go through it."

"Maybe you don't have a problem breaking the law when you drive back from fire calls, but I do. I won't run through a red light even if there is no traffic, and if you have a problem with that, then call the Chief."

He turned his head away from her, stared out the window, and let out a loud huff.

That night, Kate lay in bed trying to go back to sleep, tossing and turning, thinking about the days events and standing up to this man. *He's a jerk, and I did what was right.*

51

KATE WAS FEELING exhausted, returning home after a rough night on the station's less than fluffy beds. She could not believe her ears when Maria informed her that Drake had not come home the night before.

"I think you are going to have to take the kids to school today," Maria said tentatively.

Kate was furious to come home to yet another disappointment from Drake after dealing with the power hungry idiot at the station the day before.

Mia and Casey ran out to the car. Kate buckled them in and drove them to school.

"Have a good day! I'll pick you up later," Kate yelled from the driver's seat, watching the two climb out, eager to start their day. Both mumbled something in response as they hurried off, and although she didn't catch whatever it was, she smiled anyway.

She returned home, happy at least to find that Maria had breakfast ready. Kate sat down and enjoyed a quiet meal with Drew, Lucy, and Maria who had become sort of a savior. Just as they were clearing the dishes from the table, there was a loud knock at the door.

"Hello. Where's Drake?" A large Hispanic man with salt and pepper hair, eyes squinting from the early Texas sun, stood on the steps awaiting her response.

"No, I'm sorry, he's not here right now," Kate said, trying to remain pleasant, in spite of the frustration she felt toward her husband. "I haven't seen him for a few days."

A look of irritation grew on the man's face. "I'm here to pick up the car for payment."

Kate was completely stunned. "What?"

"Drake owes me money, so I'm here to take the car," he growled.

Kate was now a bit frightened; her heart was racing; she spouted back, "I don't know what you're talking about, but that is MY car...not his...and you aren't taking it. What does he owe you money for?"

"He owes me money..." The man's words were said with a level of fierceness that caused Kate to cross her arms over her chest in a defensive way, "for the drugs I gave him."

Kate was now furious. "That is between you and him. I don't know where he is, but that is *my* car. He has no claim to it whatsoever. If I see him, I'll tell him you came by, but you need to leave... now!" Her hands were shaking for fear of what he might do before she could close the door; but he didn't force the issue. She stood still and listened through the door. She heard the man's footsteps retreating from the front entrance. A flood of relief made her weak in the knees.

Kate was so upset she went straight to the bedroom and started pulling out everything that belonged to Drake. Clothes to cologne, toothbrush, and shoes were tossed into large black garbage bags. She put the bags in the car, scoped out the area for fear the man may still be lurking around, and said to Maria, "Lock the door and watch Drew and Lucy. I'll be back soon."

Kate drove in the direction of her mother-in-law's house and knocked on the door with bags in tow.

Teri answered, "Hi, Kate!"

"Hi, Teri!" Kate greeted the woman setting the bags at her feet. "I am dropping off all of your son's belongings. Drake and I are done. You can take back responsibility of him because I'm done being his mother."

Her words were riddled with anger. "Tell Drake I'll start making arrangements to move out of your mother's house as soon as possible," and without waiting for a response, she added a simple, "Thanks."

Teri just stood there bewildered as Kate got in her car and drove away.

The next morning, Kate got the newspaper out and began searching for an apartment. After all, she had been providing all of the financial support while Maria was taking care of the house and kids.

A drug dealer in my house! How dare he put us in this dangerous situation, she fumed inwardly, *that is the last straw!* Kate was on the phone the rest of the day setting up showings for apartments. *How could I have been so blind?* she wondered, crying herself to sleep that night.

Morning came, and she still had not heard from Drake, which was fine with her. She preferred not having to deal with him. She got the kids ready for school and then dressed Drew and Lucy while Maria prepared breakfast. She had four apartments to look at and didn't want to be late. Kate gave the kids a hug and then loaded them all into the car. She put on her happy face, and after dropping Mia and Casey at school, she headed to her first appointment.

After a morning of seeing apartment after apartment, Kate found one that would not only accommodate them, but she could afford by herself, and would allow her to keep Maria employed.

Maria joined in to help Kate pack after the kids were laid down for a nap. Kate paid her an appreciative smile and headed to the kitchen to wash the glasses before packing them away. Kate was washing the last glass when she noticed in the water blood — a lot of blood. She didn't feel anything but saw that the glass had broken. She pulled her hand out of the water and blood spurted everywhere.

"Shit," she cried out, moving quickly to put pressure on the wound. She had sliced off a portion of skin on the knuckle of her right thumb. Kate, feeling faint, immediately grabbed a towel and wrapped her hand while trying not to panic. Once she'd calmed down, she told Maria to watch Drew and Lucy while she went to the emergency room.

She waited a few hours in the ER before the doctor arrived to sew up the hole in her hand. Kate had not felt the injury because it had severed the nerve. It took the doctor a while to stitch it closed, but she was able to get back in time to pick up Mia and Casey from school.

"What happened?" Mia's face wore a look of fright when she saw at her mother's bandaged hand.

"Oh, I just cut myself but," Kate added, noting that the fear hadn't yet left her daughter's face, "the doctor said it's fine."

When they got home, Kate took the pain medication the doctor had given her and went to bed, leaving the kids in Maria's care.

Wonderful day, she thought sarcastically as she laid her head on the pillow, *what else could go wrong?*

The next morning, Kate called the administration office to inform them she'd cut her hand very badly and wouldn't be going into work until the doctor gave her a release. The Assistant Chief asked her to come in to get the form to take to the doctor. Kate agreed and hung up the phone. She dressed herself, with difficulty, while Maria made sure Mia and Casey were ready. They all ate breakfast before Kate drove them to school on her way to the administrative office.

Kate arrived only to be greeted by Assistant Chief Garza saying, "So let's see this hand you cut so badly you can't work."

She looked at him with surprise. "It was stitched in layers to close the wound, and they bandaged it tightly." Kate held her hand out for him to see.

"It doesn't look bad enough to keep you from working," he said with mild sarcasm.

"I'm telling you it is," Kate assured him.

"So show me. I don't believe it is that bad," he insisted.

Kate looked at him as if to say, *Are you kidding me?* Nevertheless, she began to unwrap her hand. She was able to take enough of the bandage off to reveal the bloody, swollen, and stitched up thumb. "Are you satisfied?"

"Umm... yeah. That's bad," he conceded. "I'm sorry I didn't take you at your word. Here is the form for your doctor. Go home and get some rest." He stood there uncomfortably, not knowing what else to say to her.

Kate snatched up the form while biting her tongue, then turned and marched out to her car. She sat there for a minute steaming, then spoke out loud, "I'll bet if I were one of the guys you wouldn't have questioned my injury!" Kate was so angry she swore she smelled smoke coming from her ears. *Why would he think I'd lie? I have so little sick time left! I'm not going to waste it. You moron!*

Kate spent the next week recovering from her injury and packing for the move. She was still coping with her decision to end her marriage. Drake kept calling, but she refused to take his calls.

Kate was helping Maria in the kitchen when she heard a knock at the door. She opened it to find Drake standing there with a confused look on his face.

"What are you doing here? I don't want to talk to you," Kate said, attempting to close the door.

He put his hand out to stop her. "We need to talk. What about Drew and Lucy? I want to see them."

"Fine…come in." She opened the door wider, turned, walked into the living room, and sat on the sofa.

Drake walked in and closed the door.

Drew had heard his voice, came running in, and slammed into Drake. "Daddy, Daddy!"

"Hey, bubba bear. I missed you," Drake said to Drew, picking him up and hugging him. "Kate, I want to see the kids. I know you have every right to be angry with me, but I miss them."

"Do you not understand the danger you put all of us in…including your own children? What kind of man…no, father…what kind of father would put their kids in danger to satisfy his own sick desires? You don't deserve to have them in your life. Why should I let you see them? Tell me why." Though Kate's anger erupted inside all over again, she tried not raise her voice so she wouldn't upset the kids.

"You're right. I didn't think, and I understand your concern for the kids. Can you at least let me visit them?" Drake pleaded.

"I'm packing for the move and have a lot going on, but once we're settled in the new place, I'll let you know," Kate said with a disconnected tone.

"Okay, that is fair enough." Drake gave Drew another hug and a kiss on the cheek "I love you, bubba bear. I'll see you soon."

"Bye, Daddy," Drew said sadly waving his little hand.

52

KATE REPORTED BACK at work the next day only to be told she was being reassigned to Station Seven. She trudged out of her station with heavy feet, and put her gear back into her car before driving over to her newly assigned station.

She was greeted by a young, slender, dark haired man with brown eyes wearing his dress blues, indicating he was an officer. He smiled at her and introduced himself as Lieutenant Peterson and welcomed her to the station. He turned to introduce the firefighter she'd be working with.

"This is Firefighter Davis. You'll be assigned here for quite a while, so I suggest you get busy studying the maps to familiarize yourself with our territory. I'll help you out for the first few weeks, but I expect you to learn the district as soon as possible."

"I am familiar with the main roads, but I'll get on the rest today," Kate replied.

She spent what spare time she had studying the maps, getting familiar with streets, house numbers, businesses, and where the hydrants were located. She wanted to do her best to get her crew to a fire scene as quickly as possible, and decided to create a book with hand drawn maps of her new district. She went a step further and went down to the local utility company to obtain maps that showed the size and location of water mains and hydrants. She color coded the size of the water mains so she would know which hydrants would supply the most water. She went to the businesses in her district to find out the location of standpipes in the building, as well as the name and phone number of the contact persons for each business.

By the time she was done, she knew her district so well that her truck was almost always the first to arrive at a fire scene. The Chief would even radio her truck for directions when he was unable to find their location. Kate also left the book at the station for other shifts to use so they could benefit from her work.

Months passed, and as she strode into the station one morning, the driver from the previous shift was headed toward her with a dumbfounded look. "What happened to the book? Do you have it?"

"Yes I have it, why?"

"We couldn't find it and we needed it."

"I had to take it home to make some updates to it," she said, still slightly confused. A smile then spread across her face, "Why? Were you lost without it? Have you guys become dependent on it?" she joked with the man.

The man shrugged off her kidding tone. "It's very helpful, and we respond much quicker with it."

"Well I updated it, and it'll be here for you to use the next time you come into work, so don't worry." Kate took the book out of her bag, plopped it on the desk, and went to put her gear on the truck.

Lieutenant Patterson overheard her talking to the other driver, and commended her, "You really have done a great job with that book and learning the district. As a matter of fact, you've done such a great job you make me look good." He smiled, patting her on her shoulder.

"Thanks, Lieutenant!" Kate said proudly. "I'm doing my best, and I'm happy to see I make you look good." She let out a snickering laugh.

"Well, keep it up 'cause it isn't just me taking notice. The higher ups are taking note as well." He turned and walked back into the office, leaving her feeling proud that her work had made a difference.

Kate walked into the station on the following duty day thinking it was beginning to feel like home, but within moments of the thought passing through her head, Lieutenant Patterson notified her that she would be assigned back to Station Six.

"The officer there has to take leave for several shifts," her superior informed her, "and you are being placed as acting lieutenant until he returns." A very brief smile passed over the man's lips.

It must have been contagious; before she knew it, Kate was smiling ear-to-ear. Kate was to be in charge of a station for the first time. No longer would she be handed the orders; instead, Kate would take command.

The day was going well, and Kate felt good to be in a position of leadership. It was a natural fit for her. The men, unbelievably, paid her a great deal more respect than she expected.

I could get used to this, Kate thought, dismissing the men for the night.

Kate retired to the dorm and climbed into the small, not-so-comfy bed to get some rest before returning home to the children the next morning. She was caught up in her thoughts, and very quickly giving up on sleep, lifted the large novel from the chair beside her bed, and opened it to the earmarked page. This was one of the many positives of the job. Though there was not a great deal of free time and though she missed her children horribly in the evenings, Kate was at least provided a bit of quiet time in the later hours during which she was able to read many books that held her interest. After all the men were sound asleep, she set the book down on her chest, still open, to rest her eyes for just a minute.

SHRIIIIIIEEEEEEEEEEEEKKKK!!!

When the call came in, she couldn't decipher the noise in her mind.

Kate was just entering that deep sleep where fantasies and nightmares could play out. The sound began to slowly register. As it did, Kate jumped from the bed startled, her book falling to the floor. The men around her chuckled, but that didn't register either. Nothing made sense. Kate could hear the details spouting from the other side of the room.

The address sounds familiar, she thought, sleepily tugging the bunker gear on. Again, the dispatcher on the radio stated the address of the fire. She tried to get her bearings, again thinking *that sounds so familiar,* but still nothing was registering with her as she made her way to the truck. Everything from the day before flooded her mind. She was lieutenant in charge. Just as that began to click, so did the address.

It's the apartment below mine! The thought turned instantly to fear, and she immediately felt her body become cold with panic. Kate felt the hair stand up on her arms with the thought of her sleeping children becoming overwhelmed with smoke.

"Hurry! My kids!" Kate knew the order did not make sense, but she didn't have time to explain. She climbed in the truck with the men and shouted to the driver, "STEP ON IT!" before she even attempted deal with of the overwhelming feeling that was now consuming her.

The engine tore out of the garage with full lights and siren. The driver turned out of the driveway to the right...

"YOU ARE GOING THE WRONG WAY!" Her scream had every set of eyes in the truck on her instantly.

Oh my God! You moron! Kate wanted to push him out of the driver's seat and take over. She had driven this route many times before and knew this was not the fastest route to her apartment, but there was no way they were going to be able to turn the truck back now. Her skin was crawling as the man kept apologizing over and over again. It took every ounce of control to keep her body motionless in her seat.

"I'm sorry! I thought this was the quickest way."

"No it's not! The apartment complex is on the north bound side of the highway and you won't be able to get to it this way. Let me think...just drive!" Kate yelled to him over the roar of the engine and the squealing of the siren.

He made quick work of righting his wrong, taking fast corners. She could hear nothing, see nothing, she could only think of her children and needing to reach them.

"Turn left on the next road. We can get there faster this way," she shouted, rubbing her chin in thought. "Yes, turn right on this street, and it will take you out onto the service road just before the apartment complex," she said, thinking, *Yes, back on track.* The driver made every turn as directed looking over at Kate occasionally for her approval.

Finally! The single thought tore through Kate's mind. Her eyes wildly searched the crowd for her children. Station Four had arrived just before them and was pulling down their hoses to attack the fire that was shooting out of the lower apartment windows. Kate jumped from the truck in a single bound almost falling from her legs being weak with fear. She raced in the direction of the building, not thinking about doing her job until she found her kids safe.

"Where are they? Where are they? Is there anyone left in there?"

53

THE STARTLED FIREFIGHTER shook his head side to side.

"Oh, thank you, thank you, thank you..."

Kate saw them, and everything in her let loose. She ran to them and grabbed at all of the young, frightened kids, and held them as tightly as she could, her hands shaking. Finally, on Maria's insistence that they were all okay, Kate ran back to help the others put out the flames.

When the chaos of the event was controlled, Kate looked at where the flames had once been. It had made its way up the side of the large building, ending just inside the window of her children's bedroom. Only days before, Drew's bed had been pushed up against that window, but for some reason Kate had decided to move it to the other side of the room. She laughed at the irony, and shook from the thought when she heard her name and turned back. The young man who had lived in the burned apartment was addressing her.

"Kate...I ran upstairs and I knocked, and knocked, and knocked. Finally Maria answered and I got them all out. I'm so sorry!" His words were filled with fear, relief, exhaustion, and sadness. She reached out and hugged him, smiled, and thanked him for what he had done for her children.

A few hours later, after returning to her home, Kate stood in the center of the living room. All around her was a blanket of black soot. It covered every surface in the room and beyond, and she knew that every moment of her two days off would be spent cleaning up after the fire she had just helped to extinguish.

At least my babies are okay, and she let out a deep sigh.

That afternoon, the apartment manager came by to tell her they were sending crews of people to not only start repairing the damage from the fire but to clean the apartment and all her belongings for her. Kate gave the woman a big hug after hearing she would not have to tackle the mess alone.

After the chaos surrounding the apartment fire, Kate was dying to have a break, but it wasn't going to happen. Kate was assigned back to the Central Station, but this time she'd be driving and operating the department's only aerial ladder truck. The thought both excited and terrified her at the same time. She'd be behind the wheel of the largest truck in the department measuring a whopping eighty-five feet in length. Although it was thrilling to be assigned to such a large truck, and it would take her off the front line again, it also meant Kate would be working only blocks from the Mexican border and the Rio Grande River. She would have to respond to drowning victims in the river, and assisting border patrol officers with opening vehicles that may contain drugs.

The first couple of weeks at the station went by rather peacefully. The only calls that came in were minor ones which did not involve the aerial truck. That, in her book, was a very good couple of weeks. On the third week, shortly after arriving, Kate learned that Engine One's driver called in sick, and she was being reassigned to replace him for the day. Kate did her morning routine check of the truck and equipment, and then went upstairs to have coffee with the rest of the crew.

Today was a field day and Kate trudged out to the front with the leaf blower. She worked her way around the edge of the building and turned the corner headed for the rear when a hand on her shoulder caught her off guard. She instinctively let her hand off the trigger and then she heard it. The alarm was blaring; a call was being announced over the intercom. She, along with Bob, who had just alerted her, ran to the garage, the leaf blower bouncing off her leg with each stride.

Kate tossed it aside as soon as she entered the huge garage and climbed aboard the truck. Only then did she catch the details of the call. They were going to be headed to the international bridge to Mexico. The department there, short on water supply, had called for assistance with a major building fire at a landmark restaurant just across the bridge. Kate and her crew were sent out to run lines across the bridge to supply them with water.

The engine roared to life; Kate pulled the truck, lights and sirens blaring, out of the station and sped away toward the bridge. This would mark the first time in history that the city of Brownsville assisted Mexico with a fire, and Kate instantly recognized the momentousness of the situation.

Kate arrived at the bridge that had now been blocked off by police. Once she had positioned the truck, they all climbed out and began pulling down the massive yellow six inch diameter hoses. Kate and her crew connected each section of hose until it reached across the international bridge to the fire truck in Mexico. She felt pride in herself, in her crew, and in her country.

They stayed all night and into the early morning hours helping the firefighters in Mexico to preserve the landmark restaurant, and it wasn't until they were rolling up the hoses that a crew from the new shift came to relieve them. All over the world, wars had happened in fights over ideas, religions, and governmental policies, but that night, Kate, along with men from two different countries, came together to battle a single evil. She felt great for having been a part of it and making history.

54

Months flew by and Kate came to fully acknowledge that her marriage was over. When Drake informed her that he was moving to Hawaii, she made an appointment with a lawyer. Divorce papers were drawn up and signed by both Kate and Drake before he left. She appeared in court alone with her attorney, since Drake was out of state, and with the slight of the pen, they were legally divorced. She left with her head low, feeling she had failed again – not for trying, but for choosing the wrong partner.

To make matters worse, the following day, while Kate was at work, Avery and Mary showed up at her apartment to pick up Mia and Casey. This time they went inside and packed all of the kids' belongings. Kate received a frantic call from Maria saying that Avery was taking the kids along with all of their clothes and toys. Kate was unable to leave work immediately and called the police to inform them that he was at her home, taking her children without permission.

The police showed up and called her back. "Ma'am, he showed us court papers stating he has legal custody."

Kate tried to remain calm in the midst of total confusion over what was happening. "That is impossible. We have not gone to court. You must be reading them wrong. There is no way he has custody of our kids."

"I'm sorry, ma'am, there's nothing we can do. He has custody papers. This is a civil legal matter, and you'll have to take this up in court."

The police then allowed Avery to take the children.

Kate hung up the phone and sat there trying to comprehend what had just happened and how helpless she was to stop it. She had trouble concentrating the rest of her shift and was thankful there were no calls that night.

The next morning, she went to see her lawyer to find out how Avery could have secured papers, shown up, walked into her home, and taken them and their belongings. Her attorney said Avery had filed with the court to obtain custody, but he had no legal right to take them out of her home until there was a court hearing. Apparently, the papers he'd shown the police officers were the ones he'd filed with the court, and the police officer misunderstood what the document said.

Kate found out that Mary had enrolled Mia and Casey in the Mercedes School District where they lived. Kate drove an hour to the school armed with the proof they'd unlawfully taken her children. She met with the principal at Casey's school, explained she had legal custody, and showed him the custody papers. He apologized, and released Casey to her immediately.

She then drove to Mia's school where Mary worked and spoke to the principal there. He was not so cooperative since he knew Mary.

Kate unloaded both barrels on the principal. "You are aiding Mary and Avery in kidnapping my children. And if you do not release Mia, I will call the police right now. And then I will file a lawsuit against you and the school district for enrolling my children without proper documentation."

The principal called Mary to the office to hear what she had to say.

"Kate, you know this is best for the kids. They need to stay here," Mary tried to explain.

Kate had no interest in Mary's point of view. "These are *my* children,

Mary…not yours. And you and Avery had no right to sneak in and take them from my home while I was at work. You need to back away, or I will call the police and have them charge you with kidnapping."

Kate was boiling inside, but tried to maintain her composure in the face of the woman who persisted in trying to take away her life and claim it as her own. *She got my husband, but she is NOT getting my children.*

"Kate, you know…" Mary continued, but was cut off by Kate.

"Stop talking, Mary. They are not your children, and you have no rights here." Kate turned to the principal. "So, are you going to release my daughter, or do I call the police?"

The principal looked at Mary, then back at Kate, "Okay, I will call her teacher and have her send Mia to the office," then said to Mary, "I'm sorry, there is nothing I can do, Mary. She is Mia's mother."

Kate returned home with Mia and Casey, who were upset and confused about what had just happened. Avery had told them that she had agreed to let them live with him and Mary. Mia and Casey were excited at this prospect after he told them how much happier they would be at his home because of all the fun things he was going to do with them.

After weeks of the kids saying they wanted to try living with their dad, who had planted the seed of fun in their heads, Kate decided to give in and let them go. She knew they needed to find out for themselves that their dad sugarcoated the life they thought they'd enjoy at his house. When they finally went to court, Kate agreed to give Avery full custody, and their roles were reversed. Kate now paid child support and carried medical coverage for her kids, while Avery and Mary took on the daily responsibility of caring for the children. As much as Kate tried to see the situation as taking the stress of raising four children alone off her shoulders, she only saw her failure as a mother.

Kate did her best to maintain a happy face for Drew and Lucy. They didn't have their father around, and now they were coping with the loss of their older brother and sister too. Deep down inside though, Kate was devastated that Mia and Casey chose their father and step-mother over her.

Kate was watching cartoons with Drew and Lucy the following Saturday when the phone rang. She ran to answer it thinking it was the kids calling, and was surprised when she heard that familiar raspy voice.

"Hello, beautiful." It was Fabian. "I was wondering if you might be free tonight." He and his band would be playing at the hotel where she used to work, and he wondered if she wanted to come out for a while for drinks and to hear his band. After everything Kate had been through, she needed to be with someone who wanted and enjoyed her company, especially since she had heard that he and his wife divorced.

"Yeah, sure. It sounds like fun," she answered, trying to hide the childlike giddiness in her voice.

Their conversation continued for several minutes, but in truth she was eager to hang up so she could be free to jump and cheer with joy.

The place she arrived at that evening was so familiar it almost felt like she was returning home. She greeted a few familiar faces while making her way to the lounge area. It was nice to think she was the one who was going to be waited on that evening, rather than carting heavy trays of assorted beverages all night.

"Hey, Kate!" Linda, a former coworker approached, smiling broadly. "I take it you have the golden ticket this evening?"

"What do you mean?"

"There's a table reserved for you," she said, pointing to the front of the room. "It's right next to the stage."

"Oh. Wow," Kate smiled, feeling her cheeks flush. "Thanks! I didn't know. One of the guys is an old friend. I was coming to see him play."

Kate headed in the direction of her reserved table. From the stage, she received a wink and a smile. Fabian was busy setting up for the show and, from the looks of it, his band was running a bit behind schedule. She took her seat, ordered a drink, and enjoyed the few moments of free time.

Fabian stepped off the stage and headed for her table. Kate stood to greet him. He smiled, gave her a hug, and softly kissed her on the cheek, "Glad you could make it. I have to finish setting up, but I'll sit with you on my break."

"Okay, sure, I'll be here," Kate said, trying not to show how tickled she was to see him.

For an hour and a half, the band played and the crowd in the hotel lounge loved it. Fabian, like the others in the group, was in his element, and Kate thoroughly enjoyed watching him. She also found that she enjoyed the attention she was getting from him paying.

Fabian sauntered over to her table during the break, with hands in his pockets, smiling ear to ear. He appeared almost like a child getting ready to cause mischief. Kate laughed and ran a hand through her hair.

"Hello, beautiful. Imagine that. All it takes is reserving a table to attract the most gorgeous woman in the room," he whispered leaning forward to plant a kiss on her cheek.

She just giggled as Linda came over to refresh her drink.

The break didn't last long, but by the time the performance was over for the evening, the two had enjoyed several moments of friendly flirting. When he suggested they head back to his place for a glass of wine, she was already on board.

Kate felt very at home as he pulled her down beside him on the couch. For a while, they just snuggled, talked, and drank the wine as promised, but there had always been an unspoken attraction between them, and it soon turned more intimate as they stared into each other's eyes.

The first kiss tasted sweet and spicy, like the wine they had moments before, but it wasn't long before she forgot about the taste and everything else when he took her hand and led her to his bedroom.

In the morning, she sat across the breakfast table from the man who had moved in and out of her life over the years, and was able to hold her interest like no one ever had. He was funny, entertaining, smart, and engaging. He made her feel like she was the only one that existed and soon the two were enthralled in a project together.

"I bought a house," he said very simply.

"What?"

"I bought a house. It needs some work, but I think I could rent it out after it's fixed up." He looked at her suggestively.

"That's great, Fabian."

"I was hoping you would say that. I was also hoping you'd want to help me with the work of getting it fixed up. You have such great ideas."

Just like that it was decided and Kate would spend her free time working with him to ready the house.

Her days were filled with happiness while in the company of Fabian. She worked her normal schedule at the fire department, but much of her free time was spent working on Fabian's new purchase.

"I really appreciate you being here... and helping me with all of this," he said, wrapping her up in his arms. She still held the paint brush, which threatened to drip at any moment. She tried to wriggle free, to prevent that from happening, and laughed when he held her tighter. After a moment, he let go so she could put the brush down, but in a flash he had her in his arms again. This time she wasn't going to fight it. The plastic which covered and protected the carpet was cold against her skin, but he was all she needed to stay warm. His lips met hers with such passion that nothing else existed. Entangled in each other, they rolled around on the floor in a heated exchange of lust.

A month had passed with working weekends on the house. They arrived at the house together to finally finish up.

"I can't believe it's almost done. It looks great," Fabian said with a huge smile, but her look didn't reflect his, so he added, "don't you think?"

"What?" She broke free from her thoughts long enough to notice the disappointment in his face. "Oh... yeah... it does. It's looks wonderful."

"What's wrong, Kate? Did I say something to upset you?"

She looked at him trying to disguise her sadness. "No. No. I'm fine."

"No you're not, Kate. You've walked around here this morning in your own little world. You haven't wanted to talk, or laugh, or do much of anything. Something's wrong. What is it?"

His prodding won her over and also opened the emotional flood gates. Her whole body visibly shrunk.

"Oh, Fabian!" She looked at the man, who she had once considered a mere friend. At some point during all of the time they'd spent together, he'd become much more than a friend. She was excited every time he called or came around – even when she was expecting it. She longed for him on the nights she had to stay at the fire station, in the small, cold, uncomfortable bed. She talked about him endlessly to her friends. She had fallen in love, but that wasn't the only truth she was facing. "There is something I have to tell you."

The look on her face must have said more than she'd intended. Fabian suddenly looked very concerned and ushered her to the makeshift chairs, upside-down crates at the center of the newly renovated living room. "What's going on? Are you okay? What did I do?"

She smirked at his last question, then was quick to explain when he looked hurt. "Fabian, I'm pregnant."

"Oh...uh...oh! I thought you were on the pill. How could this happen? Is it..." When words failed him, he pointed to himself.

"Yes! I was, but I don't know what happened...and yes, it's yours. I haven't been with anyone else." Once the sting of the question left her, the overwhelming sensation returned. "What are we going to do?"

"We'll get married." He made the statement as if it was the most obvious solution in the world.

Kate looked at him with shock, and then sadness. "I can't marry you." Her head fell.

"Why not?" His voice now sounded annoyed. He pulled her chin up until she was looking him in the eye. "Why not?"

"Fabian, I can't marry you. You didn't want to be a couple before. A baby won't change the way that you feel about me." Another tear rested in the corner of her eye, but she willed it not to fall.

Much to her disappointment, Fabian didn't argue the point. "Are you going to keep the baby?"

"Yes! Of course! Although this was not planned, a baby is a blessing. I can't..." Kate couldn't even say the words.

"Okay." It was obvious that the news was taking an emotional toll on the man. For several minutes he just sat on the hard plastic crate, trying to process what was happening. "Well, I want to help you. You can stay here!" It was as if it were the greatest epiphany.

"Fabian, you need to rent it so you can pay back the loan," she said, peering at him as her heart was breaking.

"Fine. I'll rent it to you. I'll charge you only what I pay the bank each month."

Though she wanted to tell him to leave her alone; to go away so she could sulk and sob in privacy, she knew that what he was offering would mean living in a much nicer home for far less than what she was paying for her apartment. It would also lessen the blow that would come from having to take leave without pay again.

Less than a month later, Kate and the kids and Maria were getting settled in the house she'd worked so hard on. Though he was good to her and ensured that she had what she needed to be comfortable in the couple months that followed, Fabian did not show any interest in spending time together.

As those first few months passed, Kate continued to do her job as she had with the pregnancies before. There was less energy and more hunger to contend with, but she managed.

"What's on the menu for lunch today?" Kate asked the question and laughed, propping her elbows on the firehouse kitchen counter, chin on her hands.

The guys manning the cooking area shot her a look before laughing with her. "Baked chicken, mashed potatoes, and corn," Joe answered, and then playfully asked, "how's that sound to you?"

"Mmm! Delicious! I better go get washed up," she said, patting a hand on her belly before she turned and walked away.

Kate enjoyed every bite of the meal promised along with the men, who made up her family away from home, but just as she placed her plate in the sink to wash it, the alarm bell rang. Everyone stopped what they were doing, so all could hear the information as it was relayed through the radio.

"…head-on collision… Highway 77…"

Shit! Kate and the rest of the men went running. She was the first to the truck and climbed behind the giant wheel, waiting for the others to climb aboard before putting it into gear. With lights on and sirens blaring, she sped as quickly as she could in the direction of the accident. Though she was racing to the scene, she couldn't help feeling as though they were motionless.

The men were practically out the doors before the truck came to a complete stop. The two mangled vehicles claimed a large portion of the road, and EMS was already evaluating the situation. The black SUV looked as though it would be repairable, but the same could not be said for the tiny car that had come up against it. The pale blue Ford looked more like a crumpled accordion than anything else.

There's no way anyone could have survived that, Kate thought, and a shiver passed down her spine, despite the ninety degree weather.

However, as it turned out, the driver in the mangled car showed signs of life. A teenage boy was trapped within the wreckage and needed to be forcibly removed.

"Would you mind?" asked David, an EMS responder. He looked to Kate with kind, concerned eyes and then motioned her to the car.

She walked closer to find the boy, still in his seat, with legs pinned under the dashboard. A large gash had cut part of the boy's scalp so that it hung freely. His innocent eyes cried out with fear and pain. Kate held the wound and did her best to calm him with a smile and soft spoken words, while David tried to insert the IV. The arm that was most conveniently accessible was broken so badly that there was no way David could get the line in place, thus they had to climb around to the other side in order to reach his other arm.

The IV had been inserted, and Kate tried to focus all of her attention on the boy.

"What's your name sweetheart?" she asked.

"His jaw is shattered. He can't answer you," David said promptly.

Out of the corner of her eye, she saw the IV fluid spurting out from the wound in his arm.

Her heart ached for the boy, but her stomach was crying also. Feeling horribly queasy, she tried again to distract herself. "Do you still need me here?" she asked, but didn't provide him time to respond.

"I have to get some air!" she declared. Her heart pounded, her forehead was sweating, and the world around her was ringed in yellow as she walked away.

While Kate sat with her head between her knees, she overheard another member of the EMS crew speaking with the Assistant Chief and Lieutenant Peterson.

"I think we might have to call a doctor on scene. Your crew can't get his legs free."

"What is the problem?" the Assistant Chief said, looking on.

"I don't know. It might be the best option…" answered the other paramedic, looking back at the vehicle and considering whether amputation was really the best way.

Kate, no longer able to be the silent bystander, walked over to the Assistant Chief and interrupted, "Is it really necessary? His legs are already broken. How much damage are you really going to do in trying to free them compared to amputation?"

"Kate, can you go speak with the parents and give them an update?" Lieutenant Peterson said, knowing she had the ability to find calmness in highly charged situations.

Lieutenant Peterson was obviously stressed. Kate didn't bother responding; she simply walked in the direction of the hysterical onlookers. She got closer to the couple; the woman looked at her with grief-stricken eyes, and Kate immediately recognized her. She was the attorney who had helped file her child support case years before.

Stay calm, Kate, she urged herself. *You can do this.* "Hello, Mrs. Kerns. I'm really sorry to see you under these circumstances, but I thought you should have an update about your son." Panicked thoughts filled her head. She searched for the right words to shed a slightly less gruesome light on the horrible situation

"What's going on? How is Ben? They won't let us near the car!" The woman, who was usually quite composed, now shook with terror and continuously shifted her head, trying to see what was happening.

"He has several bad injuries, and they are trying their best to stabilize him while they work to free him from the car. He is conscious and in good spirits despite the situation. I am going back over and I'll give you an update again in a few minutes, okay?" Receiving a nod in response, Kate turned and headed back to the car.

Kate walked up just in time to see them free Ben from the car using the Jaws of Life. He was placed on the stretcher and she noticed, due to multiple fractures, the boy's legs looked very short and swollen. She turned to David, who had been working to stabilize him, with a questioning look on her face.

"Both of his legs are broken in at least three places, his jaw is shattered, and his right arm is broken. He doesn't appear to have internal injuries, but we won't know until he arrives at the hospital for further evaluation. Tell the parents that we are transporting him to the BMC Hospital, and they can meet us there."

"Okay! Take care, Ben." Kate laid her hand on the boy's shoulder and then looked over at his parents. As soon as he was in the ambulance, Kate went over to Ben's parents to relay the information.

"Thank you so much, Kate... for all your help... and for being there for Ben." Mrs. Kerns said with tears in her eyes and gave Kate a hug before leaving.

Kate felt great sadness and yet satisfaction that she was there for their son during this terrible tragedy.

55

AVE YOU HEARD anything more about the boy from the head-on collision? Did he come out of the coma?" Kate asked the Captain one day during an afternoon meal. She had heard that Ben underwent massive surgery to repair the multiple injuries, but had lapsed into a coma. A month had passed, and she hadn't heard anything more.

"Yes, he did. It had to have been a week or so ago now. He spent three weeks in a coma, but last I heard he was starting to show signs of recovery."

A miracle, thought Kate, who felt proud and happy for being able to play a part in saving his life that day. She hoped that it was an omen for what the day held in store.

Kate had been pregnant for five months. Her clothes were getting tight, her belly had popped, and it was becoming near impossible to hide her condition. It was time to see the Fire Chief. Although Kate knew that nothing had changed, as far as policy was concerned; and fearing the repercussions of having already filed a lawsuit against the City, Kate trudged, heavy-hearted, toward the door of the new man in charge.

I don't even have anyone to help me this time, she thought, dreading the encounter that was about to take place as she walked into the Fire Chief's office.

"What can I do for you, Kate?"

"You have probably heard rumors that I may be pregnant...well I am, so I am here to find out if the City has changed their policy." Kate's head began to sink when she heard his answer.

"No, Kate. It hasn't changed. You will take leave as you have in the past, and return when you have a release from your doctor."

"I thought so, which is why I am here."

"Okay. You know the drill. See Miss Vicki to fill out the necessary forms."

She dragged herself out of the office to the same fate as in the past. *No job, no money, and now no husband. At least I know I can get government assistance,* she thought, trying to remain positive about all that had taken place.

Kate was due in three months, with a belly that entered a room far before she did. Kate nearly fainted when she read that the date of the Lieutenant's exam was around the same time her baby was due. This was something she'd been awaiting with impatience. It was yet another opportunity for her to prove herself within the career field she had chosen.

I don't care. Let me go into labor, she thought, as she read the date again, which happened to be just two weeks shy of her due date. *I am going to study for it anyway. More money, more respect, less risk, and no need for a second job — it's worth the try!*

With that decision, the final three months of the pregnancy passed quickly. She cared for the kids, prepared a space for the new baby, and spent every free moment pouring over the exam books.

Kate arrived at the office of Dr. Mata, her ex-sister-in-law Diedra's new husband, the Wednesday before the lieutenant's exam. Kate wasn't comfortable going back to see Dr. Marsha since she and Ronnie had broken up and chose to see Dr. Mata for her pregnancy instead. With any of the other pregnancies, she likely would have been hoping to be told that the time had come. That was not the case this time around.

"The baby is very large, Kate," Dr. Mata warned. "...and you may run into complications. I think it's best to schedule you for a cesarean section this Friday."

"Oh," she said quickly, "no, that won't work!"

"What?" He stared at her with confusion.

"I'm sorry. It can't be Friday. I'm taking a promotional exam on Friday. I need to take this exam. I have to be there." The words fell from her mouth in a flurry.

"Well, I don't really know if it's wise to wait any longer than that?" he said, giving her a look of doubt and a hanging question. She didn't respond, giving him no choice. "I suppose we can wait until Saturday."

"Yes! Perfect! Oh, yes! That'll be great. Thank you! Thank you!" Kate said, slightly embarrassed to have reacted so passionately, but sighing with relief as well.

The doctor laughed. "Okay," he said, with a shake of his head, "I'll see you on Saturday.

56

WHEN THE ALARM clock rang on the Thursday morning before the exam, Kate sprang from the bed, and the book which she had been studying from the night before fell on the floor beside her. She laughed.

I guess I was working a little too hard, she teased herself. She felt awake, refreshed and full of adrenaline. The exam wasn't until the following day, but she knew she had to review a few more things.

The first task of the day, however, was getting the kids ready for school. While Maria finished cleaning up after breakfast, Kate bent down to help Casey tie his shoe.

Ow! The word circled her head, but when she stood, the pain was gone. *Must have been the way that I was standing.*

Half an hour later, both kids were packed in the car, and Kate was headed to the school. Sitting at a red light, she felt the pang again and put a hand to her belly. She didn't say a word, didn't act on the pain, but got the kids to school and headed home again.

Damn it! Not now! She was frantic. She couldn't go into labor. *I will take that test! Even if I am in labor, I am taking that test!* As determined as she was, she decided it best to skip some of the studying and lay down.

Friday morning, Kate considered it a miracle that she had made it through the night. The pains had not subsided, but Kate found her way to the Civic Center where the exam was being held.

Be tough, she thought, grimacing one last time before she climbed from the car. *No one has to know. Just get in there, get it done, and deal with the rest later.*

Once Kate had signed in, she found a seat and pulled her chair in toward the desk until her pregnant bulge touched.

Just hold on there, little one. Just a little longer, she told the baby within her, lightly placing her hand on top of her rounded belly.

In addition to several other people in the room, the Fire Chief and the Civil Service Director were standing in opposite corners of the room. They would be certain that the exam was administered correctly.

The Civil Service Director began to talk while two other men passed out the exam papers. "Keep the exam face down until you're told to begin. From the moment that instruction is given, you'll have two hours to complete the exam. Once you're finished, please come to the front of the room and place the test on the table. You may wait for your results if you would like." His voice bellowed through the room, and the anxiety of all in attendance could be felt.

"Okay," he called out again, a few moments later, after all participants had received a copy, "you may begin!"

The first two questions were a cinch and Kate was feeling more confident. She began to silently read the third "What are the...?" *Oh my... Oh!* The pain coursed through her midsection. She couldn't sit up, and gave into it and leaning forward, trying to feign interest in the test before her, all the while trying to regain control of her breathing.

A hand touched her shoulder. "Are you okay?"

"Yes!" She realized that her answer was too forceful, and turned to the Fire Chief again, "...yes, I'm fine."

"All right," he said, uncertain, but began to pace the silent room.

Kate continued to answer questions, but found it difficult to concentrate. Just as she recovered from the first pain and found her composure, another hit her. Again, her breathing quickened and she

293

had to push her face toward the desk. And once more a hand touched her back.

"Are you sure you're okay?" The Chief's voice was barely a whisper, but his expression was demanding.

"Just having some pains…" she whispered back, "I'll be fine." Though she tried to come across as cool, calm, and collected, she was anything but that.

"Really? Are you in labor?" The man's face showed obvious uneasiness. "If you are, I can have an ambulance stand by."

"No, really. I'm fine. I am scheduled for surgery tomorrow. I just want to get through with the exam…but thanks," she said unconvincingly.

"Are you sure?" he said again.

"No," she answered honestly, "but I want to finish this test." Then she gave a nervous laugh and looked back down at her exam.

Every few questions she would stop to breathe through another pain until, finally, she had completed all of them.

"Okay, I'm going home," she whispered to the Chief when he came to the front to meet her at the table. "I don't think I did well, so I am not sticking around to see the results." She knew that her hair, her face, and everything about her gave away the discomfort she was feeling. The words were voiced with disappointment.

"Alright," the man said, and she headed for the door. On her way out, he added, "Good luck!"

Kate went home and got a few things ready for her and the baby for the next day and then lay down again. It seemed she couldn't stop looking at the clock for the rest of the day and into the night.

Come on! Morning couldn't come soon enough. Deidra drove Kate to the hospital first thing the next morning and helped her get situated. Dr. Mata agreed to perform the cesarean section on a Saturday.

Once she was all settled in, Diedra said, "I have to take off, now. I have to pick up my girls at my mom's house. Call me when you are out of recovery. Don't worry, it will all go well!" "Alright! I'll call you," Kate whimpered out with disappointment.

Kate suddenly felt all alone. She had no one to stay with her, and she was about to have major surgery.

No parents, siblings, spouse, or friends. The thoughts twirled around within her, filling her body with more anxiety and a sense of helplessness. *You can do it, Kate. You've been through tougher situations,* she kept telling herself, even as a nurse wheeled her to the operating room.

The anesthesiologist was waiting to give her an epidural.

"Hello, Kate!" a rotund little man said, flipping through the chart in his hands. "I'm Dr. Rios. I am the anesthesiologist who will be assisting Dr. Mata during the delivery of your baby today."

Karen smiled at the man, even though her insides told her to run away. She had not seen him before, and he began asking her a rapid series of questions about her health and allergies.

"All right, what I am going to do is numb the area first, and then insert the epidural into the spine. I'll need you to lie on your side with your knees tucked as close to your belly as possible. You must remain as still as possible. It'll be over very quickly." He smiled at her. "I promise." For a few moments nothing more was said, but then the same voice started to speak again. "I'm going to open the gown exposing your back." She could feel the cold air as he opened it. He continued, "Now I am going to wipe the area to sterilize it and then insert a needle around where you feel my fingers. This will numb the area. You are going to feel a sting, so try not to move."

She lay motionless in anticipation; then she felt a pinch and then burning. "OW!"

"Okay, now I'm going to insert the catheter. You will feel some pressure, but that is normal."

"OW! OW! OW! That hurts!" Kate cried out.

"It shouldn't hurt. You should only feel pressure. Where does it hurt?" he said, trying to calm her.

"It runs down my legs to the middle toes on my feet. Is that supposed to happen?" Kate said with fear in her voice.

"No. You must have moved. Let's try this again and don't move," he said with evident frustration.

"No, I did not move. Something is not right." Kate was afraid to continue, but she did anyway, clasping one hand very tightly around the other. "OW! OW! OW! It hurts and there is pressure down to my toes again. Something is not right!" This time Kate insisted in an angry tone.

"You're moving!" Dr. Rios sounded annoyed.

"No I'm not. I didn't move at all. I don't feel well. I feel like vomiting." Her stomach flip-flopped anxiously as she grew more upset with him.

"Take a few minutes to relax and breathe, then I will try one last time, and if you continue to feel the same, we'll stop and go with a local."

"Okay," she said with reluctance looking around the room as if someone would come in and rescue her. At this point, Kate wanted to cry and ask for another doctor; instead she tried to breathe and relax.

"Are you ready to continue?" the doctor said, holding back his annoyance.

"Yes," she said with a sigh.

"Hold very still."

"AHHHH!" She tried to muffle the scream as he continued, but this time was different and there was more pressure than pain.

"We got it. You're all done," he said, placing the instruments on the tray next to him. Kate felt slightly relieved when the nurse came in and draped her with sheets. Just as the nurse was finishing up, in walked Dr. Mata; but it wasn't the doctor who surprised her, following behind him was Diedra.

"I thought I'd come back to give you support and to watch my husband do what he does best." Diedra looked over and smiled at her husband.

"Okay, Kate! Let's get started," Dr. Mata said, walking around to the opposite side of the table.

Kate began to cry at the relief of having someone there for her.

"Don't cry! Everything will be alright," Diedra said, wiping the tears from Kate's eyes.

"I'm just glad you're here, and I'm not alone." Kate looked at the sheets draped over her like a tent and then back at Diedra. "Has he started cutting yet?"

"Cutting...HA! He is already taking the baby out. He's fast!" Diedra said, laughing and stroking Kate's hair.

Before Kate knew it, the pediatrician was there to take her baby. He wrapped the baby and brought him close to Kate's face.

"Here's your baby boy, Kate. He's gorgeous. Give him a kiss," Dr. Mendel said, smiling. He held the newborn as Kate gave her newborn a kiss on his forehead.

"I will take good care of him, Kate...don't worry," and then he whisked the baby away while the rest of the staff tended to Kate.

Two hours later, Kate was back in her room and was beginning to feel an itch on her face.

"I can't stop scratching," she complained to the nurse.

"Hmm," the nurse replied, "I'll let Dr. Mata know and see if he wants us to give you anything."

Hours passed after the promise was made, and Kate still hadn't heard anything. Her whole body was now itching unbearably.

"I can't take it," she said to the nurse, pleading with the woman to help her.

"Okay," the nurse gave a sympathetic look, "Dr. Mata still hasn't prescribed anything..."

The words were almost as aggravating as the incessant itch.

Kate picked up the phone to call Diedra.

"Hi, it's Kate," she listened for a moment and realizing it was Dr. Mata, she asked, "Did the nurse call you about my rash and itching?"

"No," Dr. Mata answered. The man was at home and in normal circumstances, Kate wouldn't have bothered him, but she felt as if she could tear the skin off her own body, which made it anything but a normal circumstance. "I never received a call or page. What's wrong?" The man's voice was kind, but a little annoyed.

She hoped the latter was a result of the nurse's incompetence and not her phone call. "I have a rash all over my body, and it itches real bad. It started with my face, but now it is my entire body. Can you give me something to make it stop? I'm going to scratch myself raw." Kate was too tired and frustrated to sound sane.

"It is a drug reaction." he explained. "There is something I can give you to stop it. Let me call the nurse now." Just before Kate hung up the phone, he added, "Call me first from now on. Don't wait."

About ten minutes later, the nurse walked in with a huff and said, "Why did you call Dr. Mata? I told you we were taking care of it."

"Dr. Mata is my doctor, but he's also a good friend," Kate said, through clenched teeth. "According to him…NO, you weren't taking care of it, and he never received a call from you." Kate snapped back at her.

"I'm sorry!" the nurse answered, though visibly irritated, handing Kate the medicine and a cup of water. "It has been busy. This should take care of it. Let me know if you need anything else." She finished up and then left the room.

Kate awoke the next morning with a severe headache. She alerted the nurse that she could not raise her head for fear of passing out from the pain.

"Kate?" The voice was familiar and Kate opened her eyes long enough to place it. "Hi. The nurses called me. Your headache is a result of the epidural and you are leaking spinal fluid." Dr. Mata's face was full of concern. "I'm sorry you are going through these complications, but you will have to stay a little longer until the headaches are gone and you can sit up. They will bring the baby into your room in a little while. Let me know if you have any other symptoms. I will be around all day." He patted her arm and smiled, trying to offer some comfort.

"Thank you…" she said, struggling to keep her eyes open, "…I'll."

A few days passed, and Kate was well enough to go home with Dustin. He was a large baby even though he was born two weeks early. He weighed in at eight pounds, fourteen ounces. To Kate he was perfect.

"Are you ready to go home?" Diedra surprised her, walking in the door to her room.

"Yes! Take us home," Kate gushed.

Kate arrived home to the welcoming arms of her other four children.

"Bienvenidos," said Maria, with a huge smile. She looked over at the baby and chuckled, "Hermoso Bebé!" Maria had taken care of the other children while Kate was in the hospital. The family could barely contain the excitement.

"Thank you," she answered Maria, offering a hug. "Look kids. Meet your brother, Dustin." Each took turns holding their new little brother. At that moment she felt so blessed and happy.

Another week passed, and Kate finally got the call that she'd been waiting for.

"Hi," said the faltering raspy voice. "I was wondering if it was a good time to come over?"

Kate rolled her eyes, but remained pleasant. "Of course. Come meet your son."

Fabian arrived a few hours later, looking a bit nervous. He couldn't stay still and appeared awkward when trying to hold his baby boy. There was a part of him, Kate was sure, that questioned whether or not the little bundle actually came from him.

"You know you can come by any time to see Dustin... if you like," Kate said in a reassuring manner.

"Thanks," he said, with a look of uneasiness. "Uh... I have to get going now. I have to go pick up my kids for the weekend. I will call you later." He seemed anxious to leave, and Kate walked him to the door. He didn't say "goodbye" or "see you later" or anything of the sort. He just gave her a look that said "sorry," and he was gone.

Just over a month after seeing Fabian, Kate was ready to return to her job. The new father had not returned to see his son, but Kate wasn't surprised by that. Still, it did sadden her that, being Dustin's only active parent, she had to leave him every third day and night with Maria so she could work at the station.

She was more thankful than ever for the woman who helped her maintain life and sanity around the house. Kate got ready and made her way to the station, already counting the hours until she could be back home with them.

When she returned the next morning, she got her two youngest cleaned, dressed and in the car. To give Maria a little break, they all went grocery shopping. Strapped in car seats behind her, the two seemed very content on the short drive to the store.

Perfectly happy with the way her life was and ecstatic to have time with the two little ones, Kate made no effort to rush. They meandered through the aisles, looking at the huge amounts of food, drinks, and snacks available.

She laughed as Lucy pointed to yet another item, begging. "No Lucy, Momma can't buy everything you point to," she said, but could barely resist the impending pout that was forming on the child's face. "How about if you pick one thing and I will get it for you," she offered and kissed the child's forehead.

"Candy, candy, candy!"

"Okay, but only one."

So with a tootsie pop in Lucy's hand and a grocery cart packed with the essentials, Kate stood and waited while her bill was totaled and food items were packed.

By the time the three reached the car, Dustin had fallen asleep. Kate gently lifted the car seat and buckled it in with the seat belt.

"Come on, sweetie-pie," she said to Lucy, helping her into the back seat.

"I got candy!" Lucy said stretching out her little arm, tootsie pop squeezed tight in her fist for Kate to see.

"You sure do, sweetie-pie!" Kate smiled back at Lucy as she buckled her seatbelt. Now that both kids safely in their car seats, Kate moved to the trunk to load her groceries.

The ride home promised to be even quieter. Lucy showed signs of being sleepy, so Kate travelled easily over the bumps. The double yellow faded lines kept her on course as she meandered around the many bends toward home on the narrow stretch of road.

She was approaching the street leading to her house, and turned on her signal then peeked into the backseat. Lucy was preoccupied with her tootsie pop and hadn't given in, but Dustin was sleeping peacefully. Kate then turned her attention to the rearview mirror and then back to the road. As she maneuvered the wheel to make the left turn onto her street...

WHAAAAM!

The sound of metal on metal wrenched her from the peaceful scene. Once, and then again...

WHAAAAM!

Despite all the strength, all the fortitude, and all of the resolve Kate had found in her everyday life – in that single moment she was as helpless as a person could be. The second impact sent her head lurching forward; her chest strained against the vinyl cloth strap which held tight and, just short of her forehead meeting the steering wheel, whipping her back again with the same violent force. Kate could see that the car was still moving, but it was out of her control, spinning around, whipping her back and forth in her seat once more before all was at rest. The noise behind her was deafening as she fought to release herself from the shoulder strap. Her back ached as she twisted, pushing off of the front console for leverage, but she didn't care. She had to reach them.

The adrenaline continued to drain from her body, and she found it more difficult to move on her own accord. The men – her colleagues – were forced to lift her up onto the stretcher as she cringed in agony. She looked up at them as she laid motionless, head secured in a neck brace. From experience, she knew that look of concern that flooded their eyes. She had shared it with these men before, and fear pierced her to the core as she thought that she might never share anything with them again.

EPILOGUE

TWO YEARS LATER...

"So..." The lawyer for the company, who'd been hired to represent the young boy who was driving the truck that slammed into Kate's car, looked at her harshly with his cold blue eyes. This tall, blond haired young attorney lacked experience in tact when questioning plaintiffs and clearly disconnected, because he continued, "You chose to have the surgery and quit the Fire Department?"

Kate stared back at his cold, uncaring face in disbelief. "Do you think I *wanted* this car accident?" Though anger bubbled within her, her voice remained calm. "Do you think that I *chose* to have my disc ruptured?" She paused, and then added, "I have done everything the doctors asked of me. I have made every effort to get better and nothing helped...until the surgery." She continued to speak even as a flood of tears began to fall. "I quit my job because I was no longer getting paid and...and I have five children to support." She fought the quaver in her voice. "The doctors also told me that I would never be able to continue working in such a physically demanding job."

Kate noticed the look of confusion on the attorney's face. "It was my understanding that you were still receiving pay from your job..."

His voice trailed off as he rifled quickly through a stack of paperwork. Apparently he didn't find what he was looking for because he quickly called for a recess.

Once everyone returned, the decision was made to settle out of court with Kate. The defendant's lawyers felt she had been through enough over the past year. At least, that's what she was told. *They know I have a case now,* she thought, but she knew that quickly settling would be the best thing for her and her family.

Eight months later, Kate took the City of Brownsville Fire Department. Again, she would find herself in a large, formal courtroom. After a five year battle to have the city's policies changed to stop gender discrimination, Kate's attorney directed her again to be true to who she was. This would become an even bigger nightmare. Barbara Vance, the recently elected city manager, was married to Federal Judge Fred Vance, who would be presiding over her case, which, of course, was filed against the City. Judge Vance interfered at every turn and did the job of the city attorney. Kate remembered the horrifying moment when she learned that she would not receive any pay during her pregnancy; and the day she had to drag her children into an ill-equipped house, admitting it was all she could afford. She thought back to when she walked into the women's restroom where the men had peed all over her toilet area, and then the humiliation of scrubbing the restroom floor on her hands and knees.

Judge Vance called Kate and her lawyer, Ellen Larsen, to his chambers and nonchalantly said, "You should take the City's offer of $75,000. If you don't, I will reduce it to that amount anyway."

Kate was boiling at this point; she got up and walked out of his chambers.

"What is the point of having a jury or continuing this trial if the judge has already made his decision?" Kate beseeched her attorney as they emerged from the judge's chambers. Her voice was loud and she did nothing to adjust her volume when Ms. Larsen was shushing her. "NO! This is a mockery...I had to endure ten years of gender discrimination just so I could continue to do my job and support my family. It's all about… it's all about… about who you know…not what is fair or right." Kate collapsed in the chair crying.

Her words, overheard by the bailiff, were reiterated to Judge Vance. He strode toward her, and said in a stern and careless voice, "You have the right to remove me from this case. Is that what you want?"

Yes! She thought, then changed her mind. *And then what? And then I start all over? I have to go through all of this…all of it all over again. And! And, with a new attorney!* Kate knew that Ms. Larsen wouldn't be able to help any further. She was appointed to be a judge and would no longer be a practicing attorney.

Kate realized she would never get a fair hearing, and answered him, "No," in an even tone, "No. I'll take the offer," and with that the deal was made.

Kate walked out of the courthouse feeling defeated in helping not only herself, but future women firefighters. Then her mind led her back. *The EEOC has already ruled in my favor, and I got to do something that few ever will. I exceeded everyone's expectations, including my own. I was able to save lives and now…and now I can spend every day enjoying mine, the best I can.* Kate knew in that moment what she had to do. She would write a book and share her story with others.

CPSIA information can be obtained at www.ICGtesting.com
Printed in the USA
BVOW02s0012100913

330708BV00001B/3/P

9 781477 275375